Under The Holly Moon

By

Ellen Dugan

Under The Holly Moon
Copyright @ Ellen Dugan 2016
Edited by Katherine Pace
Cover art designed by Kyle Hallemeier
Cover image: fotolia Anastasiia Kazakova
"Legacy of Magick" logo designed by Kyle Hallemeier
Copy Editing and Formatting by Libris in CAPS

This is a work of fiction. Names, characters, businesses, organizations, places, events and incidents either are the product of the author's imagination or are used fictitiously. Any resemblance to actual persons, living or dead, events, or locales is entirely coincidental.

Excerpt of: Spells Of The Heart
Copyright © Ellen Dugan 2016
Edited by Katherine Pace
Copy Editing and Formatting by Libris in CAPS

Other titles in the Legacy of Magick Series
by Ellen Dugan

Legacy of Magick, Book #1

Secret of the Rose, Book #2

Message of the Crow, Book #3

Beneath An Ivy Moon, Book #4

Spells Of The Heart (Coming June 2017)

Other Paranormal Fiction Titles

Gypsy At Heart, Welcome to Haven Harbor Anthology

ACKNOWLEDGMENTS

Thank you to the fans first and foremost. Without you this series would not be possible. A special thanks to my Beta readers: Erin, Katie, Ro and Shawna.

As always a few words of appreciation goes to my editors, and of course to the cover artist who brought Holly to life with a very witchy, sexy, broody cover!

Finally, thanks to my family and friends who put up with me when I am in the "William's Ford" head space… or who tiptoe around me when I am fighting to get back there.

I love you as certain dark things are to be loved,

In secret, between the shadow and the soul.

-Pablo Neruda

CHAPTER ONE

I stood on the front porch of the manor, my suitcases at my side. The Yuletide decorations were up, and the holiday lights glowed in bright festive colors across the porch railings. A huge fresh pine wreath hung on the front door as if to say 'welcome.' I started to open the door and thought better of it.

I hadn't been home in over two years. Would I even be welcomed?

I'd probably forfeited the right to waltz back in to the family's house as if only a few days had passed since I'd last been home. I stalled and called myself a coward. I could see my own reflection in the stained glass of the manor door. My eyes were droopy, my face was pale, and the smattering of freckles across my nose and cheeks really stood out. My hair was— as usual— sticking up all over the place. I brushed an annoying curl away from my eyes and tried to smooth my long hair back into place. I took a deep breath. *Be brave,* I told myself. The air was sharp and clear, and my breath made little white clouds against it.

While I stood shivering in my pale blue coat, I gathered my courage. Packing and loading up my car on my own and then making the four hour drive had been easy compared to what I was about to do. I'd rehearsed this reunion scene in my mind over and over as I'd driven east. Off to my right a pretty, waxing crescent moon was hanging low in the western sky. That was a good sign. The waxing crescent was a symbol for new beginnings, abundance— and also our family's magickal crest.

I didn't hazard a guess at what my family's reaction would be to my surprise visit... Though actually this wasn't a *visit* at all. Because I hadn't told anyone— not even my family— that I was moving back home. Permanently.

Behind me, parked in the long driveway, my car was stuffed full of boxes, books, clothes, and everything that I'd owned for the past two and a half years while away at school. But instead of returning to Kansas City in January, I had hoped to live at the manor and drive across town to class... That was my master plan, anyway. I had transferred to William's Ford University. My schedule was set and there was no going back now.

On an academic level, it could all work out perfectly. That is, if the family took me back in. There was a good chance they wouldn't even welcome me back. Not after the way I'd acted.

Not after the way I'd treated them.

Not after everything that I'd done.

I had run. Using the convenient excuse of a partial scholarship to a university clear across state. I had tried to live a mundane life and swore to put all magick behind me. At the time, escaping William's Ford seemed like my best option.

But I had gone overboard in my attempts to remove any temptation to practice magick. I'd ruthlessly cut off any and all attempts of contact the family had made. I took extra summer classes, visited my father and stepmother in Iowa, or claimed I was simply too busy working to come home on semester or holiday breaks.

Now I was back, and standing on the front porch of the house I'd grown up in made me realize how badly I had missed them all.

I squared my shoulders, reached out, and knocked briskly on the front door. It seemed like forever until it opened. When it did, I found myself face-to-face with my twin sister, Ivy. She wore a long, loosely knitted deep green sweater layered over a black gauzy skirt. Leggings and boots completed her outfit, and it was sort of Forest Witch meets gothic faery tale.

Her hair appeared to be its natural brown color and was cut in a cute, long bob. The front angled sharply to her collarbone while the back was shorter. Her makeup was still dramatic, but yet more subdued then I'd ever seen it. I blinked in shocked surprise

"Ivy? You look so different," I said, and then cringed at how that sounded to my own ears. *What did you expect?* My inner monologue chastised. *You haven't seen her in person for two years.*

"Well, well." Ivy looked me slowly up and down. "If it isn't Holly Irene Bishop. My twin sister who turned her back on her family and gave up Witchcraft."

"Hello, Ivy," I said, trying a smile.

Ivy leaned against the door jam. "So, how'd that all work out for you?" she said, crossing her arms over her chest and staying within the wards of the house.

"It sucked, actually," I heard myself say.

Ivy raised an eyebrow at me. "It was your choice to stay away. No one made you abjure the Craft." Ivy stopped herself and took a shaky breath. She noticed my suitcases. "Why are you here now, Holly?"

"I wanted to surprise everyone with a visit for the holidays," I said, bracing myself against the distrust that was written all over her face.

Ivy's green eyes narrowed at me. She glanced significantly towards my car and shifted her eyes back to mine. "Your car is awfully full for a holiday *visit*. Isn't it?"

Before I could answer, I saw movement in the foyer behind Ivy.

"Jeez Ivy." I could hear my cousin, Autumn. "You're letting all the cold air in," she said as she came into view, wearing jeans and a bright green sweater. She stopped suddenly and stood staring at me open mouthed. "Holly?"

"Autumn—" was all I managed to say before she

was leaping out of the front door and grabbing me up in a hug. My heart jerked once, then settled.

"You're here!" Autumn said, pressing her face along mine. "I had the weirdest dream last night about seeing a holly shrub and an ivy vine growing up the Yule tree in the foyer." She squeezed me tight, then pulled back and stared deeply into my eyes. "You're home for good. Aren't you?" she said.

I nodded. "Score another one for the Seer," I said, hugging her back.

"Oh, we've missed you!" Autumn let me go and grabbed a suitcase. "Come in! Come in." She beckoned me with one hand while she wheeled one suitcase in with the other.

"I wanted to tell you I was moving back, myself..." I picked up the second suitcase and crossed the threshold. I glanced up at the ward over the front door. To my relief the house didn't reject me.

It probably should have.

Autumn shut the door behind us and Ivy stepped back. Before I could begin to try and apologize, or even say anything meaningful to my twin, a small red-haired tornado blew through the foyer.

"My Ivy!" Morgan ran straight to Ivy.

Ivy scooped him up and planted a loud kiss on his cheek. As the little boy laughed, Ivy hitched him on her hip.

Now it was my turn to stare. The last time I'd seen my nephew in person he'd only been a baby. "Hi

Morgan."

"Who's that?" he asked Ivy, pointing at me.

Autumn ran a hand over the toddler's head. "It's your Aunt Holly," she said.

"No." Morgan shook his head and frowned at me.

It gave me a jolt to see that my pajama-clad nephew had the same strawberry blonde, curly hair that I did. As I watched, he tucked his head on Ivy's shoulder, and I found myself regarded by two very suspicious sets of eyes... One baby blue, the other a sharp green.

While Autumn called for the rest of the family, I watched as my sister and my nephew moved back and farther away from me. Even as Bran, Lexie, and Great Aunt Faye came pouring into the foyer with smiles and welcoming hugs, I willed myself not to cry.

I could feel my sister's hurt and distrust from where I stood. I had no illusions that our relationship would be repaired quickly or easily. I had more apologizing and making amends to do to with my twin than I did with anyone else.

I was back in William's Ford. For better or worse, I was home and here to stay. I could only hope that with a little luck I'd be able to start my life over. To find a way to balance the scales and to become a person worthy of love and respect.

But that would take magick.

And I'd stopped practicing magick a long time ago.

***

A few hours later, I carried the last of my boxes up the stairs and into the room I'd once shared with my sister. The bedroom had originally belonged to our mother, and it was technically the master suite of the manor. As such, the suite claimed a curving turret, a sitting area, generous bedroom and a spacious private bath. It was more than large enough to accommodate two people. Especially since one of those two people seemed determined to avoid the other.

I stood in the center of a stack of cardboard boxes and suitcases and wondered where to begin. The family's cat, Merlin, strode into the room. He stopped, and seemed to consider me as I stood there. "Hi Merlin," I said, and set down the final box on my old, antique dresser.

Merlin wandered over slowly. I bent down and offered my hand to him. He stopped and leaned tentatively in to sniff my fingers. To my shock, he hissed and arched his back. I yanked my hand back, and he spit again and then high-tailed it out of the bedroom.

I felt tears well up at his rejection. *Even the cat was avoiding me.* I pressed my fingers to my eyes and tried to focus on my breathing. *What did you expect?* I thought, fighting to keep control of my emotions. *Did you think your twin would smile, give you a hug and say, 'All is forgiven?'* I almost laughed at myself.

I didn't deserve forgiveness.

Inhaling deeply and trying for a calm that I was far from feeling, I pulled back my frustration and studied my reflection in the mirror that hung over the dresser. I pictured in my mind's eye that all of the negative emotions surrounding me would dissolve and fall harmlessly away. I blew out a cleansing breath, refocusing on my reflection once more. What I saw had me flinching.

I almost didn't recognize myself. I was once considered to be the prettiest girl in my class. But the person staring back at me today seemed like a stranger. I was much too thin, even though my face was puffy, and my complexion was completely washed out. There were circles under my eyes, and my comfortable blue sweater only seemed to make my eyes look cloudy and dim instead of bright aqua blue.

My hair— *well there was no help on that front*— It was still a massive pain-in-my-ass explosion of red-gold curls that I allowed to grow long so the weight of my hair would pull some of the curl out. A couple of photos tucked into the frame of the mirror caught my attention. I pulled them free.

The first picture was of my one-time best friend, Cypress Rousseau, and me. We stood together in our cheerleading uniforms. Cy had her hands on her hips and was throwing her head back in laughter, and I'd been grinning at her. We'd been co-captains of the squad, and the picture had been taken at Homecoming during our Senior year. I couldn't even remember what we'd been laughing about. It felt like a lifetime ago.

The second snapshot was of Ivy, me, and Cypress. It

had been taken at the Halloween Ball only a few weeks before my mother had died. The three of us were standing arm in arm and posing happily for the camera.

The photo showed Ivy puckering up her pink lips and dressed in a swath of pale peach organza. Iridescent butterflies decorated her shoulders and her tall sparkling crown. Everyone's favorite Goth-girl had gone as *Glinda the Good Witch* to the Ball, and she'd totally nailed it.

In the center of the photo, Cypress' faerie costume was stunning. Anyone else studying the picture would have seen three attractive teenage girls dressed in great Halloween costumes. What I saw was something more. I saw a true representation of each of our magickal characters.

Ivy at her core *was* good, but she covered it up with attitude and sass. Down deep, I knew that my sister was loving, kind, and fair with her Craft. Cypress, like the sprite she'd been dressed as, was an elemental force of magick. She was earthy and powerful, but yet, at her core, Cy was a *neutral* force.

And then there was me. I'd gone as a *Wicked Witch*, and had worn a long gray gown, all trimmed out in gothic black. I studied those puffy Victorian inspired sleeves, and the under-the-bust-style black velvet corset, that I'd laced up around my waist. My hair had been swept up and mostly hidden under a tall, pointed, black Witch's hat, decorated with flowers in blood red and gray. My makeup had been severe; with charcoal smoky eye shadow, ebony nail polish and deep burgundy lipstick.

I thought back to how edgy I'd felt that night. How I'd caught everyone off guard by going all gothic and 'out of character'. It made me sick to my stomach, remembering how I'd laughed at everyone's shocked reaction to my costume.

Holly Bishop, the captain of the cheerleading squad, the popular girl everyone thought was so pretty and so sweet— dressed like a Wicked Witch? The irony was that by the end of the night, I had actually ended up personifying my costume by becoming the scariest, darkest practitioner of my entire family line.

The night of the Halloween Ball had been a turning point in my life. It was the night I'd tried the dark path of magick. *No,* I shook my head at myself in the mirror and owned it. *No, I hadn't merely 'tried' dark path. It wasn't like sampling a cupcake or something...* I'd let that destructive magick rip, and I'd embraced it... enjoyed it even.

Three years later, and the memory had me quaking in reaction. I could still hear Leilah Drake Martin taunting me. She had laughed in my face when I'd realized that she'd been the one making the poppets and causing all of the injuries to my friends on the cheer squad.

And I had snapped.

My heart thudded in my chest, and I struggled against anxiety. I gripped the edge of the dresser as that night played back in my mind...

"You bitch," I said to Leilah.

Leilah sneered at me, "You deserved it! I'd have made the varsity squad if not for you! The *perfect* Holly Bishop, captain of the varsity team— thinking you're so much better than everyone else!"

"You hurt my friends to try and get on the varsity squad?" I asked, trying to be calm, even as my temper began to bubble up inside of me.

"Yeah? What are you going to do about it?" Leilah practically spit. "A perfect little princess like you?"

I surged forward and Duncan Quinn stepped between us. "Cool off, Holly." Duncan warned, steering me away from Leilah.

"I'm going to call the police," Autumn said, in response to our catching Leilah trying to break into the manor.

Leilah continued to shout insults, even as I walked away over to the edge of the patio. I turned my back on all of them, hugging my arms over my middle. I tried to breathe, tried to stay calm, but my rage tore free, and a roar of energy began to fill me up. I let it in, embraced the negative emotions, and let it fuel my magick. The force of it had my head falling back— I trembled at the incredible rush it provided and reached out to the elements. First air, and then water answered me. *I'd always had an affinity for water...*

"That's right," Leilah yelled at my back. "Walk away

you prissy little bitch! You don't have the guts to come at me with magick."

In the background I heard Autumn shouting at Leilah, telling her to shut up. But that sound was torn away as a new wind ripped through the side yard. It was unnaturally strong, and I joyously embraced the dark, reckless power that I had channeled. I smiled, standing in the night and wondered why I'd waited so long to turn my powers loose.

The howling wind that I'd called tore through my hair, and I twisted to focus on Leilah. "You wanna see magick?" I asked her, and then I tossed my hands down and out to my sides. As thunder rumbled above me, I slowly bunched my fingers closed into a fist. *Water, I call you forth.* I called the element, visualized it, and manipulated its energy into a weapon.

Instantly, Leilah fell to her knees, her hands tearing at her own throat. Her eyes bulged and her color changed dramatically.

"Holly, stop!" Duncan shouted.

With a terrible gagging sound, Leilah dropped farther down to all fours on the patio. "Help—" Leilah made an awful gurgling sound, and then she violently coughed up water— right out of her lungs.

Lost in my own spell, I was too furious and wrapped up in revenge to stop. The winds shrieked, and rain started to pelt down from the sky. I continued to focus unblinkingly on Leilah, who had collapsed to her belly and made a horrible rattling sound. Then she was quiet.

Good. Now she would never cause harm again...

The next thing I knew I was hit with a full body tackle. Autumn had taken me down and we bounced together, hard, on the lawn.

Several things seemed to happen at once. The wind stopped as if it had never been, and the rain disappeared. I came back to myself, and discovered that Autumn had me pinned to the ground and was shouting at me. Behind us, Leilah started to gag, cough, and then breathe on her own.

Autumn gave me a brisk shake. "Holly, are you back?"

With a shudder, all of the negative emotions and magick I'd invoked rushed away from me. "Leilah," I said, staring at the girl as she coughed and struggled to breathe. It was then that I understood with a real horror, exactly what I'd done.... *I'd almost killed her,* I realized. *By filling up her lungs with water as she stood on dry land.*

I came back to the present and forced myself to release my death grip on the dresser. I felt slightly nauseous at reliving the memory so vividly. I glanced at my reflection and realized that, *that* Holly Bishop, the girl who'd purposefully caused another person physical harm with magick, had disappeared a long time ago. Fate had stepped in and taught the Holly of the past some brutally hard lessons.

The cost of my actions had been horrific. The

backlash of my dark magick hadn't rebounded immediately on me— as I'd thought it would. Instead, a few weeks later, my mother had died under suspicious circumstances.

For a time I'd thought that the accident had been all my fault. A karmic punishment for the dark magick I had unleashed on Leilah Drake Martin. Had it weakened the protection spells on my family? Had the destructive energy I'd set free somehow assisted the hex that ultimately killed my mother?

There was no way to ever be sure. So, I tried to make amends. I'd studied hard to gain better control. However, instead of things settling down, in my grief, a new surprising power— telekinesis, had emerged. And the ability manifested whenever I was frustrated, or angry.

It had terrified me. If I couldn't control the powers I was used to, what sort of damage could I inflict on my remaining family accidentally with my new ones?

When I left to attend the university in Kansas City I'd promised myself I wouldn't come back until I had my magick under control. I owed it to my family to keep them safe. There would be no more mishaps. If that took cutting off my magick to accomplish it— then so be it. I'd live my life without magick, I'd be a mundane, and I would find a way to make it work. *I had to.* There could never be any magickal disasters caused by me. Not ever again.

So I'd gone away to school and pretended to be

someone new. A different Holly Bishop. A regular, ordinary girl who knew nothing about spells, magick, or Witchcraft. No one knew me, or my family's legacy of magick, on a campus clear across the state, and I liked it that way. I became the fun, popular, outgoing Holly who studied hard, and partied harder. I dated a lot of guys, slept with a few of them. Broke some hearts and didn't care. Then when I did care— well, he didn't.

I stopped my reminiscing and considered the stacks of boxes. I was home, and couldn't honestly say I was any wiser for my time away.

Because I'd learned that some tragedies could be of your own making— no magick required. Now I had to live with that sorrow too, and the strain was overwhelming.

Autumn poked her head in my room. "Want some help with the unpacking?"

I jolted at the sound of her voice. "Sure." Carefully, I replaced the photos.

Autumn strolled in and seemed to grab a box at random. "How was the drive in?"

"Uneventful," I said. "Quiet."

"Well your welcome home dinner was anything but," Autumn laughed, and tucked her shoulder length, brown hair behind her ear.

"Another peaceful night at the Bishops," I agreed, thinking on the pandemonium my surprise arrival had caused. Everyone talking at once, all the questions and excitement when I'd announced I was home to stay.

Well except from Ivy, she'd ducked out right away and had gone to meet up with her boyfriend.

"You'll need to give Ivy some time," Autumn said, as if she knew where my train of thought had headed. "You being gone was hardest on her."

"I know. I'm sorry." I picked up a suitcase and set it on my bed.

"Did you tell her that?"

"It's kind of hard to apologize when she's avoiding me like the plague."

Autumn gave a non-committal sort of hum, popped the top on a box and peered down at the contents. "You packed your clothes on their hangers." She sounded surprised.

"I figured it would be faster to put them away."

"No argument there," Autumn said, going over to the walk-in closet. "I hope there's some room in here for your stuff." She opened the door, flipped the light on and stopped.

I glanced up and saw that half of the closet was completely empty. It was as if an invisible line had been drawn down the center. The right side of the closet was jam packed with shoes, boots, purses and clothes. But the left side was completely bare.

Autumn went back, gathered up the clothes and carried them into the closet. "That was nice that Ivy cleaned out half of the closet for you. Did you tell her you were coming home?"

"No," I said. *Ivy's intuition had probably clued her*

in, I figured, and grimly unzipped my suitcase. I scooped up my personal items and a few clothes from the suitcase and carried the stack to my dresser. I opened the top drawer and the scent of roses wafted out. The hair stood up on the back of my neck.

Roses were a scent we'd come to associate with my grandma Rose— with her ghost anyway. I held my breath for a moment. Nothing happened. I sighed and wondered why I'd ever thought she'd be any more likely to communicate than my sister would. After all, she was probably ashamed of me, and everything I'd done.

Autumn hung the first batch on the rod. She went back for the second. We worked in uncomfortable silence for a good minute. "Holly, are you okay?" she asked.

I turned my face away. "Yes," I lied, and went back to my suitcase.

"Do you want to tell me why you decided to quit school halfway through your Junior year and come home?"

"I didn't *quit* school," I said, working to keep my voice calm. "I simply transferred to William's Ford University to finish my degree."

Autumn opened another box, and pulled out a pile of folded sweaters. "So nothing happened on a personal level that sent you home?" She carried the sweaters into the closet and stacked them neatly on a shelf.

I felt my stomach roll over. *There was no way she*

could know. "No, of course not."

"Holly, I love you." Autumn's announcement had me glancing up at her. "But you know what?" she said, crossing her arms over her chest.

"What?" I asked her.

"I call bullshit." And with that, Autumn marched across the room, took a hold of my arms, and forced me to sit on the bed.

"Hey!" I said pulling away. I tried to stand up, only to be strong-armed right back.

"The minute you stepped inside the manor I could see that something was seriously wrong with you," Autumn said, searching my face. "You have a dark aura, it's like you're ill, or maybe grieving."

"I'm tired, that's all."

"I'm *scared* for you," Autumn said. "Something is wrong."

"It was a stressful last few weeks," I said, meeting her eyes. "That's all."

"Wow, you just lied. Right to my face this time," Autumn said. "Impressive."

"I'm *not* sick," I argued. "Please leave this alone."

"Are you gonna tell me, Blondie, or do you want me to simply look for myself?" Autumn's tone of voice was gentle, but her grip was no-nonsense.

I wasn't strong enough to wrestle away from her, so instead I raised my eyebrows and smirked. "I see you never learned any patience while I was away at school."

"Patience may be a virtue but it's not one of mine."

Autumn smiled at me, and it wasn't a particularly friendly one.

I drew back. I had my reasons why I didn't want her to see into my thoughts. "Using your abilities to scan me without my permission would be considered unethical behavior."

"Yup," Autumn shrugged. "Them's the breaks."

"I may not practice anymore but I *can* keep you out of my head." *I was pretty sure of that.* To prove it, I laughed at her. "You'll only embarrass yourself if you try."

"You think so?" Autumn cocked her head at me.

"Autumn, please don't," I pleaded, understanding too late that I had only egged her on.

"Then talk to me, damn it," she said. "You're really scaring me."

"You won't like what you see," I warned. "I don't *want* you to see."

"Holly," Autumn's voice echoed oddly in the room. "Look at me."

Despite myself, I did. I felt an inner click as Autumn's eyes locked onto mine, and to my shock she rolled right past any resistance or shields that I *thought* I still possessed. I tried to block her out of my mind, and it was useless.

Damn, she's so much stronger than before! I quivered as I felt her shuffling through my recent memories, and when she hit on the biggest secret I'd ever kept in my life— she winced in reaction as much as I did.

I wasn't surprised to see my cousin turn pale as she relived my last few weeks for herself. My breath began to hitch in reaction, even as sweat started to pop out on her brow. "That's enough," I gritted out between my teeth.

"Only a little more..." Autumn dug her fingers into my arms and kept scanning. "Holly, give me a goddamned name."

My stomach roiled and tears welled up in my eyes. "He's not worth it."

Let me help you Holly. Autumn's voice whispered through my head. *You don't have to carry this all on your own.*

I bowed my head in defeat and surrendered. *Don't think less of me...* I sent the thought to Autumn. *Please, don't think less of me.*

Then I let her see. Everything.

***

I don't know when I became aware that I was lying on the floor of the bedroom. I blinked up at the ceiling and felt Autumn pat my arm. The next thing I knew, her concerned face filled up my line of sight.

"Are you okay? she asked.

I ran my tongue around my teeth and hesitated before answering her. "Better." I thought about it. "I feel a little better. Lighter maybe."

"Try and sit up for me," Autumn said and slowly helped me to a sitting position.

I sat up and shifted, leaning back against the side of my bed. I focused on my cousin who now sat cross-legged on the area rug opposite of me. I opened my mouth, fully intending to speak, and found I simply didn't have the words.

Autumn took a deep breath. "First let me say, that you should have called me." Tears were rolling down her face. "Honey, no one should ever have to go through something like that alone. *One* phone call Holly. One. And I would've been there."

I dropped my chin to my chest. I couldn't even look at her.

Autumn reached out and took my hand. "I saw, when I scanned your memories, that you went to an emergency room. What did the ER doctor say?"

"She said that it was one of those things..." My voice cracked and I wiped tears from my eyes. "I was only about seven weeks pregnant when I miscarried."

"I'm sorry Blondie." Autumn pulled me close. "I'm *so* sorry." She held on tight as we cried together. "And you're alright, now?" she asked after a little while.

I laid my head on her shoulder. "Yes, I'm fine. I followed up with a different doctor at a clinic a couple of days ago."

"Holly," Autumn's voice was ragged with tears, even as she rubbed my back in sympathy. "The father, did he know?"

"He did." I sniffed. "He was relieved when I told him I'd lost the baby." I squeezed her tighter. "I was planning on keeping it, and he didn't want me to."

"The selfish jackass," Autumn hissed.

Her words made me smile a little. "I had decided to come home," I admitted. "Figured I'd raise the baby here by myself... and then... Well, I started bleeding."

Autumn took my face in both of her hands. "I'm so sorry you were alone."

"I didn't think about that. I got in my car and drove to the nearest hospital. And, well, you saw the rest for yourself."

She pressed a kiss to my forehead. "Tomorrow, I'm taking you to *my* doctor."

"That's not necessary—"

"Oh yes it is!" Autumn cut me off. "This time you're going to shut up and let someone take care of you. That's non-negotiable."

I started to argue and instead pulled her close. "Thank you," I said.

Autumn ran her hand down my hair and held on. We stayed that way for a while.

"I've missed you," I finally said. "So, so much."

"Do you need anything? Can I get you anything?" Autumn wanted to know.

I knuckled away my tears. "No. I told you. Physically, I'm okay."

"Well you're just going to have to suffer through me hovering for a while," Autumn said.

"Autumn." I pulled back and studied my cousin's face. "I don't want the family to know about this."

My cousin opened her mouth to argue, stopped and seemed to think better of it. "Alright. I'll respect your wishes," she gave in.

"Thank you."

"It's the least I can do since I pushed my way into your head." Autumn sighed and stood. "You've been through enough."

I nodded, and Autumn gently helped me rise to my feet. "Do you still want to help me unpack all my stuff?" I asked.

"Of course." Autumn grabbed a nearby box. "Together we can have this done in no time. But if you need to take a break or rest, you do that. Okay?"

"I will, and Autumn?" I waited until she met my eyes. "Thanks."

"There's no need to thank me sweetie." Autumn pulled several dresses out of a box. "I'm here for you. It's what families do."

CHAPTER TWO

I padded my way down the back stairs the next morning in my plaid flannel pajama bottoms and navy long sleeved t-shirt. I'd only managed to fall asleep somewhere around five o'clock in the morning. It was the weirdest thing, but I dreamt of a woman stroking my hair. When I woke the room smelled faintly of roses, again. It was now a little before nine, and I yawned as I stepped down into the kitchen.

I rubbed my eyes and considered the pretty scene before me. I must have been more tired than I thought when I'd arrived home yesterday. I'd barely paid attention to the fact that the manor was decorated for the holidays. *Yule was only a week away,* I realized with a combination of guilt and dread. With everything that had happened lately, the holiday season hadn't been a priority.

A red poinsettia in a green basket rested on the kitchen table. White lights had been strung through deep red sprays of berries and artificial pine branches, and they illuminated the soffit area above the creamy white cabinets. I spotted a trio of glass apothecary jars filled with red and white vintage ornaments sparkling on the counter. A snowman shaped cookie jar grinned at me from the top of the fridge, and my mother's collection of carved wooden Santas had found a place of honor on a kitchen shelf. With holiday music playing in the background it was cozy, warm and picture perfect.

All that holiday cheer made me feel more isolated than ever before.

"Good Morning." Aunt Faye turned from the stove where she switched the flame off the tea kettle. She sat two mugs on the breakfast bar and poured the tea. As was her habit, my great-aunt was meticulously groomed. This morning it was a festive red sweater and dark blue slacks. Her silvery white hair hung long and loose down her back, and she clipped around the kitchen in bright red, high heeled boots.

"Morning," I said, and hitched myself onto a barstool. I yawned, shook my head to clear it and yawned again.

"I'd ask how you slept, but I can see the answer for that myself." Aunt Faye added sugar to her tea, and passed me the sugar bowl.

I added two teaspoons and stirred. "I suppose I'm too wound up to sleep, what with being back home and all." I took a sip, added a third.

She joined me at the breakfast bar. "Are you well?"

Great Aunt Faye, like Autumn, was a Seer. If I out-and-out lied to the woman, she'd know in a heartbeat. To stall, I changed subjects. "It's awfully quiet around here. Where is everybody?"

"Lexie's at work, Bran took Morgan to pre-school, and Ivy left to go and drop Nathan off at the airport—he's flying back to spend the holidays with his family in Massachusetts."

"Where's Autumn?" I said, and a second later my cousin came clattering down the back stairs.

"Good morning!" Autumn purposefully slid across the kitchen floor in her mismatched fuzzy socks. She skidded to a stop beside my chair and dropped a hand on my shoulder. "I'm thinking that since I have the day off, this calls for waffles for breakfast. How about it? Holly, are you in?"

"Sure." I set the tea down.

"I'll get the waffle iron out for you," Aunt Faye volunteered.

"That's okay." Autumn patted her shoulder. "I'll get it."

Autumn hitched up her baggy black sweatpants, crouched down and began to root around in the cupboards. She pulled out the waffle iron and several pots hit the floor, making an unholy racket.

"Darling," Aunt Faye said, pitching her voice over the sounds of the crashing.

"What?" Autumn called back. Her voice was muffled as her head was now in the cabinet.

"By the Goddess." Aunt Faye rolled her eyes to the ceiling.

"Found it!" Autumn crowed in delight pulling the glass mixing bowl out of the cabinet.

I tried to keep a straight face as Autumn stood and thumped the bowl on the counter with enough force to make Aunt Faye wince. I cleared my throat instead. "Let me give you a hand," I volunteered and got up to help.

The waffle iron came thudding down next to the bowl. "Thanks," Autumn said, and then she started to shove all the pots back in the cabinet.

The noise was deafening.

"I have to go in to the shop this morning," Aunt Faye announced over the ruckus.

"That's right, big holiday sale this week. You and Ivy will be busy," Autumn said, going to the fridge next and gathering ingredients.

"Will Ivy be at the shop today?" I asked Aunt Faye.

"All day," she said. "I'm going in to help. We expect to be busy."

"Oh." Defeated, I looked down at my tea. *I had hoped to talk to Ivy today.*

"Ladies," Aunt Faye said, rising to her feet. "This kitchen had better be spotless after Autumn destroys it making breakfast."

"Hey!" Autumn set milk and eggs on the counter. "I'm a damn good cook!"

"I never said you weren't." Aunt Faye raised her

bows. "You are however, a sloppy one."

I stepped between them. "I'll help her clean up. Don't worry, Aunt Faye."

"See that you do," Aunt Faye passed a hand over my hair. "It's good to have you back home." She smiled and let herself out the potting room door.

While Autumn dashed around measuring ingredients into her bowl, I went back to the barstool and my mug. I added some milk to the tea and sipped. *Better.*

"How're you feeling this morning, Blondie?" Autumn asked. Her hair swung brown and shiny past her shoulders. I noticed she was wearing new glasses. The frames were trendy, dark brown and edged with green on the interior. They suited her well.

"Okay. I guess."

"Did you sleep at all?" Autumn wanted to know.

"I got in a couple of hours." I heard Aunt Faye's car start. "Nice diversionary tactic, by the way." I said to my cousin. "It always did wind her up when you start crashing things around in the kitchen."

"Hey, it worked." Autumn wiggled her eyebrows at me. "Plus I was really in the mood for waffles."

"That does sound good," I admitted.

"And scrambled eggs," Autumn decided. "Let's add some extra protein to our breakfast."

I sent her a look and plugged the waffle iron in for her. "You don't have to fuss over me."

Autumn whisked the waffle batter in the bowl. "I know I don't have to. But I'm going to anyway. Go get another bowl for the eggs, will ya?"

I went to the cabinet and took out a second bowl. I cracked four eggs in the bowl and beat them with a fork. *There was no point in arguing with her.* I realized. *She was only trying to help.* "Do you have plans for the day?" I asked.

"We do." Autumn set the batter bowl down and tapped the whisk on the side. "You have a doctor's appointment at 10:30 and I'm taking you."

I huffed out a breath. "I told you last night, I followed up with a doctor a few days ago."

Autumn put her hands on her hips. "And I told you, that I was taking you to my doctor anyway."

I opened my mouth to argue and thought better of it. Instead, I put on the skillet and poured in the eggs. I grabbed a spatula out of the crock on the counter and stood there watching them. For a few moments the kitchen was silent except for the sounds of cooking. I struggled against feeling ungracious. "I do have a copy of my recent medical records," I said. "I could bring those along, I suppose."

"Good thinking." Autumn tested the waffle iron, found it to her satisfaction and poured the batter in. "After the appointment, we could do something fun. Let's say... a little holiday shopping and lunch. Then more shopping."

"That would be nice." I stirred the eggs. "I haven't had the chance to do any shopping for the family."

"Well, we can get that all sorted out today— aw

crap!" Autumn grabbed for the paper towels.

I glanced down at the waffle iron. Batter had begun to ooze out the sides and onto the counter. "You always did put too much batter in."

"Yeah, I know." Autumn tried to wipe up the spill but managed to smear even more batter on the counter instead. Then she swore when she bumped her knuckles on the hot waffle iron.

I took the eggs off the heat and covered them with a lid to keep them warm. Autumn lifted out the first waffle and poured in the batter for a second. While it cooked, I set the table while my cousin sang along to the music on the radio.

Somehow, the normality of it all helped me relax a little.

***

I muscled several shopping bags into the booth at the local restaurant Autumn had chosen for lunch. I slid in next to them and sighed in relief.

She sat across from me and blew out a breath. "God I'm starving!" She checked her phone. "No wonder, it's 1:30!"

I wasn't particularly hungry but I had to admit the smells coming out of the kitchen of the little Mexican restaurant were fabulous. I pulled my sock cap off my head and my curls exploded. "Cute place," I said, unbuttoning my winter coat.

Autumn smiled up at the waiter who slid a basket of chips and a small dish of salsa in front of us. She ordered a margarita on the rocks. I stuck to a soft drink. I wouldn't turn twenty-one for another week. I'd done more than enough drinking in college, anyway.

"Try the chimichanga," Autumn suggested as we perused the menus.

I shot her a look over the top of my menu. "You're all about the food today. Why do I get the feeling you are trying to fatten me up?"

Autumn scooped up some salsa on her chip. "You heard what the doctor said. You could stand to gain about ten pounds." She squinted at me from over the top of her glasses. "Let's make that fifteen."

"I don't know what strings you pulled to get me an appointment so quickly," I said softly. "But I wanted to say thanks for that, and for going along in the exam room with me."

Autumn reached across the table gave my hand a squeeze. "Of course."

The doctor had been kind: Also brisk, cheerful and non-judgmental. When all was said and done, I'd been given a different prescription for birth control pills, a recommendation to start taking multivitamins, *and* a firm suggestion to gain some weight.

"What are you going to order?" I asked.

"The shrimp tacos," Autumn said immediately.

I closed my menu. "Perfect. Make that two."

"So how are things with Rene?" I asked about her

gorgeous boyfriend.

"Okay," she said. "He's up in Chicago right now, on business." Autumn flashed me a smile.

My stomach dropped when I studied her face and *felt* the falseness behind her smile. After brutally squashing any and all of my gifts over the past few years, I was used to keeping that part of me locked up. Feeling them return made me flinch. *It's only clairsentience,* I told myself. *Plenty of mundane people received empathic information psychically.* I took a breath and let it out slowly. *You are in control. Be calm and let the information roll past you.*

The waiter dropped off our drinks and took our food orders. As soon as he left, I gave my cousin's shin a light kick under the table. "What's really going on?" I asked her.

Autumn sighed. "Rene wants me to relocate with him to Chicago."

My heart jerked hard at her words. "And how do you feel about that?" I said fairly calmly, considering my heart was in my throat at the thought of her leaving town.

"Torn," Autumn admitted. "William's Ford is my home. My family is here. I can't— I *won't* leave."

I nodded, cautiously observing my cousin. Once I got past my own relief that she wasn't going anywhere, I realized that I was picking up on her disappointment and panic at the thought of losing Rene.

Those emotions shimmered around her and began to

drift towards me. My own throat grew tight— just as Autumn's was. I fought back the need to push her feelings away and out of my personal space. *My hands were in my lap... she'd never even notice,* I thought. *With one simple gesture I could shield myself. It would only be a 'little' magick—*

I cut the train of thought off, dug my fingers into the bench, and struggled for control. "Maybe you can do a long distance relationship?" I suggested.

"Maybe." Autumn sipped her drink. "It's harder than I thought it would be."

I rolled my shoulders, stretched my neck and felt relief when it popped. The tension from holding back my magick eased up a bit. A few seconds later and the intensity of Autumn's emotions drifted away to be absorbed into the ambient energy inside the restaurant, making me a bit more comfortable.

I shifted my attention to the front windows and watched as shoppers hustled along Main Street. *Enchantments* was only a block down from where we were. I felt a sudden urge to go visit.

"After we eat, I'd like to drop by the family's shop." I heard myself say.

"Sure," Autumn set her drink down. "You should meet Terry, the store manager, she's great."

I picked up a chip and sampled the salsa. "That'd be nice."

Autumn folded her arms on the table. "It's been a long time since you've visited the shop."

"Mmm hmm," I said with my mouth full.

"There's a few new businesses open on our end of Main Street." Autumn helped herself to another chip.

"Really?" I asked.

"Yeah, there's a fabulous antique shop now down from *Enchantments*."

I perked up at the news. "You know I love antiques and primitives."

"That's right." Autumn passed me a chip. "Your step-mother Ruth has a little antique shop up in Iowa, doesn't she?"

"She does," I said. "I helped out there when I spent the summer with them."

"How are she and your dad?"

"They're great, going on a cruise soon for their anniversary. They're pretty excited." I nibbled on the chip. "You know Autumn, I'd really like to see that new local shop."

"Sure we can stop by, it should be open unless Ginny, the owner, is finally having her baby. She was due last week and—" Autumn stopped speaking and her green eyes jumped to mine.

I couldn't deny her words had made my stomach drop in reaction. "It's okay," I said as Autumn's eyes grew large in her face.

She reached across the table and rested her hand on mine. "I'm sorry. That was stupid of me."

I turned my hand over and gave hers a squeeze. "I'm not going to fall apart every time I see— or hear about a pregnant woman, or a baby," I said firmly.

"Still. I'm sorry if I upset you," she said.

I was saved from saying anything else as our lunch arrived. Once the waiter left I reached for my soft drink and eyeballed my cousin. "Do me a favor, will you?"

"Anything," she said.

"I admit, I've had a rough time off and on for the past couple of weeks, but for the most part I'm doing okay." I set my glass down and cleared my throat. "But *if* I need to talk about how I'm feeling over the loss— I promise, I will come to you."

"Understood." Autumn stared hard at me for a moment as if weighing my words. "Okay," she said. "Now do *me* a favor... and eat something. Those jeans you're wearing have been sliding off your ass all day."

"Stop looking at my ass," I said automatically.

"What ass?" Autumn shot back with a playful grin. "You don't even have one anymore."

I rolled my eyes at her, but picked up a shrimp taco and bit into it.

The name of the antique shop was *Obscura*. And as Autumn had predicted it was closed. I smiled slightly at the makeshift sign stuck on the front door. It read: "Shop closed. We are having a baby today!"

I peered in through the windows and my heart yearned over what I could see. It was a dream antique store, there were attractive and clever displays, and the shop was neat as a pin. I saw a row of old blue canning jars behind the counter and sighed over them a little. *I loved those old glass mason jars.*

"We can come back next week," Autumn suggested as I continued to look in through the window.

"I'd really like to," I said, cupping my gloved hands on either side of my face and pressing closer to the glass. "It's a pretty shop."

"Ready to go to *Enchantments*?"

I mentally squared my shoulders. "Sure." I tried to sound casual, but as Autumn hooked her arm through mine and led the way across the street, my heart began to beat quickly in my chest.

Cheerful sleigh bells sounded when Autumn opened the door. I stepped inside the store my mother had owned, that now technically belonged to me, Ivy and Bran.

"Lavender, sage and rosemary..." I sighed. "It still smells the same."

I found myself smiling, really smiling for the first time in weeks as I walked in. The space had been reorganized and re-arranged— and I had expected that it would be. But hearing my steps echo as I walked across the wide planked pine floor made me feel nostalgic. The old brick walls, the chunky shelves filled with jars of herbs, and the big front counter hadn't changed. The atmosphere was welcoming, warm and somehow, it healed my heart a little.

Soft, instrumental holiday music played on the speakers, and the store sparkled from white fairy lights wrapped in pine roping. The lit garland swooped around the walls and added to the holiday atmosphere. Groupings of white potted poinsettias were arranged at the base of the checkout counter, and I spotted a small tree decorated with moon and sun shaped ornaments in the front window.

Aunt Faye was deep in discussion with a customer over tarot cards, and Ivy was behind the front counter measuring out dried herbs. A middle-aged woman with blonde highlighted hair stood behind the cash register and rang up another customer.

"That's Terry, our manager," Autumn nudged me. "Come on, I'll introduce you."

"In a minute," I said and wandered off to check out the bookshelves and a cozy seating area that had been arranged in front of the shelves. I glanced over at my twin, she stood wearing a long burgundy skirt with a draping black sweater. A trio of witchy silver pendants hung around her neck. They seemed to sparkle under the lights. Ivy studied me, as I did her, but she made no move to come over.

I felt a tug on my solar plexus. It was Ivy using our psychic connection to communicate. She'd done that often when I'd first moved to Kansas City, then less and less as I'd learned how to block her out.

I'm surprised to see you. Ivy's voice sounded clearly through our connection.

I hope it's okay that I'm here. I sent back.

I felt Ivy flinch. *Why wouldn't it be? It's your shop as much as mine and Bran's.*

I set my shopping bags down on the floor, pulled off my gloves, and tucked them in my pocket. *I wasn't sure you would want me in here.*

Ivy narrowed her eyes and stepped out from around the counter. *What's that supposed to mean?* She sent the message and moved directly towards me.

"We should talk," I said out loud as she approached. "I'd hoped to catch you this morning."

"I had to take Nathan to the airport," Ivy said, crossing her arms.

"Yeah. Aunt Faye told me." I shifted my feet and tried again. "I was wondering if you could talk to me privately, for a few minutes? I have some things I need to say to you."

"I'm sort of working right now," Ivy reminded me.

"I can cover for you, Ivy." Autumn said, peeling out of her coat. "Why don't you girls use the office."

"Come on then," Ivy grabbed my coat sleeve and tugged me towards the back room and our mother's old office.

I'd barely cleared the door when Ivy's telekinesis shut it smartly behind us.

"It's different in here," I said, taking in the new wall color, and a little water cooler in the corner. There was a different desk and computer, but I recognized most of the supply catalogues. "It doesn't feel the same any longer. The vibes are different."

"Probably because Terry uses the office for the most part now." Ivy pointed at the desk chair and her years of control over her gift had the chair rolling out, and stopping in front of me. "Sit down," she said. "You don't look well."

"I'll sit only because I want to," I said, and sat. "Not because *you* told me to."

"What's wrong with you?" Ivy asked.

I twisted my hands in my lap. "I'm a little run down. It's stress from transferring schools and moving home, that's all."

Ivy leaned over and studied my face. "Frankly, you look like crap. You're too pale and I've never seen you so skinny."

Even though it was true, it still stung to hear. "Thanks," I said, wryly.

"Holly, are you sick?" Ivy demanded.

I raised my eyes to meet hers. "No. I'm not sick."

"Are you in trouble?"

I tried not to react to the unintended double entendre. "No, I haven't broken any laws. Don't be so dramatic."

"I have this gut hunch..." Ivy trailed off as she considered me. "And it's screaming at me right now. I *know* that you're hiding something."

"If I told you I wasn't ready to talk about it quite yet, would you let it go?" Our eyes locked and our gazes held.

Ivy blinked first. "Well why *did* you want to talk to me then?"

"So I could apologize to you." I wanted to reach out to her badly, but didn't know if she would accept it.

"I'm sorry I cut myself off from you and from the rest of the family."

Ivy didn't respond. She sat back on the edge of the desk and studied me.

I clasped my hands in my lap. "You were right, I was *selfish*. I moved away, became a different person, tried to pretend that William's Ford and the legacy of magick didn't exist. In the process, I hurt all of the people that I love, and I've hurt you most of all." I continued to look her in the eye. "I'm sorry for that."

"Did it ever occur to you," Ivy began, "that while you were hiding and pretending to be someone else, that you were actually hurting yourself in the process?"

"Not until very recently," I admitted.

"Well, at least you're being honest." Ivy's lips curved up, but her eyes were serious.

"I've worked very hard to gain control of my emotions and my powers while I was away."

"Control?" Ivy arched a brow. "I don't think it's *control* that you've gained at all. You simply shut off your more volatile feelings and your magick. Any strong emotion, love, lust, anger... You can't turn that off indefinitely. Eventually it's going to break away from you."

"You don't understand." I shook my head. "It can't *break away* from me ever again." I gripped the arms of the desk chair, and tried like hell to hold onto my rising temper. "The one time when I totally lost control— the dark took me over, Ivy. It sucked me in and I *reveled* in it!"

The lights above us began to flicker. "Easy," Ivy said, reaching for my hand. "Holly, calm down."

"I'm trying," I gritted out.

Like water leaking out of cracks in a vase, my magick rushed towards the weakest areas of my aura hoping to escape. I could feel the blood rush to my face as the strain of the past few weeks finally caught up with me. Everything whirled up and threatened to choke me.

Even as the adrenalin kicked in and the urge to let go rushed through me, I fought hard to not lose control. The water inside the cooler began to bubble and swirl. I focused on it and bore down. *No, no, no!* I thought. Sweat began to roll down my back from the physical effort it took to *not* tap into my favorite element, and to simultaneously rein in my emotions and magick.

The pencil cup tipped over on the desk, and a catalogue fell off a shelf. Ivy's green eyes were intense as she got up in my face. "See? This is what happens when you bottle up your emotions and your powers. It doesn't help that you're in a small, enclosed area either."

"Why's that?" I asked a little desperately.

"Because all that magick has to go *somewhere*. If you were outside, your powers wouldn't have as many small inanimate objects to pick on." She placed her hands on top of mine. "This happened the day you announced you were moving away to KC, too. Don't you remember? We were in Autumn's room with the door closed."

"I haven't had any random issues with telekinesis since that day," I said through my teeth. "I've been in plenty of small rooms since then."

"So what's the common factor?" Ivy said as if nothing unusual were occurring.

"You!" I snapped. "You always could push my buttons."

Ivy ignored the gurgling of the water cooler, and little crashes in the office. "Sure, I'm *one* of them... but the other factor is your own emotional distress. The emotions that you've squashed down are so strong, that even a non-empath could feel them boiling up." She knelt down in front of me. "Let me help you," she said, placing her hands over mine.

"I don't need your —" My words cut off as she pushed her own magick into me.

A bright sunny yellow color seemed to shoot straight up both my arms and then bloom in the center of my chest. It felt like a bright yellow rose had opened in my solar plexus.

"Breathe with me," Ivy suggested.

I attempted to synch my breathing with hers. As we inhaled and exhaled together, my chest muscles began to loosen, and my heart rate returned to a more normal pace. I stared into my twin sister's eyes and felt her power— stronger and more refined than I'd ever experienced.

The water cooler in the corner fell silent. The lights stopped their frantic flashing, and to my relief nothing else fell over. The onslaught of negative emotions I'd fought to control... simply fizzled out.

I drew in a shaky breath. "When did you learn to do that?"

Ivy patted my hands. "I've had to learn to work magick as a solitary Witch, while you've been away." She rose to her feet. "It wasn't easy for me either. I had my own demons to face, my own fears to confront... but I finally figured out a few things."

I consciously lessened my grip on the arms of the chairs. I deliberately drew in a deep breath, held it for a count of four, and blew it out in a controlled stream. "I'm sorry about all of this." I gestured to the no longer tidy office. "I'm very grateful that you were here to help me."

"I grew up with telekinesis." Ivy said, righting the pencil cup. "I've had all my life to work on control. *You* on the other hand didn't have it present itself until a few years ago. It's not a coincidence that PK pops up on you when you're trying to block or restrain yourself from experiencing your more negative emotions."

"PK?"

"PK is short for Psychokinesis— the official or scientific term for telekinesis."

"When did you get so smart?"

"Ha!" Ivy smirked at me and replaced the fallen catalogue. "I've always been smart. Plus I learned all this from Dr. Meyer at the university. He's been working privately with both Autumn and me."

"Whoa," I said. "Is that safe? Can you trust him?"

"Relax, Holly." Ivy brushed at her hair. "It's a long story, I'll tell you about it sometime. But right now you need to chill out. Your face is awfully red, I mean it's an improvement from the dead white you had going on when you first walked in the shop... but still."

It was mortifying. *Two and a half years of working on gaining control, and it was lost within twenty-four hours of my returning to William's Ford.* I dropped my eyes to my lap, drew in a shaky breath and to my humiliation, tears began to roll down my face.

"Hey," Ivy said, and then waited until I looked up to meet her eyes. "There is no shame in leaning on your family. We love you."

I sniffled and wiped away the tears. "Okay."

Ivy held out a hand and pulled me to my feet. I wobbled a second and then was steady. "Sheesh," I said. "I'm barely home, and I already fell off the wagon."

"Magick isn't a drug, Holly." My sister's green eyes seemed to blaze. "You're treating it like some sort of addiction is a big part of your problem."

"I don't do that—" I began and then shut my mouth as realization dawned. *That was exactly what I'd been doing. Treating magick like it was a drug.* I considered her as she stood in front of me. We were so different from each other. Even though we were twins, we didn't resemble each other in any physical way. I'd been the empath, Ivy was the intuitive. I'd always been the nurturer, Ivy had always been the rebel.

Funny, how our roles had changed.

She reached out and tugged on a wayward curl of my hair. "I wish I had all of the answers for you, Sis. But you're going to have to work this issue out for yourself."

"I know." I shoved some of my hair behind my ear. "Do you accept my apology?"

Ivy nodded. "I do."

"I want you to know that I'm going to work hard to be a better sister, and to earn your trust back."

"I've always trusted you Holly." Ivy rested her hand on my shoulder. "What you need to do is learn to trust *yourself* a little more."

CHAPTER THREE

The holidays seemed to pass in a colorful, noisy, and wonderful rush. Day by day I began to feel a little more 'back to normal'. My appetite slowly returned, and I started to catch up on my sleep. Every once in a while, I had rough moments thinking about the baby I'd lost, but I tried to tell myself that everything happened for a reason.

Ivy and I worked at reconnecting as sisters. She was busy with her job at *Enchantments* and with her new boyfriend, Nathan Pogue, but we managed to spend some quality time together over winter break. She shared with me her recent adventures on campus; the haunting she and Cypress had experienced, and the entity she had battled with and finally bound to its grave. When she told me our mom had contacted her from the other side, I cried.

I told her about my experiences since I'd moved back to the manor with the roses, and Ivy had suggested that I keep a journal and wait and see if Grandma Rose appeared to me. When I pointed out that I had no talent for seeing ghosts, Ivy had responded with, "Sometimes it's up to the ghost whether or not you see them, instead of the other way around."

I guessed she'd know, as she'd had an awful lot of ghostly encounters herself in the past at the dormitory.

I finally met Nathan Pogue, and was impressed. He was handsome, even though he seemed a little more serious than the sort of guy I would have figured Ivy would have gone for. But they were totally adorable together.

It was easier re-connecting with Bran. But then, sharing the manor with him and his family gave us more to talk about. Lexie hadn't changed, and little Morgan gave his parents a run for their money. Seems the family had all assumed I'd had a bad breakup while I'd been in KC and that was what had encouraged my decision to move back. I let them think that— as it was partially true.

But I hadn't told anyone else the real reason I'd come home.

Autumn stayed true to her word and kept my secret. I, in turn, tried to show her my appreciation by being supportive when Rene made the permanent move up to Chicago.

Before I knew it, the winter break was over and I was starting my new semester as a student at William's Ford University. Ivy and Cypress had moved back to their now ghost-free dorm, Crowly Hall. The first time

I'd met up with them on campus for lunch, Cypress had taken one look at me, jumped into my arms and given me a hug. It was as if the years we'd gone without seeing each other had never happened. Her friendship and generosity was more than I deserved, and I was grateful for it. I fell back into the routine of classes and was content to commute across town.

On my second week of classes I came home one blustery and cold Friday afternoon, let myself into the manor, dropped my backpack on the potting room counter, and shed my outer gear. I hung my coat on one of the pegs by the door that led into the kitchen, unwrapped my scarf from around my neck and listened for a moment to the quiet.

Now that the holiday decorations were down, the house seemed calmer, almost softer somehow. I picked up my backpack and scanned the kitchen. "Anybody home?" I called out, tugging on the hem of my soft pink cardigan. No one answered and I realized I was alone in the manor. My shoulders dropped in relief.

Merlin came trotting in and sat beside his food bowl. He meowed long and loud.

"Are you a poor, starving, kitty?" I asked him and went to the old crock we used for his cat food. I lifted up the wooden lid and the cat rubbed against my ankle. This was the first time Merlin had showed me any affection since I moved back in December.

I wanted to reach down and pet him, but figured I shouldn't push my luck. I added a scoop of kibble to his bowl, and he chowed down. Deciding this momentous occasion called for something special, I went to the fridge and decided to splurge and make myself some hot chocolate from scratch.

Once the hot chocolate was prepared I went to the family room, with the intention of snuggling on the couch. I saw that the fireplace was laid and ready for a fire so I took down a long fireplace match and lit it, happy at how the flames caught so quickly. I sat on the sofa, kicked my shoes off, stretched out my legs and watched the flames in the hearth.

Perhaps it was the fire, or the hot chocolate I'd finished, or maybe I was simply relaxed for the first time in a long time. I set my mug aside, slid down farther on the couch, crossed my legs and shut my eyes. *Only for a minute or two,* I told myself.

The next thing I knew something warm, furry and purring was sprawled across me. I discovered that Merlin had taken advantage of my afternoon nap by the fire and had made himself at home. His head rested on my chest, while one paw was stretched out across my neck. Merlin purred away, sound asleep. The fact that the cat had finally decided to be around me, let alone sleep on me, made me grin from ear to ear. Happy and content, I shut my eyes and drifted off again.

The next thing I knew, a small hand poked me in the shoulder. I cracked one eye open and discovered Morgan was standing over me.

"Holly is asleep," he attempted to whisper in his

toddler voice.

"Morgan John, let her sleep," I heard Bran say. "Come on, leave her be."

"Kitty is sleeping too," Morgan said, and before I could decide what to say or do, my nephew climbed up on the couch and flopped down.

"Ooof!" I said as Morgan landed on my upper body, and the cat woke up with a grumble. Merlin rolled over and Morgan made himself at home.

"Hi Holly." Morgan laid his head on my shoulder.

"Hi there MJ," I said. The toddler and I were still getting to know each other. He'd been slowly warming up to me, but like the cat, he'd never plopped himself on top of me so casually before.

"Ivy's at school," Morgan announced.

I yawned. "Ah, yeah she is."

"She's with Cy at crow hall." He reached over and played with my hair.

Crowly Hall, I realized.

"Sorry about the preschooler attack," Bran said from the doorway.

"No worries." I waved his concern away.

"Were you sleeping?" Morgan wanted to know.

"I was taking a cat nap."

The words had Morgan giggling. "The kitty sleeps on my bed sometimes."

"He does?" I asked, my voice sounding amazed.

"Uh huh." Morgan's blue eyes were solemn. "I have a big boy bed now."

"Well you're getting pretty big," I said.

Morgan sat up with a bounce. "You wanna come see my room?"

"Sure," I answered, rolling to my feet with Morgan in my arms. The move had him laughing. I set him down and Merlin reclaimed the warm spot on the couch.

"Come on!" Morgan grabbed my hand, and I found myself being taken to my nephew's room where he personally introduced me to all of his toys.

I spent an hour sitting on the floor with Morgan and "seeing" all of his trucks, stuffed animals and assorted action figures. His room had changed little since he'd been an infant. The room was still decorated in neutral tones of buff, cream, and tan. The new addition of a twin size bed with a navy and tan spread was tucked next to the back turret.

Merlin strolled into the room and sat next to the tower of blocks I'd built for Morgan. He lifted one white-tipped paw towards the blocks.

"Merlin," I said, narrowing my eyes at the clever familiar. "Be nice."

Merlin tucked his tail around his body and left the blocks alone. For the moment.

Autumn appeared in the doorway. "Hey guys, it's time for dinner."

"Autumn!" Morgan smiled.

"Hey ya, MJ," she said, leaning against the door in jeans and a black sweater. "Are you hungry?"

Morgan scrambled out of his room and I rose to follow.

They were waiting for me at the second floor landing, and when my nephew held out his hand, I took it.

He gave my hand a squeeze. "Are you still sad?" he asked me.

I started to respond automatically, but those big blue eyes simply slayed me. *There was some psychic ability there,* I realized as our eyes held. *It was young and mostly untried... but it was starting to grow as Morgan did.*

"I'm feeling happier," I finally said, staying where I was at the top of the stairs.

Autumn raised an eyebrow and waited silently a few steps down from us.

Morgan swung my hand. "When the new baby comes will it make you sad, Holly?"

The breath simply left my body. I sat shakily down on the top step and tried to compose myself. He'd said that so matter-of-factly that I tried to respond in kind. But, it took me a few moments to pull myself together.

Autumn bent down to the little boy's level. "What 'new baby' are you talking about, Morgan?" she asked gently.

"Mommy's new baby." He said and wiggled in to sit beside me on the step. He heaved a sigh and leaned against my arm. "That baby can't have any of my toys," he grumbled.

Autumn, started to chuckle. "Oh boy," she said,

sitting on the steps. In silent support she rested a hand on my leg.

"Lexie and Bran haven't made any announcements as of yet." I said to her.

"That's true," Autumn agreed, "However, our boy here carries not only the Bishop's legacy, but through his mother— the Proctor's magickal lineage as well.

"How do you know that a baby is coming?" I asked Morgan.

"I saw the baby in my room." Morgan insisted, reaching up to run his little fingers through a curling cable of my hair.

"Were you sleeping when you saw the baby, or were you awake?" I asked him.

Morgan frowned over my question. I wondered if a three year old would understand, but he surprised me again. "I heard a baby cryin' and I went to see. The baby was in my room. Then I got a-scared and woke up."

Precognitive dream, I decided, and fought to keep my expression bland. I put my arm around the little boy and dropped a kiss on the top of his head. "Did you see anything else?"

"There were dolls in my room," he whispered, his eyes wide.

My lips started to twitch. "I guess that was scary."

"And my room was *this* color," he said in a conspirator's whisper, and pointed at my cardigan.

"Pink," Autumn said.

"Uh-huh," Morgan nodded his head in agreement.

"Hey!" Lexie called up the stairs. "Are you guys coming, or what?"

"On our way!" Autumn called back.

"I'm hungry!" Morgan grinned at me.

"Dinner's gonna be interesting tonight," Autumn predicted, patting my leg.

"That's for sure." I managed.

"Gimme a ride!" Morgan wrapped his arms around my neck and I stood up, with an assist from Autumn, to carry him piggy-back style down the stairs. I added an extra bounce by jumping off the bottom step into the kitchen.

Hearing him chortle in delight more than made up for the fact that he almost cut off my air from holding on so tightly to my throat.

Bran took Morgan from me to settle him into his toddler booster seat. Autumn walked over to take her usual place. Aunt Faye was at the head of the table. Lexie and Bran sat across from Autumn, with Morgan sandwiched between them.

I eased down next to my cousin and bit back a laugh when she winked at me. *Here we go,* I thought and watched Bran and Lexie carefully.

"So," Autumn began. "MJ here—"

"Morgan John," Lexie and Bran corrected in unison.

"Was telling me and Holly," Autumn continued smoothly as if she hadn't been interrupted. "That he is — under no circumstances— going to share his toys with the new baby."

Lexie's eyes went large in her face and Bran froze.

Autumn leaned her elbows on the table. "Do you two have anything to say to that?"

Aunt Faye narrowed her eyes at everyone. "What's this?"

Lexie and Bran both looked down at their son, who tipped his head back and smiled innocently up at his parents.

"Don't want no dolls in my room," Morgan said, and I couldn't help but laugh at his parents' shocked expressions.

"No dolls in your—" Lexie threw back her head and laughed loud and long.

Bran shook his head and began to laugh as well. "I swear," he said. "I didn't say a word. Not to anyone."

Lexie wiped her eyes. "I was going to tell everyone next week, after I made it through my first trimester."

"How far along are you, dear?" Aunt Faye wanted to know.

"A little shy of twelve weeks," Lexie said.

"We are due in late July," Bran reached over and took Lexie's hand.

"Again?" Aunt Faye grinned. "That puts you close to Morgan's birthday."

Morgan crossed his arms over his chest. His bottom lip was out and he was pouting. "No. *My* birthday." he said.

"What?" Lexie said. "What'd you say baby?"

Morgan turned his face away from Lexie.

"I don't understand," Bran said. "How did Morgan know?"

"He told me that he saw a baby in his room," I said, and the room fell to silence.

Leaving out the part about Morgan wondering if the new baby would make me sad, I filled in the family on the conversation with Morgan.

"Precognitive dreaming at three years old..." Bran stared down at his son in wonder.

"Well," Aunt Faye began, "he is a Bishop."

"*And* a Proctor," Lexie added, dropping a kiss on her son's nose. "Do you have anything else you want to tell me Morgan John?"

"Don't like pink," Morgan said.

Lexie sighed. "We *were* wanting to be surprised with the baby's gender this time around too..."

Bran pressed a kiss to the back of his wife's hand. "I think that may be a foregone conclusion at this point."

"Aw jeez!" Lexie blew out a breath. "Now I'm going to have to know the baby's gender, as soon as possible... just to see if he's right or not."

After dinner was over and the kitchen cleaned up, I found myself sitting in my cousin's room. The walls were still the pretty robin's egg blue color, mom had painted it before Autumn had come to live with us, and now there were other touches as well. The sort that made the room more hers. The black and white bedspread was heaped with pillows in shades of azure and teal. A bold area rug covered most of the hardwood floors, and a collection of framed family photos were crowded across the mantle in the bedroom.

I leaned back against the pile of pillows at the top of her bed. "Stop worrying," I said.

Autumn swiveled towards me from her computer chair at her desk. "What do you mean?"

"I can feel you worrying. You still project your feelings when you are stressed."

"Do not," Autumn said.

"Do too."

Autumn made a face at me, and then switched her attention back to her computer. "Actually Blondie, I *am* nervous, but not for the reason you might think."

"Oh yeah?"

"Yeah, it seems like the universe is giving me a boot in the ass towards something I've been waffling on for a while... And now that we know Bran and Lexie are expanding their family, we are going to be one room short here at the manor."

"Oh." I blew a curl away from my eyes. "I hadn't thought that far ahead, but you're right."

"I'd like your opinion on something," Autumn said. "As long as you keep it between us two for the time being."

I sat up and swung my legs over the side of the bed. "Sure, what's up?"

"Come look at this," Autumn said, gesturing towards her computer.

"Is that a real estate website?" My stomach dropped. *Had she decided to relocate to Chicago to be with Rene after all?*

"I've been thinking about getting my own place, here in William's Ford." Autumn said.

"Really?" Excited and relieved, I scooted over to take a closer look.

"Yeah. There was some money that came to me, when my father's old business partner sold the nursery they'd owned. I've been talking to Aunt Faye for the last few weeks about maybe buying a house. Something small, but something that would be mine."

"Aunt Faye has a good head for investments and for business," I said.

"Yeah she does. Anyway, the older couple, next door?" Autumn hooked her thumb to the left. "They're going to put their house on the market next month. They've decided to get away from the cold winters, and to move closer to their grandchildren."

"The Greene's house right next door?" I asked. "Autumn, that'd be perfect!"

"I think so too. I'd still be close by... but I'd have my own place."

I went to her bedroom window and tugged the curtains back to view the house along the left side of ours. "It's always been such a pretty cottage," I said, admiring the bright yellow paint and white trim.

"I only hope I can afford it." Autumn ran a hand through her hair. "Technically the *cottage* you're looking at is a 1920s bungalow, and that Craftsman style of home doesn't come cheap."

"Does it need work?" I asked her.

"It does. The real estate agent took some pictures." Autumn stood and pointed to the computer screen. "If you'd like to see."

I rushed over. "Of course I want to see!" I plopped myself down at her desk.

Autumn reached past my shoulder and clicked on a file she'd saved to her desktop. "It's a three bedroom, one bath house," Autumn explained, grinning at my enthusiasm.

Her excitement was contagious. I clicked on the first photo of the living room. "Ooh, is the mantle original?"

"It is. After two more photos you'll see a large dining room and a small outdated kitchen."

"Oh, Okay." I clicked forward through the photos.

Autumn pointed at the screen. "I'm thinking, eventually, I could lose the dining room, expand the kitchen and—"

"Add another bathroom," I said.

"Exactly." Autumn nodded in agreement.

I clicked on the upper level bedroom photos next. "By the Goddess!" I cringed over the current paint colors. "What was Mrs. Greene thinking painting the walls that color?"

Autumn laughed. "The good news is that the hardwood floors in the bungalow are still in excellent shape, and well... paint is cheap."

"I'm buying you a couple gallons as a house warming present, and painting the master bedroom walls myself," I said.

"Holly, I don't have the house yet," Autumn reminded me.

"Is that *wallpaper* in the bathroom?" I scowled at the photo. "That's got to go." I glared when I heard Autumn chuckle. "What?" I asked.

"I'm really happy to see you so enthusiastic, and acting like yourself again."

I smiled back. "I'm so happy for you."

"Thanks, I'm hoping that between Aunt Faye's wheeling and dealing, and our realtor, that they can land me a good price."

I stood up and gave my cousin a hug. "I may not be a Seer like you, or an intuitive like Ivy, but I have a feeling, that cute little yellow house with its tiny kitchen and horrible wall color in the upper level will be yours. Sooner than you think."

Autumn hugged me back. "I hope so. I should know something soon."

"In the meantime we could go look at paint swatches at the hardware store tomorrow afternoon. Just for fun."

Autumn laughed. "Really? I wanted to before, but was afraid I'd jinx myself somehow."

I brushed that aside. "Don't be silly. Magick doesn't work that way."

"Okay, if you're sure you want to…"

I raised my eyebrows at her. "We could look at

bathroom fixtures, towel rods, and new cabinet drawer pulls while we're there..."

"Simply to get an idea of price— and so forth," Autumn said.

"I've always thought that ugly front porch light on the Greene's house should be replaced anyway," I said.

She went to look out the window at the bungalow to check it out. "It's not even period correct for architecture of the home." Autumn sounded somewhat horrified over the fixture, and I knew that she was actually, completely sincere. "The least they could have done was get something Craftsman inspired," she muttered to herself.

"Personally, I am outraged." I said deadpan.

"I know, right?"

I didn't bother to respond. Instead I tucked my hands in my pockets and grinned at my cousin while she stood dreaming over the possibilities next door.

***

The weather warmed up a bit and I took advantage of the clear winter day and popped by *Obscura Antiques*, the next morning. I stopped in my tracks when I noticed a 'Help Wanted" sign in the window.

Excitement surged through me. Suddenly relieved that I'd worn nice jeans and my good winter coat, I checked my reflection in the store window, decided I was presentable enough, and reached for the door. Bells above my head chimed as I entered the store.

"Let me know if I can help you with anything," a man's voice drifted from the back of the store.

"Thank you," I called back.

Pleased to have the shop to myself, I took my time and walked slowly up and down the aisles. The shop was spacious and cleverly arranged into little vignettes, and I sighed over some Jadeite on display in a white Hoosier cabinet, and then picked up an old Ball jar that was a lovely shade of soft blue.

The price was pretty decent, and I tucked the large jar in the crook of my arm. I spent a pleasant hour roaming through the shop and scouting out where I soon hoped to be working. I had a good feeling about the place. I psyched myself up, discretely powdered my nose, brushed a few stray curls out of my face, and made my way casually to the front counter to pay for my purchase, and hopefully talk to the manager.

Before I made it to the counter, a little girl came barreling towards me.

"Gracie, you come back here!" A man was in hot pursuit of the girl, and she was laughing and running down the main aisle of the shop as fast as her little legs could carry her. She was several feet ahead of him, and running unsteadily towards a display of china.

My heart lurched. *She could get seriously hurt...*

"Gracie, stop!" His voice was urgent.

I knew the man would never catch her in time, and before she could toddle headfirst into the display, I leaned out, grabbed her by the back of her denim overalls, and hoisted her off the ground. "Gotcha," I said.

"Hi!" she smiled at me, unfazed by her mid-air and captive status.

"Hi cutie." I couldn't help but grin at the short brown pigtails, and the mischief in those blue eyes.

"Airplane!" she yelled. "Play airplane!"

"How about I take you to your daddy, instead?"

"No Daddy, Unca Rik," she said.

I shifted towards the man and focused on him. My first thought was: *Oh wow.* My second was: *I had no business even looking.*

I judged him to be in his mid to late twenties. His hair was light brown, and short. The sides were a medium length and the top was full, tousled and casually combed over. A pair of startlingly blue eyes regarded me from behind a pair of classic, black frame glasses. He had a medium stubble beard, and when he smiled, I felt a little hitch in my chest.

"Did you lose something?" I asked him, holding out the toddler.

The little girl began to belly laugh as I held her up in the air with one hand.

"Thank you," the man said, taking her from me. "My sister would kill me if she broke something." He hitched the girl on his denim-clad hip, and she tipped her head over, sending the man a devastating smile. With his soft plaid shirt, jeans and boots he put me immediately in mind of a cowboy.

"Airplane!" she pleaded.

"You little demon," he said to the girl affectionately.

A second girl, who appeared to be around five years old, peeked out from around the front counter. "She got away. Sorry, Uncle Erik,"

He walked to her and rubbed his hand over her shoulder. "It wasn't your fault Gabby."

I set the jar on the counter. "Looks like you have your hands full." I sent the trio a friendly smile.

The older girl went back around the counter. I spotted a child's size chair and a few coloring books on the back counter. She smiled shyly at me. "Do you shoot a bow?"

"What?" I asked.

She pointed to my hair. "Are you Merida?"

I rolled my eyes up to my curls, "Oh." I got it. *The Scottish, Disney princess with the wild red curly hair.* "No. Sorry," I said, smiling down at her. "Actually, my name is Holly."

"I'm Gabby, that's my sister Gracie." She pointed to the man. "This is our uncle."

"I'm Erik," he said, and moved behind the counter with the girls. Keeping the little one on his hip, he competently rang up my purchase.

While he did that, Gabby took out a piece of newspaper and began to wrap the jar up. "You have quite the assistant," I said to Erik.

"Gabby's the boss around here," he said, in a stage

whisper.

Mommy and Daddy are the bosses of us," Gabby said, as she pulled open a plastic shopping bag and put the jar inside.

"I see." I tried to keep from smiling at her matter-of-fact tone.

"My sister is on maternity leave." Erik took the bag from his niece and passed it to me. "She had a doctor's appointment today, so my brother-in-law took her, and I got drafted to hold down the fort and monster-sit."

Gabby nudged her uncle in the thigh. "Here, you forgot to give her the receipt." She held it up.

Erik took it from Gabby and handed it to me. "See what I mean?" His dark, arched eyebrows went up, and I smiled at how remarkably expressive they were.

I tucked the receipt in my bag. "Well, it's a good thing she's here to keep things under control."

I supposed I would have to wait until the parents came back to ask about the job. But as Gracie bounced on Erik's hip, I felt a little inner nudge. Not magick, but something... or someone familiar. *You are in the right place at the right time.*

The words rolled through my mind, making me wonder, if somehow, Mom was watching over me from the other side. Unlike my cousin and my twin, I'd had no contact with my mother's spirit after her passing, at least not yet. But something was pushing me.

I took a deep breath and went for it. "Well Gabby, since you seem to be the boss around here today, maybe

I should talk to you about that help wanted sign you have in the window."

Erik chuckled, but before he could do or say anything. Gabby pulled a piece of paper out from under the counter.

"Dad says you're supposed to fill this out." She handed me an application.

CHAPTER FOUR

I suppose I had made a good impression on the little girl. I was called in for an interview with Gary and Ginny Chandler, the owners of the store, the following Monday afternoon. After a brief interview where we talked about my experience working at Enchantments and my step-mother's antique store in Iowa, I became the newest employee of *Obscura Antiques*. After a few days of training, I found myself behind the counter, surrounded by beautiful and interesting items filled with history.

Outside the store's front windows it was cold and gloomy. February had arrived and Valentine's Day was right around the corner. The jewelry case that was on the right of the counter was filled with sparkly pendants, rings, and brooches. Some were set with real stones, and others were costume. At this time of year the rings were center stage in case a bride-to-be was of the sentimental heirloom type. The display shelves behind the front counter featured a lot of red, pink and lace at the moment. A china tea set in pale pink decorated with rosebuds was arranged with some depression-era pink glassware. On the top shelf, an old cherub statue with a weathered patina held court and was surrounded by framed vintage Valentine's Day cards.

In the past couple of weeks, Ginny had started coming in for a few hours in the afternoons— while Gary stayed home with Gabby and Gracie. Ginny claimed she needed to get out of the house if only to reclaim what little was left of her sanity.

The Five G's as I'd started to think of them— since everyone's first name began with a G— were a charming family, and I thoroughly enjoyed working for the Chandlers.

I had just finished with a phone call from the university's theater group. Ginny came out from the back room with her new son snuggled against her chest in an ingenious baby carrier. It was like a big scarf, cleverly arranged around the two of them, that comfortably supported the baby so he was facing his mother, and it left her hands free.

"Ginny, I've got that list from the costume and prop departments at the university."

"What are they looking for this time?" Ginny asked as she pushed an old grocery cart loaded with red and rose colored Fiesta ware.

I waved the list. "Hats, ladies dress coats, costume jewelry and a rotary telephone."

She steered the cart along. "Happy hunting."

"I think a few of the items might be in the consignment area," I said. "I'll go check it out. See what I can pull for the theater's costume assistant to come and look at."

"Thanks, Holly." Ginny smiled. "I'm going to go and re-arrange that Hoosier cabinet's display."

"Leave this to me." I took my list and smoothed my tunic length gray sweater down over my hips. It was edged with a lace flounce and appealed to my girly side. Today I'd worn the sweater with black jeans, and I was delighted that my pants fit me again. It was nice having my clothes stay in place instead of sliding down my backside. I walked over to the far right side of the store where the consignment booth spaces were. One of the booths in particular was filled with vintage clothing and costume jewelry.

A short time later, I was making my way back to the front counter. Several ladies hats and more accessories were stacked on top of four coats I had draped over my arms. Ginny was sitting behind the front desk, speaking in her cell phone. Her tone was low, but as I approached, I could hear the frustration in her voice.

"For god's sakes, Mom!" she said. "You need to talk to Erik... That girl is selfish, bad-mannered, and spoiled. He can't still be thinking of going through with the wedding can he?"

I stopped and ducked behind a display, blew at the curls that seemed determined to hang in my eyes, and listened. I knew it was rude, but I was curious. Erik McBriar— Ginny's brother, was the man I'd met the day I filled out the application. And he was engaged. From the comments I'd heard over the past few weeks, I'd gathered that the wedding was scheduled for sometime in the coming fall months.

Now, I realized not everyone in the family was thrilled with the upcoming nuptials.

"I'm telling you, it won't last." Ginny sighed, loudly. "She's going to break his heart *and* try and take him for every penny he has."

From where I stood hidden behind a tall wooden bookshelf, I could feel Ginny's distress. The negative emotions rolled out and permeated the atmosphere. *Anger, stress, mistrust,* and to my shock, *loathing.* This wasn't a catty type of 'that girl isn't good enough for my little brother', thing. She was unhappy, and genuinely concerned for her brother.

Ginny McBriar-Chandler was an easy going woman, cheerful and charming to the customers, a loving and devoted mother to her children, and was obviously smitten with her husband. The conversation and the destructive sentiments flooding the store were completely out of character to the woman I'd begun to know.

If she keeps up that level of anger and anxiety, it's going to affect the baby, I thought.

And sure enough, the baby began to fuss.

"I know, mom," Ginny argued in the phone. "But

you mark my words... they won't last any longer than a year. That is unless she gets pregnant, and tries to trap him."

Unless she gets pregnant... tries to trap him... At her words, I flinched hard enough that I bobbled the hats I was carrying.

"Damn it," I swore under my breath, and scrambled for the items I'd stacked up in my arms. After a quick shuffle, I managed to hang on to all of them. To my horror, I saw the old leather books next to me were beginning to quiver on their shelf. One hardback slid forward, and another fell over. *Calm. I* thought a little desperately, as my telekinesis fought to break free. *Stay calm.* I reminded myself. *Do not react to her careless choice of words. Don't take it personally.*

I attempted to ground and center, hoping to reduce my chances of any more stray magick affecting my environment. Slowly, the books on the shelf stopped trembling, and while I had continued to struggle out of sight with my emotions and powers, Baby George went from fussing to wailing.

"Mom," Ginny said over the cries, "I've gotta go."

I couldn't stay hidden forever, and after my talk with Ivy I knew that staying cooped up in a little area was probably not my best idea. I set my jaw and stepped out into the main aisle of the store. Ginny never even noticed me as she had her hands full with the baby—who was red faced and shrieking. Determined to act normal, I marched forward and draped the items over the jewelry case. "Wow, somebody's mad." I said, trying to sound casual.

"I have no idea what set him off," Ginny said, trying to unwrap herself and the baby from the carrier. But Ginny was having a hard time getting herself and an angry, squirming baby free. To add to the chaos, the delivery-man arrived with a stack of boxes, the store phone began to ring, and a group of customers walked in.

The delivery guy wheeled his boxes up on a red dolly. "Kid's got a good set of lungs," he said cheerfully over the noise.

The baby's cries had cranked up to ear piercing, and it was a toss up as to what made me the most uncomfortable: The crying baby, or his mother's negative emotions regarding her future sister-in-law.

I didn't give myself too much time to think it over. Instead, I simply followed my gut. I reached out, took the infant gently under his arms, and lifted him free. I turned the baby, and cradled him in my arms. "George," I said firmly. "That's enough, now." I focused on his eyes and intentionally made an empathic link.

It had been a few years since I'd tried to initiate an empathic link with anyone. I didn't know if it would even work; but I felt the connection *click* home, and the baby stopped crying. He took a shuddering breath, waved his arms once, and settled.

Delighted that I hadn't completely lost my touch, I grinned. I heard a gasp, and glanced up to find that

Ginny, the delivery man, and the group of ladies were all staring at me.

"How in the world did you do that?" Ginny asked.

"Practice," I said, patting the baby's diaper covered bottom. I swayed slightly from side to side as I'd once done for Morgan when he'd been an infant.

"Girl's got a magic touch." The driver grinned and began to unload the boxes.

Buddy, you have no idea, I thought ruefully.

"Do you have kids?" Ginny asked, signing for the shipment.

Her words had my heart aching. "No. I don't, but when my nephew was an infant he would shout the walls down when he was hungry or wet." I smiled down at baby George as he'd begun to coo. "I've had a little practice calming a fussy baby."

"Do you mind holding him for a few more minutes?" Ginny asked, reaching for the still ringing phone.

"No, I don't mind." I stepped out from around the counter and approached the group of women who had stood gawking at the baby meltdown. "Ladies," I said calmly, "can George or I help you find anything today?"

As I expected, the women all gathered around the baby to admire him. One of them wearing a navy coat pointed at me. "You're Holly Bishop."

"Yes Ma'am." I nodded in reply.

"I know your Aunt Faye," she said. "I'm Sharon Waterman. We're both members of the Historical

Society."

"Nice to meet you." I steered them towards the sales floor, walked along with the group for a few moments, and then left them to shop.

I made my way to the back area of the store, and George lay contentedly in my arms. I hummed along to the oldies station that was playing on the store's stereo system, and the baby seemed relaxed. He waved his hands in the air and stretched his legs. I glanced around, saw that I was alone, and connected to the baby again. "Take a nap, George," I suggested.

The baby yawned, closed his eyes, and was out like a light. I smiled down at that sweet little face, thrilled that I'd successfully used my powers to help another, and then the loss of my own baby hit me unexpectedly, like a ton of bricks.

How long was this going to hurt? I shut my eyes and allowed the grief to roll past. I tried to conjure up that visualization of the yellow rose— the magick Ivy had shown me, and imagined it blooming in my solar plexus area. It helped a little. I was starting to feel more in control when a noise had me opening my eyes. I shifted my gaze to the right and discovered that a thick, glass vase had begun to shake.

I considered the vase as it wobbled dramatically back and forth where it was displayed on a farmhouse table. "Stop. Be still," I whispered. Conscious of the infant in my arms, I focused my powers for the first time with a calm intention— instead of fear or anger.

The vase ceased rocking back and forth, then finally rested and was still.

Wow. It actually worked! I blew out a relieved breath, and then a rush of new emotions hit me from behind. Someone *else* was in the back of the store. Perhaps it was from using my powers deliberately for the first time in years... but my senses were hyper alert at the moment, and I felt the person's emotions as surely as if they had jumped up and shouted them out loud.

Longing, confusion, and a reluctant admiration... I squared my shoulders and deliberately spun slowly around to confront the owner of those emotions.

Erik McBriar stood at the door to the back room, watching me. "Hi Holly."

When did he get here? I thought with alarm. "Hello Erik, how are you?" I forced myself to speak as calmly as possible. *How much had he seen?* I wondered, and then, *Why had I felt those emotions aimed at me— from him?* No matter how attractive he was— he was engaged, and I was swearing off men.

He tucked his hands in the pockets of his fleece-lined jacket. "Are you alright?" His voice was casual, but those cobalt blue eyes held mine, and his face gave away his concern.

"Yes, I'm fine." I shifted the baby slightly. "Just taking George for a stroll around the store." To cover the fib, I started walking towards the front desk.

Ginny had things under control as I returned. I

gently placed George in the little vintage bassinet that was behind the counter. He slept away and I covered his legs with a light blanket.

"Hey Ginny." Erik greeted his sister and leaned on the counter. "I'm here to pick up the stuff for the barn."

Ginny's smile for her brother lit up the front counter. "I've got it set aside," she told him, and then addressed me. "I don't know how you got the baby to quiet down so quickly," Ginny said, "but thank you."

"No problem." I waved it away. *Don't panic.* I told myself. *No one in the store is going to start pointing and shouting, 'Witch!' They're mundanes... they would never even consider the possibility of magick. Stay calm.*

The stack of items that I'd pulled for the theatre department still lay draped across the jewelry case, and they allowed me the perfect escape. "I'll go put these in the 'Hold' section in the back room." I scooped everything up, nodded politely to Erik and fled.

I nudged the back door open with my hip and went directly to the rack and shelves the Chandler's had designated for their hold section. I pulled several large tags out of an old wooden box and began to meticulously fill out the hold slips for the theater department.

By the time I'd done the third tag my hands had stopped shaking. I sat at the desk in the back room and rubbed my hands over my face. I wasn't sure whether I should congratulate myself for my successful use of positive magick, and controlling my telekinesis, *or* panic over the near miss of having Erik McBriar see me using my empathic powers to link with the baby.

Then there was the matter of those emotions he'd been broadcasting... Erik had been nothing but polite to me. I must have been wrong about those emotions I'd picked up on. Maybe he'd simply been thinking about his fiancée. The fiancée that his sister detested. Maybe that was where all his conflicting emotions came from...

That had to be it.

Satisfied that I had figured it out, I finished my task and made my way back to the front counter. Ginny would be heading home soon, and I would need to lock up the store within the hour.

Ginny had her self and the baby bundled up as I approached. "I'm going to leave for the day," she said, slinging her diaper bag over her shoulder. "Could you finish the Fiesta ware display for me?"

Determined to be cheerful, I nodded. "Sure, I'd love to. I'll get to work on it right away."

"Thanks, Holly." Ginny headed for the front door. "Oh," she called back. "Erik will be in and out. He's picking up a few pieces for the barn."

Why would he need antiques for a barn? I wondered, but shrugged it off and went to finish up the display. The store was currently empty of customers, and I considered the rose and red dishes still in the cart and began to arrange them on the Hoosier cabinet shelves. As I worked, I saw Erik carrying wooden chairs towards the front door. Back and forth he went several times singing along to *Bad Moon Rising*. His voice wasn't bad, and eventually my curiosity got the better of me.

My task finished, I rolled the empty cart towards the back room. "Do you need a hand?" I asked as he passed me.

"Nope, I've got it." He smiled and kept going.

I dropped off the empty cart and followed him to the front. "Mind if I ask why you need wooden chairs for a *barn*?"

"It's chairs for the reception tables," Erik said, and carried a pair outside.

"Reception tables?" I asked.

A heavy duty truck with a towing trailer was parked at the curb. I could see him through the front window placing chairs inside the trailer.

Around me more than a dozen mismatched antique chairs waited. The chairs were all wooden and in a variety of vintage styles, finishes and colors. I held open the door for him when he came back.

"Didn't Ginny tell you?" he asked, grabbing two more chairs at random.

"Tell me what?"

"God, usually no one is safe." Back out the door he went.

"Safe from what?" I asked as soon as he came back inside.

"Last year we renovated our old wooden barn on the

property, making it into a wedding venue." He grabbed more chairs.

"Really? That's cool," I said. *And financially smart.* I realized. The whole Rustic Chic thing was big for weddings these days. The McBriars were probably making bank branching out into the wedding venue business.

"Yeah, it was my mom's idea," Erik said. "The McBriar Farm has been a working farm in some capacity for three generations. My grandfather grew fruit, and my grandmother ran the farm stand. We still have their apple and peach orchards. In the 1970s Dad talked my grandpa into growing pumpkins commercially for the fall... next thing you know Dad and Grandpa started offering hayrides every October, taking families out to the field to pick their own pumpkins for Halloween, and that added to the business even more."

Oh, yeah... I remembered now. *The big farm outside of town.* "I remember going out to your farm to pick pumpkins when I was little," I said. "Do you guys still build the big maze out of hay bales?"

"We do." Erik leaned against the doorframe.

"And the scarecrow that talks to the kids?" I couldn't help but grin. "That always amazed me when I was little."

"Yeah, we rig it up with a walkie talkie and the employees take turns talking to the kids who are looking for a pumpkin," Erik explained.

"I didn't realize it was your family's farm. We always called it *The Halloween Farm*." The autumnal displays had been incredible to me as a child. With the hay bales, colorful chrysanthemums, cornstalks, a maze, and the pumpkins. There'd been hundreds of pumpkins in all shapes and sizes arranged, stacked and piled... everywhere.

"A lot of the kids in town still call it that." Erik's lips kicked up in a lopsided grin. He grabbed two more chairs and let himself out.

I picked up a chair and followed him. "Oh man, I loved that place at Halloween!" I said over the wind. I waited until he had climbed into the trailer and then passed him one of the chairs.

"You should go inside, get out of the wind," Erik said.

"I'm fine," I insisted, and went to fetch a few more chairs.

We worked together and the chairs were loaded quickly. I scampered inside and out of the cold while he locked up the trailer.

I blew on my hands to warm them. Erik knocked on the door and gave me a casual wave. He hopped in his big truck and left.

It was fifteen minutes until closing time, and I straightened up the front counter area. I decided to give the jewelry case a quick wipe down, it habitually was full of smudges and fingerprints by the end of the day from folks looking in the case. I spritzed glass cleaner and wiped the glass clean. I was kneeling down to clean the front when I noticed, on the bottom shelf, a crescent moon shaped jeweled pin.

"That looks like a similar design as Aunt Faye's garnet pin," I said to myself.

I went around, unlocked the case and took it out. The brooch was maybe three inches long, and soft purple stones were set in old gold. I flipped over the price tag and winced over the four hundred dollar price. As I held it, I felt a little tingle shoot from the palm of my hand all the way to my heart.

Now, where did you come from? I wondered. There was a time when I could have read the history of the jewelry using my clairtangency, but I hadn't practiced psychometry— the psychic reading of an object— in three years, and my skills were rusty. What I could pick up on was that the brooch was definitely owned at one time by a magickal practitioner. *Hmm, I wonder what Witch owned you?*

I studied the piece and counted thirteen amethysts in total, all oval cut. The largest stone was centered with the rest of the stones decreasing in size as they worked out to each point of the brooch. While the amethysts didn't appear to be high quality— their color was too pastel for that— it was a striking piece nonetheless.

I pulled out my cell phone, took a quick photo and texted it to Aunt Faye. I typed a quick message.

Looks like something you would wear. Has some interesting vibes coming from it. At Obscura $400 *bucks.*

I sent the message, replaced the brooch, re-locked the cabinet, and did my final walk through of the store. At five o'clock on the dot I locked the front door and started the end of the day paperwork.

I zipped up the change bag, locked it up in the safe in the back room, and flicked off the lights. I was buttoning up my coat when the store's phone began to ring. I picked up the extension in the back room. "Obscura Antiques," I said.

"Is Erik still there?' a woman asked.

"No," I told her. "I'm sorry, he left about twenty minutes ago."

"Is this Holly?" she asked.

"Yes it is. Can I help you?"

"Holly, this is Diane McBriar, Ginny's mother."

"Hello Mrs. McBriar."

"Do you know if Erik picked up two large metal milking cans when he got the chairs?"

I thought back. "I didn't see him take any milking cans, only chairs."

"They are large galvanized cans— a matching pair. Ginny told me they would've been in the back room."

I swung my gaze around and saw next to the holding shelves the milking cans she was looking for. "Hang on Mrs. McBriar." I walked over and checked the tags. 'McBriar Farms' was written on the tags. "I've got them both right here."

"Well, damn it," she said mildly. "Holly, can I ask

you a favor?"

"Sure."

"Do you think you could drive those out to the farm for me?"

"Ah..." I began.

"The florist is coming to consult with the Bride in an hour, and I need those to help stage an area for an upcoming wedding."

I had to admit, the idea of seeing their barn made into a wedding venue appealed to me. "Sure," I said. "I'm getting ready to leave now. I'll load them up in my car and drive out."

"Do you need directions?"

"Just an address," I told her.

While my car warmed up, I loaded up the milking cans. They weren't heavy, and I set them in the backseat and used the seatbelts to secure them. I sent a quick text to Aunt Faye informing her that I would be home later, and then plugged the address into my phone.

It wasn't a long drive to the McBriar Farm. Less than twenty minutes outside of William's Ford. It was relaxing driving through the dusky light, down a pretty stretch of winter-bare fields. I'd always loved the peace and quiet of the country no matter what the season, which was one of the reasons why I'd spent the past two summers in Iowa, on my father and stepmother's farm. Staying with them over the summer break had instilled an appreciation for how demanding farming was and what it took to run a successful one.

The GPS alerted me that my turn was in 500 feet. I slowed down and made the turn onto a gravel road. Up ahead, at the top of a gentle hill, I could see the McBriar farm. The old farmhouse was still painted white and was surrounded by a mixture of pines and deciduous trees. The house was at the top of a gentle slope, well back from the commercial area in the front. Off to the far left sat the barn. It appeared freshly painted in a classic dark red, and landscape lighting illuminated the front.

I slowly drove through the parking lot and took the first gravel lane to the left. I pulled up in front of the barn and parked my car next to three other vehicles. I noted Erik's truck and trailer were parked off to the side of the building.

I retrieved the milking cans by the handles and carried them towards the decorated double door of the barn. Large, glass paned wrought iron lanterns were used as outdoor lighting on either side of the double doors, and a garland of silk ivy was swaged above the main entrance as well. White tulle and tiny fairy lights twinkled above and around the barn doors, adding to the ambiance. A small bed of evergreen shrubs and boxwoods studded with solar lights ensured that the front of the barn was pretty no matter what the season.

"Nice," I said, and before I could knock, the door slid open.

The woman who stood there looked to be in her fifties. She was dressed in dark jeans, a charcoal sweater and wore bright blue, cat-eye shaped glasses. "Oh thank god," she said. "You're finally here." She held a large bolt of burlap fabric, and annoyance and nerves simply radiated off the woman.

"Mrs. McBriar?" I asked.

"Diane," she said. "Come in, come in." And without further ado, she wrapped an arm around my shoulders and tugged me inside.

"Do me a favor and arrange those over by that oak barrel, and other pails, will you?" She pointed to an area to the left of the inside of the double doors. "Consider it a favor to a desperate woman."

Before I could speak, she was muttering under her breath. "Damn indecisive Bride is going to be the death of me..." She dumped the bolt of fabric on a nearby table. "If I don't kill her myself, first." And with that, she took off across the barn at a run.

I bit my lip to keep from laughing as she hustled off, and got my first look at the space. "Wow," I breathed. *No wonder people were into holding their wedding receptions inside of a barn.*

It was a two story barn, and the majority of the interior was open all the way to the wooden roof. The massive beams were cleverly lit, and that tall ceiling added to the impression of space. I walked in and tipped my head back. At the far end there appeared to be a partial second floor. Making me wonder if it had been a hay loft at one time, and there on the other three sides there was a sort of— balcony, I supposed, that went around the rest of the second level. The balcony was narrow, the railing was attractive and rustic, and it was large enough to allow room for people to safely walk around and view the space below.

Strings of clear globe lights swooped down from the rafters, and I admired a trio of clever rustic chandeliers positioned over the central open area. The chandeliers were made from old wagon wheels and suspended by chains from thick beams. Edison bulbs glowed inside of several glass jar shades from each chandelier, and the jars were hung from the wheels by varying heights.

I counted a dozen rustic, wooden tables arranged along the outer perimeter of the barn's smoothly worn pine floors. The long tables were charmingly set with mismatched wooden chairs. Scattered down the center of the long tables were glass paned lanterns again in various finishes and designs, and even old birdcages that held LED pillar candles. What appeared to be a head table was set at the far end, sans chairs, and there was plenty of space for a buffet or a dance floor in the center of the room.

I shifted my gaze and considered a rustic library table arranged on the right side of the double doors. *For gifts and cards,* I supposed. To the left of the door was an oak barrel, several bales of hay, and a few galvanized tubs. Feeling guilty for gawking when I'd been asked— or dragooned into helping, I went over and set up a little display with the tall milk pails and the other items.

I was finishing up when Diane McBride ran back into the room. "Erik!" she shouted. "I need the rest of those chairs set up!"

"Jesus, Mom." I heard his voice from somewhere up above. "Relax woman!"

"I don't have time to relax!" She dragged a hand through her silver and brown hair. "I didn't get to set the head table and the bride and her mother are pulling up the lane!"

She jogged over to where I was. "Hey, that looks great. Thank you." She gave me a thumbs-up.

"You're welcome," I said.

"You have a good eye. I may have to steal you from Ginny." Then she cast her eyes up towards the loft. "Erik!" she called. "Get down here now!"

Erik dropped down behind us, seemingly from out of nowhere, and I squeaked. "Where did you come from?" I demanded.

"From the balcony." He grinned, holding onto a rope.

His mother gave him the stink eye. "You did *not* swing down here on that, did you?"

"Hey, it got me down here fast."

He laughed when his mother reached out and twisted his ear.

I could hear a car approaching. "Well, I guess I should get out of your way..." I began to ease away from the McBriars and towards the door.

"Oh god," she said, turning to me. "They're here. I

never got the head table set and... Oh screw it. How do I look? Do I look professional?"

I couldn't help but like her. "Here," I said, and reached up to brush her bangs back into place. "You look great."

A knock at the main door had Diane McBriar almost jumping out of her shoes. "Oh-my-god," she whispered. "Here we go." She blew out a breath walked to the door and slid it open with a smile. "Hello," she said, in a completely different tone. "Welcome to McBriar Farms."

Erik took my elbow. "Let's get out of the way of the tour," he said softly. "Come with me."

I balked. "I'm not swinging out of here on a rope, Tarzan."

Erik laughed. "No, come back here and help me set up the rest of the chairs, before my mom finds something else for either of us to do."

CHAPTER FIVE

"Sorry that you got dragged into all of this," Erik said as we set the chairs from the antique shop in place, at what I had come to discover was indeed the head table. "My dad has a cold and he was supposed to help mom finish the set up. So she fell behind in her schedule."

I had peeled out of my coat and left it and my purse draped over a nearby chair. "That's okay, it's fun helping."

"You almost sound like you mean it."

I nodded. "I generally say what I mean."

"Mom's normally not such a spaz." He shrugged. "But she's a little stressed. The bride that's here tonight? If she books the venue it will be the biggest wedding we've done so far." Erik carried a box over and pulled out soft beige chair cushions. He placed a stack down on the table and reached in the box for more.

"You want me to tie these on the chairs for you?" I

asked, picking up a few cushions and setting them in place.

"You don't have to do that," he said.

"I don't mind at all." I bent over and started to attach the ties to the backs of the chairs.

The two of us worked on the chair cushions while Erik filled me in on the prospective client. The barn could hold up to two hundred guests I was told, and the bride was considering booking for a large August wedding. But the bride had been waffling back and forth, and that had been driving Erik's mom nuts.

I straightened up. "So your mom is giving her a tour. That way the bride can get a feel for everything, and hopefully book the venue?"

"That's the plan," Erik answered distractedly. He'd been texting back and forth with someone the entire time.

I suspected that it was the fiancée. There was a strong mixture of emotions: impatience, aggravation, and suspicion coming off him in waves. The suspicion concerned me most of all. *They were supposed to be getting married, right? Shouldn't he trust her?* Mentally I shrugged it off. Erik was a nice guy, and his personal life was none of my business... It did, however, make me feel a little sad for him.

"Is that your fiancée that keeps texting you?" I couldn't believe the words had come out of my mouth, and I blushed.

"Yeah." He slapped a cushion on a chair with a bit

more force than was necessary.

I shouldn't ask... "Is everything okay?" And I did anyway.

He ignored my question, and silently tucked the phone in his back pocket. I decided to keep my mouth shut as he picked up the empty box and moved it out of the way.

I looked out over the barn. "You know," I said, "the globe lights hanging from the ceiling are very pretty all lit up... but I wonder if it *would* help if the bride and her mother got the full effect of a decorated head table."

"Hmm..." Erik ran a hand through his hair." I'm not usually here when mom does this."

A woman in a vibrant purple coat walked into the main doors. I recognized her and smiled. "That's Violet O'Connell, I've known her family all my life. She's a talented florist." Violet slid the door shut behind her and clipped off in the direction that Erik's mother had taken the Bride and her mother.

"Yeah, the chick with the purple in her hair. She's cool," Erik said, and then cringed when his phone started to signal another text.

"So we have what, maybe a half hour before they all come out and walk the room?"

"I guess," Erik frowned. "Why, what are you thinking?"

A picture was forming in my mind. "I have an idea, and if you gave me a hand, you would be a hero to your mom."

"Hang on a second." He pulled out his phone, switched it to silent. "I'm in. The money this wedding could bring in would go a long way to helping the farm financially."

"I'm going to need some branches off the boxwood bushes outside and that bolt of burlap fabric," I said, and then explained to him what I wanted to do.

We unrolled the burlap fabric, and Erik cut it to length with his pocket knife. I covered the head table with it, while Erik announced there were a few odds and ends in the supply closet. He unearthed a long swath of ivory lace and a dozen bronze colored chargers. The lace was narrow, more like a table runner, so I flicked it open and arranged it down the center of the burlap. I quickly set the table with the chargers that he'd given me.

"I don't suppose you have any cloth napkins, do you?" I asked.

The long suffering male look had my lips twitching. "I don't know, I can check the supply closet again."

While Erik rooted around in the closet, I gathered up a few lanterns and candles from the other guest tables. He found several lace napkins, tossed them to me, and ducked outside. I began clicking on the LED candles and started arranging them in groupings of odd numbers along the far ends of the head table. The family had been clever to invest in the LED candles, I thought. This way they had the 'look' of a flame without the fire hazard.

Erik brought in the greenery that I'd asked for. "Is this what you wanted?"

"Yes," I said. "Can I borrow your knife?"

"Sure." Erik passed it over. "I'll go get the rest of the candles turned on." He began to work his way down all the guest tables.

While he worked his way around the barn, I took the knife and quickly cut little sprays of greenery, then arranged it around the bases of the LED candles and the lanterns on the head table.

"That looks great," he said, when he came back.

"I kept it simple, I hope your mom approves." I cut several long pieces of the flexible boxwood and tied one stem around a lace napkin, making a natural napkin ring. I held it up for Erik. "See how I did that?"

"That's slick." He reached for a couple and tied a few more.

I set mine in the center of a charger. "I'll finish with these if you want to put the boxes away."

"Holly," Erik dropped his hand on my shoulder. "My mom's going to love this."

"Hero status, guaranteed," I told him, setting the last of the napkins on the chargers. I was taking one last critical look when we heard the office door open up.

"Come on!" Erik grabbed the empty boxes, the left over boxwood, and shoved it in the supply closet.

I scooped up my coat and purse, and we scrambled up to the stairs to the loft.

We sat at a little table, out of sight, on the upper

level and listened as the bride and her mother walked the room with his mom and Violet O'Connell. Actually, I listened while Erik answered his fiancée's many, many text messages.

I heard the women approach the head table area, and it took everything I had not to peek down the stairs to see their reactions.

"Mom, look at this!" A young woman said.

"It's that Rustic Chic look you wanted, sweetheart." That comment had to be from the mother of the bride. "It's absolutely charming."

Charming. Ha! I tried to keep a straight face at overhearing the mother-of-the-bride's comment.

"Yes, well..." Diane McBriar said. "We wanted to give you a little idea of what your head table could look like."

"We could easily do a variation of this with dried wheat and sunflowers, for your August wedding," Violet told the bride.

I nudged Erik. "They like it!" I mouthed the words to him. Erik grinned at me, and

I sat back in the chair and considered him as he sat with his long legs stretched out in front of him, reading through the messages on his cell phone. I hoped things would work out with him and the fiancée. But the emotions I was picking up on made me think he had a rocky road ahead of him.

Finally, a short time later, I was able to make a discreet exit from the barn. The ladies had returned to the office to sign contracts, from what I could hear, and Erik had walked me down to the main doors. I smiled, said goodnight and left the McBriar Farm.

***

My hours at *Obscura Antiques* were Thursday afternoons, all day Saturday, and from noon to five on Sunday. For the most part I worked alone. During the winter months traffic was slower on Main Street, and with me holding down the fort this allowed Ginny more time with her family. Now the couple could have the weekends off for going to estate sales to purchase items for the shop, and for spending time with their brood.

I enjoyed being alone. I could work on my class assignments between customers, and the people who strolled in and out of the shop were interesting. To my relief Erik didn't come by the shop for the next couple of days. I'd learned from Ginny that the family *had* landed the big wedding for August, and now Ginny and Gary were on the hunt for even more rustic items to decorate the wedding barn with.

The Thursday afternoon after my visit to the McBriar's Farm was a mellow one. A few inches of snow had fallen, and foot traffic was light on Main Street. We'd only had two shoppers today, and they were currently over to the side debating on a farmhouse style table. I was trying to give them some privacy and let them make up their mind over the antique.

So while they debated the pros and cons of the piece, I stayed busy by dusting the glass shelves in the mirror-backed display cases that stood behind the front counter.

I caught my reflection and grimaced. I'd attempted to tame my unruly hair into a loose bun on the top of my head today, and I'd been only partially successful. I tucked a few wayward curls back into place and tightened a few bobby pins.

I took a critical look at my reflection. *My color was better, my eyes were clearer*, I decided. Comfortable in my sweater, jeans, and sneakers, I adjusted the reversible enameled crescent moon pendant that hung around my neck.

The simple necklace had once belonged to my mother and wasn't particularly valuable monetarily, it was, however, still priceless to me. I'd been wearing the pendant pretty regularly ever since she'd passed away. Today it was rotated to show the black, waning side of the moon. In another week I'd flip it over, and the crescent would face the opposite direction, appear to be waxing, and the white side would be on display.

The pendant was one of my favorites because the symbol didn't automatically register to most folks as an occult one. It was hidden in plain sight, not unlike I'd been for the past few years. I touched the pendant where it was framed by the V-neck of my dark purple sweater, gave up on trying to tame my hair, and went back to work.

The phone rang a moment later, and I hopped down off the step stool to answer it. "Obscura Antiques, may I help you?"

"Hello dear," said a familiar female voice.

"Hi Aunt Faye, what's up?" *No one said 'dear' with quite the same vocal inflection as Aunt Faye did.*

"That crescent moon pin that you sent me a picture of the other day, is that still for sale?"

I leaned over and double-checked the jewelry case. There it was, sparkling a soft purple in the case. "It sure is."

Aunt Faye sighed in what sounded like relief. "I'd like you to hold that for me."

"Oh, sure." I pulled a hold slip from under the counter and began to fill one out. "I'll do that now."

"Tell the Chandler's I'll be in to pick it up on Saturday."

"Saturday." I noted the date on the ticket. "No problem. I'm sure they'll be thrilled with the sale."

"Yes, it's a very intriguing piece. And now your cousin has something she wants to talk to you about."

"Oh, okay." I smiled as I heard Autumn take the phone.

"Holly?" Her excitement radiated through the receiver.

"Autumn? What's going on?"

"I got the house!" she cried. "They accepted my offer!"

"That's great!" I exclaimed. "Oh I'm so happy for

you!" I gave a fist pump, caught myself and lowered my voice.

"If everything goes well after the inspections, I'll take possession in thirty days!"

I nodded over at the young couple. They smiled back at me and continued to shop. "I get off at five. I want to hear all about it when I get home."

"There's an inspection on Tuesday morning at eleven," Autumn said. "Do you want to come with me?"

I thought about my schedule. "I don't have any classes on Tuesday. I am *so* there!"

"Okay! It's a date! I'll talk to you later," Autumn said.

The couple approached the counter, I told Autumn goodbye, and hung up the phone. After explaining to the couple that the prices on the items were firm, the couple took a business card and promised to come back after they'd gone home and measured their kitchen space and thought it over.

As soon as they left, I jumped up and went across the store to a booth that held lots of different light fixtures. There were a few that dated to the 1920s, and now that Autumn had the house— I was going to take advantage of my employee discount and grab one of them for her. I knew exactly which fixture I wanted.

I picked it up. The metal, semi flush mount was bright red. The milk white glass shade was in the schoolhouse style, and it featured a thin red stripe around the glass. I carefully took the fixture to the back room, nestled it in a box and packed paper around it. I filled out the hold tag and slid it on the shelf.

I didn't care that it was expensive. I wanted it, and by the Goddess, that was going to hang in my cousin's bungalow. I grinned the whole way back to the front counter and did a little happy dance in my running shoes.

When the front door opened I aimed that grin towards the customer. "Hello," I called out cheerfully.

A young woman with dark hair approached the front counter. Her stylish, hip length burgundy coat had black leather sleeves, a dark infinity scarf was looped around her neck, and the handbag she carried was designer. Affluent shoppers often meant big sales, so I continued to smile at her even though her expression was set.

The closer she walked to the counter, the more the vibe in the shop went from positive to negative. My smile faded away and then, to my shock, I got hit with a blast of hatred. I took an automatic step backward. *What the hell?*

"I'd heard you were back in town." The voice was smoky, dramatic and unfamiliar to me.

My heart started to beat faster, and I lifted a hand to my mother's pendant for comfort. "I'm sorry, do I know you?"

"What, you don't recognize the person that you tried to kill?" Her leather gloved hand slowly reached up and pulled her sunglasses off.

Leilah Drake Martin. I realized with a sick dread. In an instant, she was suddenly around the counter and up in my face.

"Boo, bitch," she said.

I flinched, hard in reaction, and bumped into the step ladder. *I hadn't even seen her move!*

"Nothing to say?" Leilah smiled down at me. "I'm kind of disappointed."

The shock of seeing her was beginning to fade, and I squared my shoulders and held my ground. She always had been a bully and the stereotypical mean girl. "What are you doing here?" I tried to sound unconcerned.

Leilah tucked her glasses in her coat pocket. "I came in to pick up the items on hold for the theater department." Leilah's voice was raspier, and deeper than I remembered.

Did I do that? I wondered. *Had the magick I'd done on Leilah when I'd almost drowned her left a lasting mark? Had it changed her voice?* My stomach churned at the thought. When she continued to stand too close, I cleared my throat. "You'll have to step back, and let me pass if you want the clothes, Leilah."

She shifted slightly, but still kept me boxed in behind the counter and the jewelry case. "Let you pass? I don't fucking think so."

"I'm not going to argue with you here, Leilah."

"Funny how I happened to bump into you today." She glanced significantly around the store. "And look at that... you're all alone too."

The lock on the front door turned by itself with a loud click. I realized fatalistically, that Leilah was here for revenge.

Shit. Mentally, I could try and defend myself with magick, but I didn't think I'd be able to pull it off. Her powers had grown, and I'd spent the last three years denying mine. Which meant I was going to have to fight a pissed off Witch— who was set on vengeance— with my bare hands.

Or maybe... I could bluff and make her think I wasn't afraid.

"I've waited years for a little one-on-one time with you," Leilah said as power began to crackle around her. While she drew up her magick, the overhead lights started flickering and the music system faded in and out with static.

"There are two things you should know Leilah," I said. "One: There are security cameras everywhere in here. So smile pretty, because you are currently being recorded."

Leilah laughed, and stepped back a few paces. She pointed up, and a popping sound sent a shower of sparks down from the security cameras. She'd fried them.

"And two?" she asked.

"Unfortunately, we don't carry the plastic dolls your low-rent ass seems to prefer to use for hexing." I smiled sweetly. "That was your favorite method back in high school... wasn't it?"

Leilah's face went red. "I've learned a few things since high school." She flicked her fingers in my direction, and the glass display shelves behind me imploded.

I automatically tossed up my arms to protect my eyes even as I felt the shards hit my neck and back. Everything that had been on those shelves tumbled down, and the noise was incredibly loud. I lowered my arms and discovered that the glass— that should have gone straight at Leilah— had instead fallen all around her, leaving her untouched.

"Aren't you going to fight back?" Leilah asked softly. "I don't imagine your employers are going to be too happy with what you've let happen to their store."

"You want your revenge?" I said. "Fine, take it out on *me*, then."

"Oh I will. But first I want to see you *try* and use your magick against me!"

"You're going to have a long wait," I said. "I wont strike at you with magick again, Leilah. You are *not* worth the karma."

"Bet I can make you," she said, and with the flick of her wrist, the jewelry case shattered.

I cringed from the racket as more glass showered me and jewelry tumbled to the floor. "You bitch!" I shook my glass off my clothes, shocked at the destruction.

She snapped her fingers, and an entire display of ceramic and metal vintage advertising crashed down behind her. "Oops," she said, as they too joined the carnage on the floor. "I hope those weren't valuable."

"Leilah, Stop!" I yelled.

"Make me," she sneered. "Because I can do this all day."

The signs had been worth hundreds of dollars. I *had* to stop her from destroying anything else. "At least you didn't get the expensive one," I said as if relieved, and when Leilah turned to look— I jumped over the glass and fallen jewelry, grabbing her from behind.

We struggled, and her energy burned me wherever her hands landed. Leilah grasped my arms, and putting her magick behind it, she swung me hard. I flew into a wooden church bench that was filled with heavy ceramic crocks. My ribs hit the bench first and I flipped over the back. The bench fell over with me and came down on my head. The antique crocks went everywhere. They landed with an earsplitting racket and shattered into pieces.

"You're pathetic," she sneered.

I rolled over, shoved at the bench, and managed to gain my feet. "Afraid to fight me without magick?"

"But magick makes this so much more fun!" she said.

I wheezed as I stepped over the fallen bench. "What's the matter Leilah?" I held up my fists, and staggered. "Scared you can't take a punch?"

"I'm more interested to see if *you* can." She pushed her hand palm out— sending a flash of energy straight at me.

I threw up my hands trying to shield myself, but she was too quick, and I was way out of practice. Her magick hit me square in the chest, and I landed hard on the floor in the middle of shards of pottery. It took me a moment or two to get my eyes to focus. When they did I saw that she had leaned over what was left of the jewelry display case. I forced myself to stand, it hurt like hell, but I struggled to my feet anyway.

"Well..." She brushed her hands together. "This was fun!" With a laugh she started towards the door then paused as if to consider. "You know Holly," she said, turning back to me. "I think you're right. I *did* miss one." She pointed slowly towards the tall hutch I'd once rescued Gracie from. The one filled with very expensive china.

"Don't!" I said, realizing what she intended to do. I took a step. Wobbled. Took another.

"Oh, the least I can do is make sure you get fired."

She slanted her eyes away from me to focus on the cabinet, and with a primal yell, I jumped onto her back, grabbing her hair with both hands, and yanked as hard as I could.

"Bitch!" she screamed, as I pulled her down by her hair to the floor with me.

I'd hoped to foul her aim by tackling her, but there was another crash, and I knew that the old china inside the hutch had been destroyed, anyway.

We were rolling over the floor when a third pair of hands was suddenly there, and they reached in and yanked us apart. I fell back and peered up to see Leilah suspended in air by the back of her coat. Her feet were a couple of feet off the ground.

My eyes traveled from a pair of fancy brown leather shoes, up to a pair of tailored navy blue slacks. The man had his back to me, and was tall, dark and built. His broad shoulders didn't seem to strain at all against his overcoat, even as he held Leilah up in the air.

Stunned, I blinked up at my rescuer. It was Julian Drake.

"You never learn, do you Leilah?" he said conversationally.

I scrabbled backwards, through the broken pottery, and away from the pair of them as fast as I could.

"Get out." He threw his half-sister towards the now open door and somehow Leilah managed to land on her feet in a cat-like crouch.

"Stay out of this, Julian!" Leilah snapped.

"Our father is not going to be happy when I tell him about your latest stunt." His voice was soft, elegant and controlled... and it scared the crap out of me.

Leilah rose to her feet and looked daggers at me. "We're even now, you bitch." She adjusted her coat, and the bag that was somehow still over her shoulder, and stalked towards the front door. "Have fun explaining this mess to your Cowan employers," she said, and slammed the door behind her, making the glass shatter.

The next thing I knew, Julian had knelt down in front

of me. "Are you alright?" he reached a hand out and offered a snowy white handkerchief.

I automatically cringed back away from him.

"You're hurt," he said dabbing at my face. "Let me help you, Holly."

I surveyed the destruction of the store. "What am I going to do?" My vision blurred. "Oh the Chandler's are going to be so upset!" I pulled a piece of crockery out from under my thigh, and let it drop. "Leilah blew up the display shelves... the jewelry case is destroyed. Wedgewood china is all smashed... the glass advertising signs... Are the metal ones ruined too?" I started to cry and a shooting pain had me gasping for breath.

"Holly," Julian tipped my chin up.

"I broke the crocks... I think the bench is broken too... there's *so much* damage."

"...going to need an ambulance."

"Huh?" I belatedly became aware that Julian had been talking while I'd been rambling.

"Yes, thank you," he said, and tucked his cell phone in his coat's breast pocket.

"What'd you say?" I squinted up at him.

"Holly, be still." Julian's voice was calm and his hands were gentle as he set them on my shoulders. "You're all cut up and bleeding."

"I am?" I scowled down at my purple sweater and discovered several burn marks. Now I could smell the burnt fabric. "Shit, she ruined my sweater."

"Look at me now." His voice was so compelling that

I met his gaze, and he connected with me energetically.

I felt a falling sensation and a warm, fuzzy sort of wave rolled over me. His magick was earnest and soothing and it caught me completely off guard. *That's Julian Drake you're letting bewitch you...* And even as the warning shouted in my mind, I continued to stare up at his handsome face. I could *feel* his concern for me. I could *sense* his compassion and his attempt to offer comfort and healing on a magickal level.

That could only mean one thing. Julian was an empath. Like I was.

"Enough," I said, trying to break the link between us. I pulled back, shook my head, and immediately regretted it. I moaned when my head throbbed.

"Holly, can you hear me?" he asked.

His hand was in my hair, and I reached up and caught it. "What are you doing?"

He froze. "You have glass in your hair," he said.

"Oh." I released his hand.

"Does anything hurt anywhere?" he asked, picking more glass out of my hair.

"My ribs." I said, and now that I was thinking about it. "My hands." I suddenly realized that they were bleeding.

He inspected my hands, and gently wrapped his handkerchief around my right hand, tying it firmly. "May I see?" he asked. When I nodded my consent, he impersonally ran his hands over my ribs. I felt a healing energy from him, and was surprised. Again.

I winced. "Right side."

"Easy," he murmured. "She really did a number on you," Julian took his hands away. "Try and relax, help is on the way."

I studied his face, and for the first time I saw that he had very unusual eyes. "Hey, you have a little blue in your eyes." I smiled. "It's like a sky blue ring around the brown. *Julian Drake was kind of hot!* I thought, and then, I giggled. "You're pretty, Julian," I said while another laugh bubbled up. "I never noticed that you were so sexy, before."

Julian shook his head. "Holly, I think you have a concussion." He picked me up slowly from the floor, stood carefully, and the room went on a slow spin.

I probably should have been afraid. I'd managed to survive a magickal attack, and now Julian Drake was holding me in his arms. But it wasn't fear I was experiencing... it was attraction. *If he kissed me now, what would it be like?* As I realized where my thoughts were heading, I jolted, hard, trying to yank them back in line. My ribs immediately protested. "Shit." I hissed out a breath while my ears rang, and my ribs throbbed.

"Did I hurt your ribs?" he said, his face close to mine. "My apologies."

"No, you didn't hurt me... It's just that you don't have to rescue me, or try and heal me. I really don't deserve it."

"You don't feel you're worthy of a rescue, is that it?" He smiled down into my face and my mouth went dry.

"We've both gone down a dark path," he said. "And we both bear the scars."

I frowned at him, trying to follow the conversation. "That's true, I suppose."

"The *truth,* is that the opportunity for redemption is sometimes given to us, angel, whether we feel we deserve it or not."

"I'm no angel." I sighed unhappily.

Julian grinned. "If it makes you feel any better, I'm no white knight."

I heard police sirens and saw the flash of lights coming down Main Street. "Is that the police?"

"I called them," Julian said.

"What the hell am I going to tell them?" I surveyed the destruction of what *had* been a charming store filled with high-end antiques.

"Leave it to me," Julian tried to reassure me. "I'll tell the police that I was walking by when I saw you fighting off a robber."

"This is never going to work." I felt punch-drunk and drowsy. "I am *so* going to get fired. The Chandler's didn't deserve this happening to their store."

"Trust me," Julian said. "I'll take care of everything."

"Okay," I yawned and leaned my head against his shoulder. *He smelled so nice...*

"Holly!" Julian's voice was sharp. Don't fall asleep!"

I jerked awake, and then swore at the pain. "Do me a

favor Julian," I said. "Keep talking to me."

"I'm not going anywhere," he said. "I'll stay with you."

The squad car came screeching up to the curb. I saw Lexie's father, John Proctor, leap out of the car and run towards us. "I'm going to hold you to that," I whispered to Julian.

CHAPTER SIX

To my humiliation, the doctors at the emergency room decided to keep me overnight for observation. I tried to talk my way out of it, but Julian spoke to the ER doctor privately and whatever he'd said to her seemed to tip the scale over to my being admitted.

It was official. Leilah Drake Martin had kicked my ass.

I had bruised ribs, not cracked, a mild concussion and assorted cuts on my face, the back of my neck, and my hands. Between my family and then Gary Chandler, they had all made such a fuss in the ER that eventually the nurses had to clear them *all* out of the treatment room so they could patch me up. I don't know what embarrassed me more. The ass-kicking or the scene they all made.

A short time later, I sat in the treatment room, alone, and waited for them to get a bed ready upstairs. I'd convinced the family *not* to call my father and stepmother. He was out of the country on his anniversary cruise and I didn't want to spoil the vacation for Dad and Ruth. Relieved that I'd gotten that concession out of them, I held onto my ribs and scowled down at the ugly hospital gown they'd put me in, feeling slightly loopy from whatever they'd given me for pain. The curtain swished open, and I swung my head around to see Julian Drake.

His lips bowed up. "The look on your face..." he chuckled.

"Is it bad?" I pointed to my face.

"No," Julian reassured me. "You'll be relieved to know they used steri strips on your face." He gently touched a spot to the side of my left eyebrow.

"I got a few stitches in my hand and on my neck," I told him, scratching at the gauze and tape they'd used to cover my neck. I only had a few bandages on my left hand, but my right had stitches in the palm, and was wrapped up in gauze.

"Holly." Julian reached out and captured my fingers. "Try not to scratch at the bandages."

"Yeah, you're right." I leaned back against the pillow. "The worst part about stitches is the shot, you know," I said to Julian. Then realizing that I'd probably sounded a little random, I sighed.

"Are you in pain?"

"The numbness hasn't worn off from the shots yet," I said. "My ribs hurt worst of all, and I bet I'll be covered in bruises tomorrow." I shut my eyes. "This sucks."

"I spoke privately to Faye and Bran," Julian said.

I snapped my eyes open. "So they know?"

He nodded. "Yes, and they are willing to let my father take care of Leilah."

I sighed again. "What about Mr. Chandler. What about the damage to his store?"

"He's a little distraught over you going after a *robber*," Julian said firmly. "At the moment he's talking to the police, but he is genuinely concerned for your well being, Holly. He doesn't seem to be angry at all..."

"No." I heard an angry voice coming through the curtain. "By the Goddess she *will* talk to me."

"Oh shit," I whispered, and flinched at the angry emotions radiating my way.

Julian tensed up beside me. "What's wrong?"

"Brace yourself," I said. "Cranky, pregnant, police officer alert."

Lexie shoved the curtain aside, pulled up an empty chair and sat beside the bed. "Julian," she nodded to him, and then switched her attention to me. "What's this bullshit about you not wanting to press charges?" she demanded.

"Let it drop, Lexie," I said.

"The hell I will!" she shot back.

"Lexie," I lowered my voice. "I'm the one who dove after her, and got tossed aside. I fell into the bench and hit my head. Even without the magick, there's no way to file charges for assault. She never physically touched me. *I* jumped on *her*. Twice."

"Now you listen to me..." Lexie said, firing up. "Whether she used her fists, or hit you with magick, the results are the same... this is *wrong* Holly."

"No," I cut her off with a furious whisper. "You listen to me! Almost three years ago I damn-near killed Leilah with magick. Duncan Quinn had to give her mouth-to-mouth, it was that bad. No one 'pressed charges' then, and everyone in the family acted like it was only a little misunderstanding, or an *accident*."

"This is different," Lexie insisted.

"No, it's not." I said. "Stop making me out to be a victim. Today, she kicked my ass, put me in the hospital and the score is settled." I cleared my throat. "The *only* thing I'm upset about is that the Chandler's store was damaged in the process."

"So what, you're a martyr now?" Lexie rolled her eyes.

"Hardly." I snapped back. "I think I got off easy, karma-wise. As far as I'm concerned balance has been reset, and the slate is wiped clean between Leilah and me. She said we were even— so it's over. And it's going to stay that way."

"Maybe you should let her rest," Julian suggested softly. "She's been through a lot."

"We're not done with this conversation," Lexie warned me.

"Go away, Lexie," I sighed and shut my eyes. "And take your angry energy with you, It's only making me hurt worse."

Lexie stomped out and I struggled against tears. I felt Julian's hand take mine. He gave my fingers a supportive pat.

"Don't go," I said to him. With all the rampaging emotions around me, I was extremely overwhelmed on a psychic level. Julian was composed and serene, and as a fellow empath, he was like a calming lifeline— one that I was reluctant to let go of.

"I'll stay for as long as you want me to," he said.

After I'd been assigned to a room, my family descended in force and Julian had made a discreet exit — not that I blamed him. Autumn sat in a chair beside my bed, Aunt Faye had somehow commandeered a rocking chair and sat across the room, Bran had taken Lexie and Morgan home— I supposed she was still angry with me. Ivy perched at the foot of my bed, and Cypress sat with her. Ivy and Cypress had come straight from campus as soon as they'd heard.

All of them seemed to be talking so loudly. *God their voices made my head throb*! I sipped my water and told my inner bitchiness to shut up.

"Damn girlfriend!" Cypress whistled. "You look like you went a few rounds with the champ."

"So you took her on bare handed, with no magick?" Ivy grinned and patted my foot.

I tried to raise my eyebrows and winced when it pulled on the steri strips. "I did."

Ivy began to pantomime a few boxing moves. She hummed the theme song from Rocky, making Cypress laugh.

My lips twitched at her antics. "I probably look like Rocky, *after* the fight," I said.

"Adrian!" Ivy said in a passible imitation.

"Girls," Aunt Faye said, "you might want to keep it down."

"Do you need anything, Holly?" Autumn wanted to know.

Yes, I thought. *A dark room, and some peace and quiet for a couple of hours would be fabulous...*

I saw movement in the doorway and Ginny Chandler rushed in. She took one look at me and promptly burst into tears.

Oh god, I thought as her emotions smothered me. *Somebody just shoot me now.*

"Holly!" Ginny ran across the room and grabbed my hand.

Ow, I thought as she accidentally squeezed on top of the bandages, applying pressure exactly where I had stitches.

"Are you going to be alright?"

I gently extricated my hand. "Yes. I'm sorry about the damage to the store."

"Don't you even worry about that!" she insisted, wiping her eyes. "I couldn't believe it when the police called."

"I'm sorry if you were frightened—"

"What were you *thinking,* taking on a robber all by yourself?" she demanded.

"Well—"

"Gary keeps a baseball bat under the front counter," Ginny went on. "Is that what you went after that scumbag with?"

"Damn Holly," Ivy piped up. "You could have laid a Harley Quinn style smack-down on their ass!"

"Harley who?" Ginny stopped crying long enough to glance at Ivy in confusion.

"It's a comic book character," I tried to tell her.

"I'm so glad you're alright!" Ginny reached out and pulled me in for a hug.

Now I was being smothered for real, and when she added a squeeze to the hug, I literally saw stars.

To my relief Autumn gently pulled her off me. "Her ribs are bruised, Ginny," she explained.

"Oh, I didn't know." Ginny blanched. "Did I hurt you?"

I shook my head no, gripped the side of the bed with my good hand and tried for a smile.

"Hey, Mrs. Chandler," Ivy said, taking her by the hand, "why don't you and I go get a magazine for Holly from the gift shop?" She tugged Ginny to her feet.

I'll keep her busy and check on you tomorrow. Ivy sent to me telepathically.

Thank you. I sent back the same way.

Ivy slanted me a concerned look as she maneuvered Ginny towards the door. *Try and rest.*

Cypress eased off the end of my bed. "Girlfriend, you're an interesting shade of pale right about now."

"Hey," Autumn said, "Holly, how bad are you hurting?"

I shook my head and struggled not to cry at the pain from the grab and hug.

"You're white as a sheet," Autumn muttered and then turned to our great-aunt. "Aunt Faye, call the nurse."

"Drugs would be nice right now," I finally managed to say.

"That's enough visitors for today, I think." Aunt Faye pressed the call button, and leaned on it. "I'm going to ask that they let you rest, and keep visitors out for the remainder of the evening."

"Thank you, Aunt Faye," I said and meant it.

The nurse popped in and left with a promise to come back with a pain pill. Cypress pressed a kiss to my head and told me she'd work some healing magick for me. She waved at me from the door, while Aunt Faye and Autumn gathered up their things and prepared to leave as well.

Aunt Faye bent over the bed and pressed a gentle kiss to my cheek. "Rest well my dear, I'll be back in the morning to bring you home."

"Love you," I told her.

"Try and relax," Aunt Faye said, shutting off most of the lights in the room.

"Do you want me to stay with you, Holly?" Autumn gently ran her hand over my hair.

I managed to smile up at her. "No, I'm okay."

"Liar." Autumn grinned. "I bet some quiet is all you really want." She handed me the nurse call button and my cell phone. "Here's the call button, and your phone. Call me if you get lonely or want to talk."

I tucked the phone along my side. "I will, thanks."

They went out, shutting the door behind them. I managed about fifteen minutes of solitude until the nurse was back with my medication. Gratefully I took it, adjusted the bed and tried to get comfortable.

I reached up for the crescent moon pendant around my neck and closed my good hand over it. I had started to doze off when a volunteer from the gift shop brought in a huge bouquet of balloons and a basket of pink tulips. The balloons were from the Chandler family, and the tulips were from Ivy, Cypress and Autumn. I shut my eyes and tried to rest, but the confrontation with Leilah kept replaying over and over in my mind.

There was a soft knock on the door and Julian Drake poked his gorgeous head in the room. "They told me you weren't receiving any more visitors today."

"No, it's okay. Come in, Julian," I said.

Julian left the door slightly ajar and walked over. "I wanted to check and see if you were settled before I went home." He draped his coat over the chair Autumn had vacated and took a seat.

I shifted slightly so I could better see his face. "In case I didn't say so before, thank you for helping me today."

"It was the least I could do."

The light splashed across his face and illuminated his eyes. I was struck again by how unusual they were. One of his eyes had a ring of blue against the brown center and the other eye was brown with patches of blue "You do have brown *and* blue eyes. That's crazy," I said, continuing to stare at him. "I thought maybe I'd imagined it..."

"It's called *sectoral heterochromia*." Julian stood, and eased me back against the pillows. "One part of the eye is different from the other. For me, it's blue mixed in randomly with the brown pigment."

"Okay," I was suddenly very sleepy. "They're pretty."

Competently, Julian reclined the hospital bed a bit lower. "Try and rest, Holly."

"Thanks, that's better. More comfortable," I yawned.

He took my phone. "I'm going to leave you my phone number. In a few days when you feel better, call me. We can meet for coffee and talk."

"Sure thing. Sounds great." I said, and wondered why he was smiling at me as if I'd said something funny.

He set the phone on the table beside me. "I'll see you soon."

I dozed off before I could answer him.

***

I was back home before noon the next day. Aunt

Faye told me to rest, and set me up in my room with a lot of pillows and a stack of DVDs to watch on her laptop. She tied the balloon bouquet to the iron footboard of my bed and set the basket of tulips on my nightstand. The tulips were only starting to open, but they smelled like spring, and made me smile.

I tried to watch the movies, but ended up napping off and on for most of the day. A combination of fatigue, being in the hospital and not sleeping well, and the various healing spells I knew my family and friends were working on my behalf. Merlin added his own particular brand of feline enchantment. He sprawled over my legs, burrowed in the blankets, and purred away, keeping me company when I dozed off again.

I had the most vivid dreams about Julian Drake. In my dreams he called me *angel* and I'd told him he was sexy. I woke up from my nap, feeling groggy, flustered and wondered how much was a dream and how much was a memory.

Besides my ribs being sore, and the mild discomfort of the stitches in my hand and neck, I felt pretty good. By Saturday I was up and around, only moving a bit slower than normal. After taking a bath, I felt almost like myself again. Washing my hair was a bit trickier with the stitches, but Autumn helped me out.

We sat on the hearth in the family room while she worked a wide tooth comb through my wet curls. "I had no idea curly hair was this much work." Autumn said.

"Use the leave-in conditioner, next," I said.

Autumn followed my directions, and when she'd worked through the conditioner, she began to finger comb my hair. "So you let this air dry?"

"I do."

She wiped her hands on the towel I'd used. "Okay, I'll go put this hair stuff away for you. Sit tight and enjoy the fire."

She strolled out of the room and before I could decide if I should stay on the hearth or relax in the big comfy chair Aunt Faye preferred, there was a knock at the front door. Bran and his family were out, Aunt Faye was working at the shop, so I went to answer the door myself.

"I'll get it!" Autumn called from the back of the house.

I rolled my eyes. "I can handle answering the door."

I checked the spy hole and saw a deliveryman. I opened the door. "Good morning," I said.

"Floral delivery for Holly Bishop," he said, holding a huge wrapped vase full of flowers.

"I've got it." Autumn reached past me to take the large arrangement. "Thank you," she told the delivery man who was already turning and walking off the porch. She carried the flowers into the family room and set them on the coffee table.

I eased down to the sofa and gently tore the paper away to reveal the flowers. Clusters of peachy-orange roses were arranged with white daisies and yellow mini carnations. The arrangement was lush, full and cheerful.

"I wonder who they're from?" I leaned over and buried my face in the blossoms.

"Here's the card." Autumn found it stapled to the outer wrapping. She tugged it off and passed it over.

I opened up the envelope and pulled the enclosure card free. "They reminded me of you." I read out loud. Then I saw who had signed the card and I felt a little flutter in my chest.

"Who sent them?" Autumn wanted to know.

"Julian Drake," I said, blandly.

Autumn held out her hand for the card, and I passed it over. There was silence in the room for a good five seconds as she considered the note written there. "Be careful, Holly," she finally said.

Angry at the comment, I snatched the card back. "Correct me if I'm wrong," I said, "but according to what I was told, Julian once *helped* you and Aunt Faye. He put himself in harm's way, and got the both of you out of the Drake mansion, and to safety."

Autumn met my gaze and didn't flinch. "Yes, that's exactly right. The grimoire almost destroyed him a few years ago, and he's worked hard to find his way back." She sighed. "He actually asked me to read him once, and I did."

"And what did you discover?"

"That he came out of that experience a very different person. He's much more controlled and cautious with his magick now. He works hard for the museum and is spearheading the fundraising for the expansion. I work with him quite a bit, and it's impressive how he's changed for the better." Autumn admitted.

"So why the warning?"

"Are you really in a place to be getting involved with another practitioner? A practitioner who has struggled with the dark himself?"

"I'm not *involved*." I picked up the flowers. "He rescued me. If he hadn't stepped in when he did with Leilah, I'm not sure what would have happened." I shuddered, remembering.

"I wasn't trying to upset you," Autumn insisted.

"You didn't," I assured her. "What happened Thursday, has had me re-evaluating some things," I said. "I've actually been doing a lot of serious thinking over the past few days."

"About?"

"I shut my magick down three years ago, thinking I could keep everyone else safe. I turned away from the Goddess to punish myself and I did a damn fine job of it. Now I have to live with the fact that because of my own childish behavior, and my refusal to accept who and what I am, another magickal disaster has happened."

"You truly think that?" Autumn asked.

"I *know* that," I said. "I was so out of practice, and incapable of defending myself from a magickal attack, and now the Chandler's are suffering a loss to their business today. Their store became collateral damage. Because of me. "

"But that's *not* your fault!" Autumn argued.

"I might have been loopy, but I still got a look at the store before the ambulance arrived." I frowned over the memory. "There was thousands of dollars worth of destruction, Autumn. And I have to live with knowing that the financial losses of that sweet family *are* my fault."

"The *fault* falls squarely at the feet of Leilah Drake Martin. The little bitch did this so you would suffer more!" Autumn said, tossing her hands in the air. "She knows you're an empath, and she's twisted enough to take advantage of the fact that if the people you care about are hurting... then you'd feel their pain too."

"I've considered that." I nodded, and held the flowers close to my chest. They acted as a sort of shield from my cousin's frustration. "I'm going to go lay down for a while. I'm tired."

Autumn waited until I was halfway up the stairs before she spoke. "Holly, what are you going to do?"

I stopped and focused on Autumn where she stood. Her concern radiated off her and made me more determined than ever, to become stronger. "You know, I used to be able to shield myself from the psychic overwhelm that comes from sensing everyone else's emotions." I took a stabilizing breath. "But I've only been blocking for the past few years... and when you are injured or tired, the blocking thing, it doesn't work very well."

"Is there anything I can do to help you?"

I smiled at her. "No but I appreciate the offer. Right now, I need some solitude to rest and recover from my injuries," I said. "After I heal, I'm going to recoup my energy, study, practice my Craft, and get my magickal abilities back on track."

Autumn raised an eyebrow. "In other words... the Witch is back."

"You bet your ass," I said, determinedly.

Autumn grinned. "There's the Holly Bishop I used to know."

I nodded to her, and took the flowers up to my room. I placed them on my dresser, running my fingertips over the flowers and trying to sense their energy.

According to the language of flowers, the white daisies brought cheer and happiness. The carnations traditionally lent healing energy to a bouquet, and the yellow hue was aligned to the element of air, new beginnings and communication. The clusters of roses infused the arrangement with a warm-fuzzy vibration. Peach colored roses traditionally meant friendship, but orange was customarily a color that signified passions.

However, I bet that Julian had chosen the color of the roses more because it was close to my hair color than for any romantic message. With a smile, I went over to my phone and sent him a text. I tried to decide what would be the best thing to say, and went for the obvious.

Thank you for the flowers. They're beautiful.

I stretched out on my back on the bed and focused

on getting my muscles to relax. Holding myself tight was not helping with the sore ribs. My phone signaled a new text message and I checked it. I tapped the screen, and there was a message from Julian.

You're welcome. I hope you're feeling better.

I thought about what Autumn had said. I sat up and typed a reply. *Is that offer of a coffee still open?* I hit send.

It is.

I considered my class schedule. *Tuesday at 4:00 pm?*

That would work.

Want to meet at the Black Cat Coffee House on Main Street?

Perfect.

See you then.

Looking forward to it.

I watched my phone for a moment, waiting to see if he would send any other messages. When there wasn't one, I dropped the phone to the bed and walked over to the round marble topped table that had once served as my mother's altar.

I trusted my instincts and went to the bookshelves. There was a mood, a feeling of sorts in the air. Excitement and hope, combined with a sort of expectancy... I supposed. I reached up and took down a small, old wooden chest. My mother had always stored spell supplies in there. I set it on the altar and opened the lid. Inside were several small candles, glass holders, and a lighter. I chose a blue candle for healing, and to represent my favorite element, water.

I placed the candle holder in the center of the table and tucked the candle inside. I headed over to Ivy's dresser and considered her dish of tumbled stones next. I selected a bloodstone for healing, a moonstone for the Goddess and moon magick, and finally a snowflake obsidian to help remove any lingering negativity that I might be carrying around from Leilah's magickal attack. I arranged the trio of stones around the candle and removed my crescent moon pendant, laying it neatly down in front of the candles and stones.

I set the chest back on the bookshelf, locked my bedroom door, and prepared to work my first spell in three years. Typically, a magickal practitioner would deliberately check astrological influences and the phase of the moon, before casting a spell. It's wise to coordinate those energies with your intention for the best possible outcome... but then there are those times when you're moved to cast a spell spontaneously. Trusting your own instincts and taking that leap of faith.

This was one of those times.

Silently I cast a circle. Beginning in the east, I moved clockwise, pointing my finger down and envisioned drawing a circle of shining blue light on the floor. Once I walked the boundary of my circle I clapped my hands once. "The circle is cast," I said.

I felt the shift in the energy of the room immediately.

Determinedly, I strode to the center of the circle and stood by my mother's altar. "By the powers of earth, air, fire and water," I chanted. "Goddess please hear the call of your daughter." I lit the candle, and then held my hands out to my sides, palms facing up.

Taking a deep breath, I spoke from my heart. "Mother Goddess I stand before you, battered in mind, body, and spirit. I am attempting to reclaim my..." *Nope, I thought. Not 'attempt'. Say what you mean.*

I cleared my throat. "I now *reclaim* my powers, and my strength. I have not practiced in three years, but that time of denial, and of mourning has passed. The legacy of magick is a gift and I am going to work hard to be worthy of it, and all the responsibilities that it entails."

I ran a fingertip along the side of the blue candle. "May the energy of water flow through my life and allow me to heal. May it wash away the sadness from my loss." I set my fingers on the tumbled stones. "By the powers of these crystals, allow me to experience your magicks once again, to recover quickly from my injuries, and to be protected from any further energetic or magickal attack."

Emotions swirled up unexpectedly, and I blinked a few tears from my eyes. I could feel the Goddess close to me. And my heart beat fast in my chest at her acceptance of me, once again.

"She's always been there, child." A feminine voice shimmered through the room. I glanced to my right, and there stood my grandmother within the boundaries of the circle I had cast. "I'll say this," she said. "You certainly are stubborn."

My jaw dropped. "Grandma Rose."

When my grandmother's spirit had manifested before, she'd appeared in her favorite gardening apparel. Today, instead of the straw hat, jeans and pink sweater, she seemed to be wearing a long shimmering sort of dress. Her trademark scent of roses flooded the turret.

"I... I'm surprised to see you," I managed to say.

I saw her reach out, and felt a hand pass over my curls. "You shouldn't be. You needed me, so here I am."

"You've been watching over me at night, haven't you?" I asked, thinking of the times I'd woken up smelling roses.

"Of course. I'm sorry for your loss, sweetheart." Tears seemed to shimmer in her eyes.

I had no words, and tears spilled over.

"You need to share this burden with your family," Grandma Rose said. "They would understand, and support you. There's no need to carry this alone."

"I'm too ashamed."

"Holly Irene Bishop." Her voice sounded impatient, and I glanced at her warily. "That is the most ridiculous thing I've ever heard."

"Is it?" I sniffled and wiped my eyes. "Three years ago I attacked Leilah with magick— almost killed her, and then I ran away to school. I rejected my legacy, ignored my family, was careless, and got pregnant." I pulled in a shaky breath. "Maybe I deserved to lose the baby."

My grandmother's ghost grew so bright I shielded my eyes. "Young lady, you stop talking like that! I've never been so tempted to whack anyone upside the head before in my entire after-life!"

She'd said 'in my entire after-life'... Maybe it was the strain, but I ducked my head, hiding the smile that threatened. "Yes Ma'am," I said, respectfully. Considering that I was dealing with a peeved ghost, I didn't want to push my luck.

She moved directly in front of me. "Do you think you are the first member of this family to struggle with the dark side of magick?"

I snapped my head up. "Well, I..."

She set her hands on her hips and leveled her gaze on me. "You're not the first Bishop woman to fight this particular battle, and sweetheart, you won't be the last."

"Still, I'm sorry," I said.

"I know you are, and you've done your best to make reparation. But Holly... letting yourself be attacked was *not* the answer."

"I didn't want to give in, and let her goad me into using magick against her. Don't you understand?"

"Yes, actually, I do." My grandmother nodded. "So what are you going to do now?"

"Reclaim my power and vow to do better."

Now, she smiled. "I have no doubts you will do so. Splendidly."

"Hearing you say that makes me start to really believe it."

My grandmother rolled her eyes. "Stubborn. Just like your grandfather. You've simply refused to see, or feel the love that was all around you. It's right there. Waiting for you to tap into it. You're an Empath, girl! That is your gift from the Goddess. If anyone would know how to work with that positive emotion— it's you!"

I felt my skin raise in goose bumps, and I bowed my head in gratitude for my grandmother's message. *Even though I had turned away from the Goddess, she had never abandoned me,* I realized. A rush of sensation ran from the top of my head to my toes. Joy and peace filled me up. Now standing in Her presence, I smiled.

"There you go," my grandmother said with satisfaction. "Remember, the Goddess is always with you, and so am I."

I faced my grandmother and saw that her image was fading. "Thanks Grandma," I said.

"Blessed be," her voice whispered through the room, and she was gone.

I took a moment for myself and searched for composure as the scent of roses began to fade. Purposefully, I picked up the enameled pendant that had once belonged to my mother and continued with my spell.

"By the crescent moon— symbol of my family line, I now rededicate myself to the Goddess, the Craft, and to the magickal path my mother taught me." I refastened the necklace around my throat, lowered my hands, and shut my eyes to stand silently for a few moments, thinking over everything I'd experienced.

When it felt like the right time to do so, I opened my eyes and finished my impromptu spell. "My loving thanks to the spirit of my grandmother who assisted me today. My gratitude to the Lady and her many blessings. I now close this ritual with a charm that rhymes; by all the power of the crescent moon that shines."

A bright light spilled across my face. I waited for my eyes to adjust to the brightness, and discovered that a beam of winter sunlight had come in through the turret windows. It illuminated the entire area, and the temperature noticeably rose. A blue crescent moon shimmered to life across the marble table top. It completely enveloped the spell candle and crystals and was dead center on the round altar. My heart slammed into my throat at the image. It took me a second to realize that the stained glass sun-catcher in the window had created a little crescent shaped beam of color in the center of the table.

I'd been home for two months and I'd never even paid attention to the sun-catcher before. I smiled at the synchronicity of the moon's appearance, and took it as a very good sign, and blessing of the Goddess.

"Blessed be," I whispered.

CHAPTER SEVEN

At noon on Tuesday, I pulled my bright red rubber boots on, buttoned up my good winter coat and walked out the door of the manor. The temperatures were currently above freezing, and the few inches of snow we had was beginning to melt. I slipped my hands into my coat pockets, delighted to be down to one large bandage to cover the stitches on my palm and a few sheer adhesive bandages on my other hand. I strolled down to the end of the driveway and let myself out of the big metal gate. I followed the high wrought iron fence crunching through the snow on the sidewalk and headed to the bungalow next door.

I knocked on the front door and let myself in when I heard Autumn's voice. She and Aunt Faye stood talking to the inspector.

Aunt Faye was dressed to impress with a pale gray coat, charcoal slacks and her long silver hair flowing over her shoulders. Autumn had tossed her royal blue coat over the newel post at the bottom of the stairs and was standing off to the side in jeans and a pumpkin orange shirt, while the inspector checked the outlets around the kitchen sink area.

The stress level coming off my cousin had me taking an automatic step back. I dug down deep and reminded myself that stress while buying a home was *normal* and to let the emotions roll past me. Having reclaimed my gifts, I had to keep reminding myself to work *with* my clairsentience again, instead of recoiling at every empathic experience.

I squared my shoulder and went to my great aunt. "How's it going?" I asked.

"Very well," she said. "I imagine the outlets will need to be changed over to CGI, and a few other minor fixes, but that's not unusual for a home of this age." Aunt Faye had been a realtor before she'd retired. Only now she was wheeling and dealing in investment properties instead of showing houses for a living. I suspected she did the buying and selling more for entertainment these days.

"Is it okay if I look around?" I asked her.

"Of course," Aunt Faye said. "I think I'll go stand with Autumn, before she passes out from the anxiety."

I glanced over at my cousin. She did appear more than a little wound up. "Ah, that's probably a good idea."

I nosed around for a while. The stairs were solid wood and fortunately had never been painted. I walked up and checked out the three bedrooms. For the most part, they were in good shape, but if anything the current colors they were painted were even uglier in person than they were online. The lone bathroom still had its original tile on the floor, and I could see potential there. I knew Autumn dreamed of stripping out the outdated wallpaper and restoring the bath with reproduction fixtures.

The wooden staircase was in the craftsman style, and charming. I trailed my fingers along the banister as I started back down. I smiled at the dozen or so family pictures in mismatched frames that the Greenes were exhibiting on the stairwell wall. The wall itself was painted in a deep rose color, and weddings, graduations, snapshots of family vacations and portraits of grandchildren were proudly displayed. There was nothing planned or organized about the arrangement. If there was an empty spot, there was a picture.

Houses often have an energy, or a spirit of sorts. The vibration in this old house was a vital, loving and positive one. As I smiled over the family photos, reality melted away from me, and the present was replaced by a scene from the future.

The walls of the stairwell were painted a warm ivory color with three large, simple, black frames placed strategically on the wall. I focused on the black and white photo closest to me and saw that it was of my cousin. Autumn wore a long gown and her back was resting against a willow tree. Her face was luminous as she beamed up at a man in a tuxedo.

A wedding photo... I was staring at a framed wedding portrait. Autumn's gown had an illusion neckline top with a long and fluid skirt. She wore no veil, and there was a casual hand-tied bouquet in her hands... and the groom? The groom's features weren't easy to distinguish. As the mystery groom smiled down at Autumn, I couldn't make out who he was.

The grandfather clock in the foyer sounded unnaturally loud as I stood there, trapped in the present, while viewing the future. I hadn't had a vision in years, and as an empath, they were rare for me. To experience one, I typically had to be in an environment ripe with emotions. And clearly I'd stumbled upon one today. The Greene's happy memories of raising their children in the house, and Autumn's hopes and dreams for a home all of her very own, were all combining and creating a strong emotional environment.

I felt pulled onwards, even as I walked down the stairs in real time. I traveled down two more steps and stopped. The second photo in the vision had me smiling. *Autumn in profile, with her hands clasped around and under her very pregnant belly.*

Still in the vision, I felt myself travel down two more steps. *This third framed photo was of my cousin pushing a toddler in a baby swing. Again the photo appeared to have been taken with an almost full profile of Autumn's face, but the child was viewed from behind. I tried to focus on details... Autumn's hair was longer and she was grinning at... two children, in identical baby swings.*

While their faces weren't visible, I could see sandals on their feet, matching romper dresses and short pigtails sticking out on both of the toddlers.

Girls. Twin girls.

The vision of the future faded away. My breath left my body in a rush. I grabbed onto the handrail, struggling to maintain my composure. I shook my head, discovered that my great-aunt was standing before me on the stairs and that we were eye to eye.

"Holly." Her silver eyes seemed lit up as she studied me.

"Aunt Faye," I said. "The strangest thing happened." Delighted by what I'd seen, I started to laugh. "I don't usually have visions, but this one... Wow."

Her hand closed over mine on the railing. "Yes, I saw and felt something too the first time I walked down these stairs with your cousin."

I peered over the handrail to check, and saw Autumn standing in the dining room, speaking to the inspector. "Did you see three framed pictures?" I whispered.

Aunt Faye brushed her long silver hair behind her shoulder. "Yes, black and white photos. Of three very defining moments in life, you might say."

"In the vision, I could only see Autumn's face clearly in the photos," I said. "Does that mean that the outcome of those pictures is still in flux?"

"Possibly." She smiled then, beautifully. "I've decided to keep what I saw to myself. Because even a Seer, like Autumn, deserves a couple of surprises. Don't you think?"

A couple of surprises. "I understand." I winked at her. "And I totally agree."

Faye looped her arm through mine, and we started down the stairs together. "This home was meant for your cousin," she said.

"I'm so happy she'll be close by."

"I'll be happy to see the bungalow back in the hands of family again, where it belongs."

"Wait, what?" I said. "*Back* in the hands of family?"

Aunt Faye adjusted the collar of her coat. "This property originally belonged to the Bishops, and they built this house for Franklin in 1920."

"And Franklin was?" I asked.

"Franklin Bishop was the brother of your great-grandfather, Walter."

"Walter was married to Esther," I said, remembering the family tree. "She was the artist of the magickal herbal prints."

"Exactly," Aunt Faye beamed at me. "Now, Franklin Bishop and his wife lived here in the bungalow until they died. As they had no children, my sister Irene took over the house in 1967."

"I've seen the picture of you, Irene, and Grandpa Morgan, I wish I could have met the woman."

Aunt Faye grimaced and patted my arm. "Irene was

an interesting character. Difficult, you might say. Which explains why she never married."

My middle name was *Irene,* and I'd always assumed that my mother had named me after her other great aunt. "So you weren't close to your sister?" I asked, feeling suddenly sad for Aunt Faye.

"No, I wasn't, we didn't see eye to eye on a great many things." Aunt Faye sighed and continued her story. "Irene lived here until she died in 1990. After that, your grandparents sold the house to the Greenes."

"The Greene's have lived here for a very long time," I said. "I didn't realize."

"Almost thirty years," Aunt Faye said. "Their family has been wonderful for this house, it deserved to see some happiness again."

I frowned. "What do you mean, deserved to see— "

"Excuse me, dear," Aunt Faye cut me off. The relator wants a word with me."

The inspector was letting himself out, and Autumn stood with paperwork in hand, speaking to the real estate agent. Aunt Faye went over to talk to them, and I stayed out of the way.

As they discussed the seller's responsibilities for repairs and what Autumn could expect in the negotiations, I looked around the house again and marveled that it had been built by the Bishops, and was yet another part of our family history.

I went and stood at the big window in the living room and tried to imagine the space empty of furniture and ready for Autumn to put her stamp on it. I let my gaze travel back up to the stairwell. In the here and now, it was still painted an outdated rose color and jam-packed with the family photos of the Greenes.

It took everything I had *not* to start grinning over what the future held in store for my cousin. A new generation of Bishops would soon be living in the bungalow. But I had to wonder, *who was the groom/baby daddy to those twin girls that I'd seen?*

"So what do you think?" Autumn asked, bouncing over.

"I *love* the house," I said.

"So, the real estate agent does her mojo, and hopefully in a week or so the repairs get started."

"How soon do you think you'll take possession of the house?"

"Three weeks," Autumn said on a long exhale.

I did a little mental calculation. "Close to the Spring Equinox, then?"

"Yeah."

"Aunt Faye was telling me about the relatives that first lived in the house."

Autumn grinned. "Oh yeah, the family history of the bungalow. That makes it even sweeter."

"History nerd," I teased.

"What'd she tell you about her sister, Irene, that lived here?" Autumn wiggled her eyebrows.

"Not much," I said, gazing over at my great-aunt where she was talking to the real estate agent. "Doesn't sound like they got along with each other."

"Did you know that it was Irene Bishop who put up the big wrought iron fence *between* the two houses?" Autumn whispered, conspiratorially. "Originally, the fencing went around the perimeter of both properties... But at some point Irene added to it, dividing the land in half, and closing off her yard."

I pulled back the front curtains and looked out across the snowy lawn at the fence. "Really? I wonder why she would put up a barrier between herself and the rest of the family?"

"I don't know," Autumn said, joining me at the window. "But as soon as spring comes I'm taking out a big section." She pointed to the side yard. "Right over there, and we are going to make an entrance from my yard to the manor's."

I leaned into her arm. "That sounds great."

"I already have ideas for landscaping..."

I started to smile. "Of course you do."

***

At the far end of Main Street, a short drive from campus proper, sat Black Cat Coffee House. The coffee shop owners had taken full advantage of the local history and had combined it with a play on their surname. Even though the owners, Mr. and Mrs. Black, were mundanes and not practitioners, they were Halloween enthusiasts, and frequent shoppers at our family store.

I'd lucked out today and had found a parking spot only a few doors down. I made my way carefully through slush and puddles of melted snow and walked in the door ten minutes before four o'clock. I scanned the room, smiling over the interior of the café. It featured old pine floors, exposed brick walls and a front counter made from reclaimed wood, with a stainless steel top and a backsplash of white subway tile. There were framed vintage Halloween prints of cats, displayed year round, as well as a huge reproduction poster of *Chat Noir,* by Steinlen.

Julian hadn't arrived yet, and I was early on purpose, to avoid any of the whole, *is this a date or not?* Type of scenario. I went straight to the counter and considered the menu written on an old chalkboard. "Caramel macchiato, please," I said to the barista, and moved down to the end of the line to pay for my drink.

After paying for the coffee, I cast an eye over the space for a good spot to talk that would afford a little privacy and noted a small table and two chairs tucked up in the far corner. It was a bit closer to the counter but farther away from the rest of the customers. I headed over, peeled out of my coat and draped it over the back of my chair. My drink was delivered and I couldn't resist swiping a finger through all of the whipped cream and caramel. I leaned back against the brick wall and sipped.

To my surprise, Erik McBriar walked in. He was

wearing a heavy serviceable camouflage jacket, jeans and work boot. It was interesting to watch every female in the café stand up a little straighter when he entered the coffee shop. Erik appeared not to notice the attention and instead he went straight to the counter and placed an order for several coffees. Impatient and aggravated vibrations poured off him.

I sincerely hoped that I would go unnoticed, and was considering attempting— out of practice or not— a reluctance spell, when he glanced casually around the café and spotted me.

"Holly." He walked over, pulled out a chair, and made himself comfortable. "How are you feeling?"

He'd brought his negativity with him, and the considering look he gave me had my heart rapping hard against my ribs. I gripped my oversized mug with both hands and tried for casual. "I'm feeling better, thanks."

Those deep blue eyes took inventory of the bandages on my hands, and then slid over my face. He frowned over the steri strips at my left eyebrow. "So you actually did get some stitches?"

Confused at the skeptical tone of voice, I answered him cautiously. "Yes, I did on the back of my neck and palm of my hand."

"And they still haven't got any leads on the bastard that stole some jewelry and trashed my sister's store?"

Jewelry was missing? "What's missing?" I asked him.

"Didn't you see what the thief took?" Erik frowned

at me. "Several of the more expensive pieces in the case were stolen. Rings, an amethyst brooch..."

Leilah. She'd stolen baubles from my family in the past. I felt my face go red— the curse of a redhead— even as I scrambled to think of something to say that wouldn't contradict Julian's fabricated explanation... Which now, as it ended up, wasn't a made-up cover story at all.

"I didn't see the thief take any particular items, Erik," I said, honestly. "As I was sort of busy getting my ass handed to me at the time."

Erik reached out and took my right hand. He turned it over and frowned over the large bandage covering the stitches in my palm. "I'm sorry this happened to you." His eyes flicked up to mine and, because of the physical contact, I clearly sensed his emotions. *Impatience, determination, and... apprehension.*

Flustered at the conflicting emotions coming from him, I tried for a little humor. "Oh, I'll be fine. The scar will probably make it interesting the next time I go in for a palm reading, though."

Erik jerked slightly in his chair and dropped my hand immediately. Now his shoulders were set and his mouth had thinned. "Yeah, right," he scoffed at me.

Whoa! There were some very scornful vibes coming off of him at my joke about having my palm read. *Some genuine anger is brewing there...* I realized, and frowned over it. For a split second I considered trying to get to the bottom of his reactions... He was sitting close enough, but now his anger had shut him down good and tight. I could *feel* more than I could see that he'd pulled his energy close around him, and he glanced impatiently up at the clock on the wall.

The barista called his name, and he stood.

"I guess I'll see you at *Obscura*. That is if your sister ever decides to let me come back to work." I brushed back the curls from the side of my face, and tried a smile. "She wants me to take off a few weeks. I've told her I'm feeling fine... but she's being pretty insistent."

"Hang on a second," he said, and went to retrieve the cups in a travel tray. "I'd like to talk to you about that," he said when he came back.

"Talk to me about what?" I asked as he sat across from me again.

He slid the tray across the table. "I've been hearing some things about you and your family..." He trailed off as if searching for the right words. "It concerns me."

I flinched at his words. "Excuse me?"

"Look, you seem like a nice person." His eyes met mine. "My sister adores you, even my mother likes you, but the truth is... trouble seems to follow your family, wherever they go."

At a loss for words, I simply sat there.

"My sister doesn't know that I planned to talk to you about this," he admitted. "But between your family's reputation for being, well... *different*, and the damages to the antique store, I don't know how Ginny and her family will recover the losses to their business."

"I thought their insurance would cover the loss of any merchandise," I said.

"Not all, and the deductible they are paying for your medical bills is pretty stiff."

I bristled. "Then have them send the medical bills to me. I'll pay it myself." A nasty little combination of embarrassment and anger began to make my heart beat faster.

"No, no. That's not what I meant." He rubbed his forehead. "Holly, to be honest, my family doesn't need the drama or any more trouble. Neither the antique store, or the new wedding venue, can afford to be associated with—"

"Associated with what?"

He stopped and seemed to choose his next words with care. "We can't afford negative press of *any* kind. I hope you can understand that. To each his own. It's nothing personal."

Nothing personal, I thought, studying him as he sat there. There had been no cruelty in his words, nor did I detect any malice in his intent. What I did pick up on was concern for his family, discomfort at speaking to me in public about this topic, and... *fear.* He was worried about what I would do, and anxious over how I would react.

He truly was uneasy being around me. The realization had my stomach turning over.

I cleared my throat. "Just so we are clear, I'm not looking for any publicity over what happened, Erik."

"There was a story in the Gazette."

"I had no idea. I certainly never spoke to any reporters."

He held up his hands. "This is coming out all wrong." He shut his eyes for a moment and tried again. "I simply wanted to talk to you privately, and ask you to please consider *not* returning to work at the antique store. So things can settle down."

"Do Ginny and Gary share your sentiments?" I worked hard to keep my voice low.

"I know they've talked about the damage to the store's reputation after the incident, and they're struggling to cover the bills from your trip to the hospital."

"Workman's comp—"

"There is a deductible. And as I said, it's high."

I crossed my arms over my chest, the better to shield myself from the emotions coming off him. "I think it would be best if I spoke to Ginny myself."

"And I think it would be *best* for you to stay away from my sister. The kids are often in the store with her, I wouldn't want them to be upset."

I hissed in a breath at the insult. *Now, I was pissed.* "I would never do anything— in any way to harm those children." I struggled with my temper, and was slightly alarmed when one of the lids on the cups in his tray came off with a little *pop*.

Unaware, Erik leaned forward across the table. "I'm not trying to offend you. I love my sister and her family, and I'm only asking you to really think about what I've said."

As I glared at him, the coffee began to bubble over the sides of the cup like a little volcano. "Are you asking me, or *telling* me to quit?"

"I'm only saying, that if you were to quit on your own... that it would be the best outcome for everyone involved."

"I see." *And I did see.* Obviously, he'd heard something about the family's legacy of magick, and now, he was suspicious. In modern times mundanes didn't come after Witches with torches and pitchforks... but I wouldn't be the first Witch to find herself 'encouraged' to leave a job, because someone was uncomfortable with the Craft, or afraid of what they didn't understand.

"You can always get another job," he said. "Gary and Ginny will have a much harder time rebuilding their store's reputation, and recovering from the monetary losses."

I gestured to his tray with a nasty smile. "It looks like you are going to have to get another coffee." It was a small, petty satisfaction to see him do a double take at the bubbling mess.

"What the hell?" He jumped back when a second lid popped off the cups. The coffee actually shot up an inch or so above the top, boiled over the side, and flooded the drink tray.

"Don't worry Erik,' I purred, while he grabbed for

the napkin dispenser on the table. "You can always get another coffee."

"Holly." Julian stepped up. His voice was smooth, but he clamped a hand down on my shoulder in a warning. "Introduce me to your friend."

"He's not my friend, Julian," I snapped. "And he was just leaving."

The men studied each other over, but neither offered a hand.

Erik narrowed his eyes at Julian even as he stood. "You're Julian Drake. The guy who witnessed the *robbery*, and called the police." Erik's emphasis on the word left no doubt in my mind that he didn't believe the story.

"That's correct." Julian said. "And you are?" His tone of voice was extremely polite, even as the men sized each other up.

"Erik McBriar," he said. "It was my sister's store that was damaged."

"Ah, you and your family run a farm, isn't that right?" Julian smiled, but it never reached his eyes.

"We do." Erik stuck his chin out.

"Well don't let us keep you." He stepped back, allowing Erik to pass.

I flinched slightly when Erik snatched up the drinks. Coffee sloshed, and barely stayed within the to-go tray. He slapped the tray on a nearby empty table and stalked out of the coffee shop empty handed.

I watched him leave, and still the coffee in the tray

bubbled over and ran onto the table.

Julian gave my shoulder a squeeze. "Holly, rein it in."

I stared unblinkingly at Erik's back as he stormed off down the sidewalk, and I fought an internal struggle to yank my powers back under control. As I watched, he stepped off the sidewalk, headed towards his truck, and promptly tripped over thin air.

"Serves you right," I muttered.

"Holly." Julian sat across from me, and laid a gentle hand over mine. I felt a little tingle at the contact, and automatically, I glanced down at his hand, which broke my eye contact with Erik McBriar.

Shit! I'd jinxed Erik McBriar! I blew out a long breath and shook off the magick my temper had brought on. "Shit," I said, and had the presence of mind to keep my voice down. "I can't believe I did that."

"I thought it was Ivy who had telekinesis?" Julian asked, his voice low.

I grimaced. "It first manifested for me a few years ago, and if I'm angry or frustrated, it pops up on me. I'm still struggling to control it."

Julian slid his hand away. "I only caught the tail end of your conversation. What did he say that made you angry enough to lose control?"

Before I could answer, someone else approached the table. "Here's your flat white coffee," the barista said to Julian.

He smiled at the blonde ponytailed barista. "Thank

you, Donna."

She beamed and fluttered. "I remembered, it's your favorite."

He took a sip. "Perfect. You're the best barista in town. How are your classes going?"

I thought maybe for a moment the barista might swoon over his good looks and charm, hard to blame her really, but she seemed to pull herself together. "They're going great. A couple more months and I'll be ready for the bar exam. Can I get you anything else?"

"Perhaps a new coffee for the lady, there seems to be something wrong with the topping."

I glanced down and discovered that the whipped cream had curdled. The barista scooped it up, made several apologies, and rushed off to re-make the macchiato.

"I guess that was a side effect of making *his* coffee boil over."

"And making him trip." Julian raised his eyebrows.

I rolled my shoulders and popped my neck, trying to release the tension that had gathered there. "Guess curdled milk was the least I deserved." I sighed. "At least I didn't hurt him."

Julian sipped his coffee. "That was very mild, more of a prank than a hex. Don't be so hard on yourself."

I thought about it. "That's true, I've seen Ivy do worse."

"I'll bet." He smiled. "Now, tell me everything McBriar said."

I told him, and when I shared my suspicions that Leilah had helped herself to the jewelry in the case, Julian shook his head in disgust. But when I explained that it had been firmly suggested that I find another job — he was outraged. And that made me feel so much better.

"That's ridiculous," he said.

"I sort of lost it when he made the comment about the kids." I tossed my hair over my shoulder. "I would never do anything to— " I stopped talking as the barista approached.

Donna slid a new caramel macchiato across the table, and I noticed that she'd added a cookie.

"Thank you," I said and reached for my purse to pay.

"It's on the house." She waved me off. "You're Holly Bishop, right?"

"I am." I answered cautiously. I felt strong emotions coming from her: Outrage, a need for justice, and even support.

"I read about what happened to you in the paper," she said. "That's scary that you were robbed and attacked in the store right down the street."

"Oh." I managed. *Erik had said there'd been an article in the Gazette. I wondered what it'd said?*

"That guy who was in here? I couldn't help but overhear the conversation." Donna tossed her head. "But legally, they can't fire you. You know that, right?"

I felt myself blush. *By the Goddess, the gossip was going to fly fast and furious around town about this.* I considered the pretty blonde. She said she was studying for the bar exam... I supposed she was about to become an attorney. Now the emotions radiating from her made sense. "Yes, I know they can't," I said. "Thanks for the support."

"You hang in there." She patted my shoulder. "I'll leave you two to enjoy your coffee." She aimed a slow smile at Julian and headed back to the counter.

"She seems nice." I sent Julian a considering look.

"She is nice," he agreed. "Donna Black is an intern at my lawyer's office. I've known her for a few years."

I broke the sugar cookie in half, passed it to Julian. "She's totally crushing on you."

Julian smiled and sampled the cookie.

"Nothing to say, Drake?" I asked, and watched him over my coffee. He sat there, elegant and sophisticated in some designer suit, like he'd stepped off the cover of a men's fashion magazine.

"What are you going to do about your job?" he said instead.

I sighed. "I'm not sure. But the idea of going back in that store, knowing I'll have that disapproval and suspicion hanging over me makes it less than an ideal situation."

"The curse of an empath." Julian murmured. "Physically being around that much negativity would make you sick in the long run, or..."

"Boom," I said, and splayed my fingers wide.

"You could have more mishaps with magick." Julian

finished with a chuckle.

"Exactly." I nodded, pleased that he understood.

"Your major is art history, correct?"

"It is."

"We have a position open at the museum. Filing, phones, some light computer work."

I set the cup down. "Really? You'd do that for me?"

Julian raised his eyebrows. "Think of it as a way for me to balance the scales. The job is yours if you want it. The pay is nine dollars an hour to start. I believe we can easily work the hours around your class schedule."

I thought about it. I would be working in town, on campus even, at a job that could help me build my résumé in the future. I could save face by telling Ginny and Gary Chandler that I'd had a job opportunity that tied in with my major. I'd be working with a fellow magician, even if he was sexy as hell, so I'd be safe from more magickal attacks... and I would be in the same building as Autumn.

"This could be a smart solution to a lot of problems," I said.

"You think it over." Julian sipped his coffee. "And let me know in a couple of days. There's no pressure, or expectations."

"I don't need a couple of days to think it over. I'll take the job." I lifted the oversized mug in toast. "Thanks Julian," I said, and grinned when he tapped his coffee to mine.

CHAPTER EIGHT

I waited a few days before I called Ginny Chandler and told her that I had taken a new job on campus. To my chagrin, she seemed relieved, and I tried not to have my feelings hurt over that. When she asked me to let Aunt Faye know that the brooch she'd been interested in was among the stolen items, I sensed suspicion coming from her. Offended all over again, I struggled to remain polite, and I reminded myself that her business had taken a big enough hit because of me, and the last thing I needed was to work in a place where they were distrustful of me, and uneasy about what I was. So I bowed out gracefully.

Even if it burned my ass more than a little bit.

I called Ivy and tried to get some advice on the random PK as she referred to it. Once she stopped laughing about the coffee mishap, and me making Erik trip, she pointed out that it could have been a lot worse and that I should be pleased with my progress.

Autumn, Bran, Lexie and Aunt Faye were outraged

over Erik McBriar's actions, but my great-aunt went very still when I passed along the information on the jeweled crescent moon pin.

"Oh my," Aunt Faye said. "That's not good. That's not good at all."

"You're telling me," I said, firing up again. "I think the Chandlers and Erik McBriar suspect me of stealing it!"

Lexie snapped her head up. "There's been nothing said at the precinct."

"I think it may have been Leilah." I said to the family. "I remember her leaning over what was left of the jewelry case..."

"She's taken things from the manor in the past, hasn't she?" Lexie wanted to know.

Bran rubbed his eyes. "Yes, she has. Thomas Drake made sure his daughter returned the jewelry that she'd stolen from mom."

Autumn shook her head. "He needs to get a tighter leash on that little bitch."

I snorted out a laugh. "Bitch. Leash. Nice analogy, Autumn."

Bran made this little growling noise of frustration, and Lexie ranted on about the legalities of it all. I sat, listened, and let her get it out of her system. She and I had an uneasy truce at the moment, and she always was grouchy when she was pregnant. I finally distracted Lexie by asking about her upcoming ultrasound—when they were hoping to find out the gender of the new baby.

Autumn was pleased we would be working in the same building, and to my relief had no warnings or caveats about my taking a job offer from Julian.

Her closing date for the bungalow was coming up fast, and then there would be a shuffle of rooms at the manor when she moved out. Morgan would be taking Autumn's old room. The nursery would remain the nursery— but if Morgan was correct, it would probably have a new paint color.

I trooped along to the hardware store with my cousin and poured over paint swatches for the bungalow, and considered bathroom fixtures. Autumn had a list and a notebook filled with ideas. Her happiness made it hard to feel sorry for myself.

I got my stitches out and started the job at the museum the following week, and it was an easy job. I was basically Julian's assistant. I organized his schedule, took his phone calls, and as he'd described, filed and did office work. It was a little nerve wracking working closely with Julian four days a week. Maybe it was pheromones or something, but I kept holding my breath every time he got close to me. I couldn't ever recall having such a strong physical reaction to a guy. I continually reminded myself that he was much older than me, my boss, *and* that I needed to curb my silly infatuation.

He was an empath as well, so whenever I was in close proximity to him I tried like hell to project a casually friendly *vibe*. I guessed it was working, since he never acted in the least bit anything other than professional and casually friendly... yet as each day passed I found myself attracted to him, more and more. My intense reaction to him aside, I was happy to have the job.

If he had any idea where my thoughts had been going lately... he'd probably be mortified. *Yes,* he was gorgeous. *Yes,* he was sophisticated, and kind, *Yes,* he had a dry sense of humor that was sexy as hell... and the one time he'd bent over in front of me to pick up a file from the floor, I'd sucked in an appreciative breath having finally gotten my first clear look at his very fine butt.

Wait where was I going with this?

He'd rescued me, and had been nothing but kind and supportive since. So, I tried to focus instead on how he'd sat with me in the ER. Supporting me as a friend, and helping me shield when my empathy had made everyone else's emotions unbearable. He was a kind and casual *friend*, and I'd be smart to remember that.

I became a regular at *The Black Cat Coffee House* when I was sent out by the other department head on the occasional coffee run. That gave me the opportunity to develop a casual friendship with Donna Black. She was still helping her parents out part time even as she interned for a law office in town. She was, however, a goldmine of information. She overheard a lot of gossip at the coffee shop, and through her I learned that

Obscura Antiques had reopened, but apparently some of the older established families in town were quietly boycotting the store, because word had gotten out of their treatment of me.

I had to wonder if Erik McBriar had figured on *that* outcome, when he'd suggested I stay away from his family and their business.

So February rolled into March. Bran and Lexie were indeed having a girl, and now there was a major debate at the manor on names, *and* on the perfect shade of pink paint for the nursery. Morgan wasn't too happy about that, but he was intrigued at the prospect of getting a different room. As the semester rolled on, I was content and working hard on my classes. I'd also started practicing with Ivy once a week, trying to get a handle on my telekinesis.

I was in the University library checking out a few books for an upcoming paper on the Art Deco period, when my cell phone signaled a text. I pulled my phone out of my purse and checked. It was Ivy.

Hello Daniel-san.

I smiled and texted back: *Greetings Mr. Miyagi.*

Still coming to the dorm for practice?

I'll be there in 30.

Wax off.

I chuckled and rolled my eyes at her silliness. I strolled towards the counter, comfortable in my denim jacket, pale blue shirt, and dark jeans. I wondered what new things Ivy would throw (via telekinesis) at me today? Last week it had been pillows. She'd actually tied my arms to my sides with a couple of long scarfs, and then sent several throw pillows shooting through the air— straight at my head.

Her master plan was that I was only allowed to defend myself with my PK and nothing else. Once I'd gotten over my surprise, and Cypress laughing at Ivy's training tactics, I had eventually managed to deflect a few and stop the rest.

"It's all Holly Bishop's fault!" hissed a woman's voice.

My stomach tightened painfully in reaction to the feeling of hatred being directed at me, and I stopped in my tracks. I had *felt* the words as much as I'd heard them, so I cast my clairsentience out before me like a net. *Where, where, exactly was it coming from?* I asked myself. I felt a definite tug to my left, so I backtracked, as silently as possible, used the bookshelves for cover and made my way closer to the source.

Leaning slowly around the shelves, I found two female college students sitting at a nearby study table and talking— about me. One had dark blonde, straight hair with some bad highlights, and the other was a brunette. Their backs were to me, and I stayed where I was and eavesdropped without a qualm. I recognized that husky voice of the brunette immediately, and surprise, surprise, it was Leilah Drake Martin.

Leilah nodded to the blonde. "I'm not surprised, Raelyn. She's a trouble making, devious little Witch."

My mouth dropped open. Leilah sat there describing *me* as a troublemaker and devious? *Said the pot to the cauldron,* I thought. *And what the hell kind of a name is Raelyn?*

"It's all I've heard him and his family talk about for weeks!" Raelyn complained. "Holly Bishop this, and Holly Bishop that!"

I shifted to get a better look at the two. *This had to be Erik's fiancée.*

"Holly's wonderful working at the antique store." Raelyn simpered to Leilah, obviously making fun of me. "Holly helped with the wedding barn... She's so nice, she's *so* talented... even those little brats of his sister's liked her." She tossed her hair. "Oooh! I've never even met Holly Bishop and I hate her guts!"

"That's why I helped you *make* Erik get rid of her." Leilah patted her arm. "They're not singing her praises any more. Are they?"

Raelyn laughed. "No they aren't. And you were right, getting her away from Erik... Well, that was the best money I ever spent. That spell worked great."

My ears perked up at that statement. *Raelyn had obviously paid Leilah to work magick on Erik. Did that mean he was also compelled into talking to me about quitting?* I frowned over the thought.

"No one is better at magick than me, Raelyn," Leilah bragged. "And the bitch is gone, isn't she?" Leilah smirked.

"Yeah, but now Erik says we have to postpone the

wedding. Something about money and his stupid sister's store!"

Oh ho! What's this? Trouble in paradise? I smiled and continued to listen.

"Postponing the wedding?" Leilah sounded shocked. "He can't be serious!"

"I know his family is paying for everything, but it's not fair!" Raelyn pouted. "And he's being so mean to me about sticking to the wedding budget, and Erik doesn't think I should go on spring break with y'all."

"You need to show him who's in control, and go anyway." Leilah suggested.

"I even went and got a tan, like you said, so I'd look good before we go..."

"Your tan does look nice," Leilah agreed.

Raelyn continued to whine about how 'mean' and unfair Erik was, and then to my surprise she stopped in mid rant, pulled out her cell phone, held it up high, made a "duck face" and took a selfie.

I struggled not to laugh.

"I'm going to Fort Lauderdale anyway!" Raelyn announced. "I just posted online that I *am* going! He can stay here on the farm and sulk. It would serve him right, and he'll be miserable without me."

"Well if you decide that you need that other spell, you be sure and let me know," Leilah said, *sotto voice*. "All I need is a few things of his. A lock of his hair, a few other personal items, and by the time we're finished with your fiancé, Erik will be bound to you so tightly that he'll do *whatever* you want. And he'll never be able to even think about anyone else."

My stomach roiled in revulsion. Leilah was talking about the nastiest sort of magickal manipulation imaginable. To take away another person's free will, and force them to be bound emotionally to another... There wasn't anything darker, or more cruel. Yet there Leilah sat, talking prices and what Raelyn could expect from the spellwork, as if they were discussing the purchase and estimated MPG of a car.

I eased away from the two of them and went to check out my books. If I wanted to be on time, then I needed to get across campus to Crowly Hall for my training with Ivy. I shook my head over everything I had heard, and almost felt sorry for Erik McBriar.

Almost.

***

"Hey, girl." Cypress opened the door. Even barefoot in jeans and an old ratty t-shirt she was stunning. Her thick black hair hung down to her shoulders, and her hazel eyes sparkled.

"Cy," I said, giving her a one armed hug.

Cypress tapped her own eyebrow. "That looks good since the steri-strips came off."

"Thanks," I said, dropping my things on Ivy's desk and peeling out of my coat.

Ivy was seated on the top bunk, wearing purple

sweatpants, in a full lotus position. "Ommmm..." she chanted, with her eyes closed. Her gray t-shirt read, *Namaste, Bitches.*

I slanted a look at Cypress. She shrugged and shook her head at her roommate's antics.

"Okay Ivy," I said. "If you've balanced your chakras, perhaps we could get on with today's lesson—"

A book shot across the room straight at me so quickly that it was a blur. I squeaked in reaction, but I still managed to make the book freeze in mid-air, about three inches away from my face.

"Nice job," Cypress said appreciatively, straightening up from where she'd ducked out of the way.

My heart pounded in alarm as I considered the heavy book. I blew out a shaky breath, pointed a finger at the hardback, and concentrated. It zipped back across the room and dropped back on my sister's desk. "Damn it, Ivy!" I exploded. "You could have really hurt me with that!"

Ivy's eyes slowly opened. "But you didn't let that happen, did you?" She uncrossed her legs, slid off the bunk, and dropped to the floor. "You used your powers, and you did it well. You maintained control over your PK. There were no other random events, nothing fell over, and the *only* thing effected by your powers *was* in fact, the book."

"I'm going to start wearing a football helmet when

you invite Holly over," Cypress said, and sat in her desk chair. "Safer for me that way."

While I sputtered, Ivy got up in my face. "What? Did you think me making pillows fly at your head last week was for the hell of it?"

"Well, I..."

"It was *training*." Ivy insisted. "That's why I wouldn't let you use your hands. Sure, getting whapped upside the head with a pillow is pretty mild... but by the end of the afternoon, you were stopping anything I threw at you with your own PK ability."

"Even when I tossed those stuffed animals at you, to try and distract you— you put everything down on the floor," Cypress chimed in.

Suddenly it dawned on me. "You want to make sure I can defend myself from another attack."

"Exactly." Ivy wrapped her arms around me, pulling me in close for a hug. "I don't want to see you in the hospital again, because you didn't know how to use your powers to protect yourself."

"Thank you," was all I could think to say, as I embraced her.

"Besides, we know you," Cypress spoke from her chair. "And we figured that if you focused your telekinetic ability and put it to work, instead of letting it yank you around, you'd be happier in the long run."

"That's true, and pretty smart of you both," I said. "In an underhanded, sneaky sort of way."

Ivy let me go. "Yeah, I'm devious like that."

"Now try and do something on purpose this time," Cypress said. "The water bottle on the far side of my desk. Try and make it slide over here to me."

"It doesn't work for me, in the way it works for Ivy," I explained to her. "I've tried over and over again. Strained until I gave myself a nosebleed, but for me there has to be intense emotions like anger, or fear before the telekinesis turns on."

"Or," Ivy interjected, "a strong need for self preservation."

I blew a random curl out of my face. "Apparently."

Ivy put her hands on her hips. "That makes sense. You're primarily an empath. Your magick comes from your heart and from the emotions that you can sense from others. This new ability didn't manifest for you until you denied your other gifts."

"Once I allowed the empathy back into my life, I'd sort of expected that the new ability would dissipate," I admitted.

"But?" Cypress tilted her head.

"It didn't," I said.

"So," Ivy said, "you learn to deal with what you have on board now."

"Before I forget," I said to the both of them, "I overheard something very interesting a little while ago."

Ivy rolled her eyes. "Don't change the subject."

"I'm not. Not really," I insisted. "Do either of you know a girl named Raelyn?"

Ivy grunted. "Yeah, she hangs out with your arch-nemesis, Leilah Drake Martin."

"Describe her to me," Cypress said.

"Dark blonde hair, bad highlights, has a thing for selfies apparently." I smirked.

"Duck face." Ivy said, puckering up and doing a spot on imitation of Raelyn.

"That would be her." I nodded, and proceeded to fill Cypress and Ivy in on what I'd overheard.

Ivy shuddered dramatically. "Wow. I'm not sure what horrifies me more. The thought of Leilah Drake Martin pimping out her magickal - er - talents, or that she's planning on putting a love slave whammy on Erik McDouchebag."

"Thanks for that." I laughed. "Now I'm going to think that every time I hear his name."

"He got off easy," Ivy said. "You shoulda made him go face first into a snow bank."

"Ivy!" I gasped. "That's not funny, I used my powers to—"

"Teach him a lesson." Ivy cut me off. "Jeez relax, you didn't choke him, he *tripped*. If little Morgan would have done something like that do you suppose Bran would have a melt down, or firmly warn him to be more careful with his temper?"

"Well, I..." I trailed off thinking about it. "I suppose he'd give him a lecture, maybe a light swat on the butt, and send him to his room."

"Exactly," Ivy said. "Can I see your hands?"

"Sure, I guess." Confused, I held them out. Quicker than I could blink, Ivy reached out and gave me a slap on the back of both my hands. "Hey!" I yanked them back.

"There, you were punished for tripping Erik McDouchebag. Feel better now?" Ivy asked, as Cypress burst out laughing.

A laugh bubbled up. "Bitch," I said half-heartedly and rubbed my hands.

"I can throw heavier things at you, if you still feel the need to be corrected." Ivy yawned.

"No," I said. "Thanks, I'm good. You've made your point."

Cypress stood up and stretched. "So how's your new job at the museum working out?"

"It's fine," I said, working very hard to sound casual. The last thing Ivy or Cypress needed to know about was my current fascination with my boss. "I mostly answer the phones, file and keep Julian's schedule organized. He's busier with the museum than I realized." I risked a quick peek at Ivy to gauge her reaction.

"Stop worrying," she said firmly. "Look, Holly, what happened was a long time ago. Julian was totally messed up by the magick of the grimoire when he roughed me up and abducted me. Since then he's been through a pretty intensive round of counselling, and he's a different person these days."

Cypress dropped a supportive hand on my shoulder. "Did you know that he went out of his way with the

University to have Ivy's photography considered for the scholarship that she won?"

"I had no idea," I said. *How was I supposed to keep my feelings in check when I found out stuff like that?* I wondered.

"Yeah he did," Ivy said. "Autumn told me that he pushed through a bunch of red tape so my photo entry would make the deadline."

"You weren't here when the final show-down happened over the BMG," Cypress said. "But I know that your Aunt Faye told you how Julian got her and Autumn to safety when things were pretty fucking grim."

"And if that wasn't enough to convince me that he's changed," Ivy said, "he recently came to the heroic rescue of my twin sister."

"He'd probably be embarrassed to hear you say that," I said. "Julian told me himself, that he's no white knight."

"No, I don't think that he is," Ivy agreed. "Besides, we're pretty much even."

"Even?" I asked, my thoughts bouncing to what Leilah had said to me that day in the antique shop.

"Did you forget, that I nailed him with a garden trowel during the BMG caper?" Ivy raised an eyebrow. "He may have smacked me and dumped me in the trunk of his car, but I *stabbed* him in the thigh."

"That's right," Cypress threw back her head and laughed. "I forgot."

Ivy buffed her nails on her shirt. "It bled like a son of a bitch too. I heard he needed stitches."

"Wow," I said, tongue in cheek. "My sister is so spiritually evolved. Like Gandhi, almost. I had no idea."

"Namaste," Ivy said, pressing her hands together in a prayer pose.

***

When I walked into the manor, Aunt Faye was waiting for me in the kitchen.

"Dear, can we talk?"

"Sure." I took off my coat and laid it over a kitchen chair. Her face was set and the vibes coming off my great-aunt had me struggling to remain calm.

Aunt Faye rested her hands on the oak table. "There's a few things I want to show you."

"Is something wrong?" I glanced down at her manicured hands and noted that they were resting on top of a jewelry box, and an old photo.

Aunt Faye wasted no time telling me what was on her mind. "I have reason to believe that the amethyst pin, the one you texted me a picture of the other day, may have been an heirloom that belongs to our family." She passed me an old photograph of three women.

"Who are these people?" I asked.

"That is my mother, Esther." She pointed to each person. "My older sister, Irene, and me."

I studied the black and white snapshot carefully. My great grandmother Esther was standing in the center. Aunt Faye was a pretty teenager, her long dark hair pulled back in a ponytail, she had high bangs in the classic 1950s style. Her older sister, however, was not smiling at the camera. She appeared unhappy and angry. As I studied the photo I noticed something else. Each of the women was wearing a crescent moon shaped pin.

Aunt Faye opened the box, turned it so I could see inside. "This crescent was given to me by my father. Each of the women in our family had one."

I ran my fingertips across the deep red stones. "You wore this brooch to Mom's funeral."

"Yes, I did, *and* to your brother's wedding. As you can see, each of the brooches has different stones and slightly different settings. My mother's pin was diamonds and sapphires set in white gold. Mine is made of garnets and is set in yellow gold.

I considered the brooch pictured on Irene's dress, pulled out my cell phone and scrolled through my photos. The quick picture I had snapped that day in the antique store was still there. Silently I compared it to the black and white photo. It was identical to the one I'd seen in the shop. "I take it that Irene's pin was set in amethyst?"

"It was, but it's been missing since she passed away. We were never sure what had happened to the piece: If it was stolen, If she sold it, or if it was lost."

"I'm sorry you weren't able to get the pin back. I could feel vibrations coming from it back at the store, but I'm so out of practice using psychometry that I didn't realize the brooch had belonged to family."

"What exactly did you sense that day when you held the brooch?"

I tried to think back. "I could tell it had been owned by a magickal practitioner in the past. But other than that, not too much."

Aunt Faye leaned across the table, and her pale gray eyes were intense. "Did the energy feel positive or negative?"

"It gave me a little zap. I felt it run all the way up my arm and to the center of my chest."

"Was it light or dark?" she snapped.

I flinched back a bit in surprise from her vehemence. "I truly don't know," I said.

"Damn it."

"What aren't you telling me?"

To my astonishment Aunt Faye pushed back from the table and began to pace the kitchen floor. "If that brooch is the same one that once belonged to my sister Irene, and my instincts tell me that it is, then we have a bit of a situation on our hands."

My stomach twisted at the level of anxiety radiating from my great aunt. "In other words... shit just got real."

She stopped pacing and looked at me. "Correct."

"Tell me why."

"I'm not sure how my sister's brooch ended up at *Obscura*. But Irene was a complicated woman. I'm very concerned that the brooch could enhance the abilities of whoever holds it, especially if they lean towards darker magicks."

Suddenly what my grandmother had said to me seemed very important. *"Do you think you are the first member of this family to struggle with the dark side of magick?"*

I folded my hands on the table. "Are you saying that Irene was a dark practitioner?"

"Irene dabbled." Aunt Faye sighed. "The magick she worked was borderline, and our parents were never happy with the choices Irene made with her Craft."

"Is that what drove you apart?" I asked. "Your different ethics when it came to magick?"

"That was partly it." Faye sighed. "Also, she was ten years older, and actually, we were never close to begin with."

I went ahead and said what I was thinking. "I think we can safely assume Leilah Drake Martin has the brooch."

Aunt Faye nodded in agreement. "We need to find a way to get it back. By whatever means necessary."

"I hope you're not expecting me to break into Leilah's place and go riffling through her things looking for the pin?" I joked.

Aunt Faye marched to the kitchen cabinet, pulled down a bottle of our expensive Irish whiskey and poured herself a shot. "I'm ruling nothing out." She toasted me with the glass, and tossed the whiskey back.

I gaped at her. I wasn't sure what shocked me more, the casual comment about breaking into the Drake mansion, or seeing her do a shot and not even react. "Ivy's your B and E girl," I said. "That's how she found those poppets Leilah made when we were all still back in high school. She broke into lockers."

Aunt Faye set the shot glass on the counter with a little snap. "Perfect. She can access the other dorms easily enough. I'll call your sister this evening and speak to her."

"Hold up," I warned her. "Leilah doesn't live on campus. She lives with her father now."

"That's right," Aunt Faye said. "She did move in with her father, Julian and Duncan last year..." She stared off into space for a moment. "Hmm, I wonder..."

I was getting a bad feeling about all of this. "You're not actually plotting to break in to the Drake family mansion, are you?" I asked, horrified. "That's a really bad idea!"

"On the contrary, it's a brilliant idea!"

I rubbed my forehead. "Lexie would skin us both if she found out. Cops don't take this kind of thing too casually."

"Then we simply won't tell her." Aunt Faye waved my concerns away. "She shouldn't be upset. Especially during her pregnancy."

"Before you go all, 'Wanda the Felon' on me," I

said, "maybe I should call Julian and ask him to check and see if she's got it stashed at her room at the Drake mansion."

"You could. But I have an even *better* idea," Aunt Faye announced.

"Which is?" I dared to ask.

"The Historical Society has been trying to talk Thomas Drake into participating in the local historic home tour, this coming summer."

"And?" I said, not following her.

"Thomas has invited several of the board members for tea next week, so they could discuss it... and I think I could persuade the women for you and I to go along."

"You're going to go have tea... With Thomas Drake?"

"Not me, dear. *Us*."

"You have got to be kidding!" I said, shocked.

Aunt Faye tapped a finger to her lips and started to smile. "No I'm not joking. As a matter of fact, this is a *brilliant* cover. While the ladies and I keep Thomas distracted with the tour— you could go and search Leilah's room."

I dropped my head to the table and groaned.

Aunt Faye patted my head. "Won't this be fun?" She sounded absolutely delighted. "Maybe I'll wear a trench coat to tea, to get myself in a sleuthing mood."

"You're killing me, Aunt Faye."

"Where's your spirit of adventure?" Aunt Faye wanted to know.

"I think I need a drink." I said to the tabletop.

"I'll pour you one." she laughed. "And we'll toast to our success."

I raised my head and glared at her. "I really, *really* don't want to go to jail, Aunt Faye."

"Nonsense," she said. "I have an excellent attorney. He'd bail us out in no time." Aunt Faye poured two shots. She strolled over and set them on the table.

"Oh good, I'll only be in the hoosegow for a little while," I said, picking up my shot glass. "That makes me feel so much better."

She picked up her own glass. "*Sláinte*," she said, and together, we tossed back the whiskey.

CHAPTER NINE

Which is how I found myself a week later, sitting in the Drake family parlor, drinking tea with a half dozen ladies from the historical society. Aunt Faye had indeed worn her camel colored trench coat over tailored navy slacks and a beige twin set. She was also wearing her pearls and had announced on the way over, the double strand made her feel much more Agatha Christie.

After she'd dropped that unbelievable statement I'd shook my head, prayed to the Goddess for strength, and stayed silent for the remainder of the brief car ride. Julian had promised to meet me at the house and would help me search through Leilah's room.

Apparently he liked his half-sister even less than I did.

Now, I sat stiffly on the edge of a fancy sofa, sipped tea out of my fancy cup and nibbled on a blueberry scone. I wore a soft and swingy royal blue wrap-around dress that came to my knees. I'd paired it with a black cardigan, but it was warm enough that I'd skipped wearing tights, which had apparently scandalized my Agatha Christie-channeling, Aunt Faye.

Listening to the ladies and Thomas Drake make polite small talk was making me twitchy. I mean, you'd never guess that once in the not so distant past our families had been sworn enemies. Not to mention that his darling little psychopath of a daughter had put me in the hospital a few weeks before.

Apparently bringing that topic up during tea was simply *not* to be done, and good news? Leilah was off on Spring Break with a bunch of her college pals. So if Julian showed up, and if we could manage to get away from the group... I might have a chance to search her room.

Another twenty minutes passed, and after listening to the grandfather clock tick, and the bunch of them all discussing architecture, tiger's eye maple, and crown molding, I was seriously considering stabbing myself in the eye with a teaspoon, if only to break the monotony.

Before I gave in to my desperation, Julian walked into the parlor. I smiled in relief, did my best to ignore the little flutter in my stomach and the fact that he was sexy as hell. Today he wore a dark suit jacket, tailored slacks and pale gray dress shirt that was unbuttoned at the throat.

He sat across from me in an overstuffed chair and showed his impeccable manners by greeting Aunt Faye and chatting smoothly with all of the ladies that were present. I watched in amusement as several of the ladies began to flirt unashamedly with him. He took all of it in stride, poured himself a cup of coffee, and it gave me yet another chance to watch the effect that he had on people. There was something about that quiet demeanor with those intense eyes. He moved slowly, almost lazily, with a sort of restrained power...

And I was obsessing.

Again.

What was it about him?

As if he sensed my thoughts, he shifted his eyes to mine. I set my teacup down too fast and the clacking sound it made when it hit the saucer was loud.

"Holly, how are you?" His eyes traveled from the top of my head, down my blue dress, over my legs and finally to my sensible flats. His face was neutral, but the look in his eyes had my heart stuttering in my chest.

Oh my goddess. I licked my lips nervously and told myself to get a grip. *That's your boss,* I reminded myself. *He's just being polite and making small talk. He offered to help you look for the brooch. Don't act like an idiot around him...*

Julian stood. "If you'll excuse us." He held out a hand to me. "I promised Holly a tour of the family library."

Around us the ladies chatted on, and I saw Aunt Faye give me a slight nod. I set my cup and saucer down, picked up my clutch bag and stood. I walked to Julian's side, and he rested his hand at the small of my back, guiding from the room.

Without a word we walked out into the main foyer, and my flats were noiseless against the black and white checkered floor. "Follow me," Julian said, and we quickly went up the main staircase of the mansion.

I could see why the Historical Society was so eager to get a tour. There were huge stained glass panels, marble floors, rich, dark wooden paneling, detailed wainscoting, and the main staircase had newel posts elaborately carved into the shape of a dragon. The mansion reminded me more of a museum, and it blew my mind that he actually lived there.

When we reached the second floor landing Julian led me down a long winding hall. "Here," he stopped in front of a carved door. "Leilah's taken this room in the section of the house we usually reserve for guests."

He opened the door and we slipped inside. Even though Leilah was gone and on Spring Break, her presence filled up the room. The room was all done in shades of pale blue and cream. There were lots of sorority knick knacks displayed around the room, and it was surprisingly tidy. But I was betting that was because of a housekeeper.

"I've searched through her things in her dresser a few times since she left," Julian said, flipping the lock on the door. "I checked the obvious places, such as her jewelry box... but I haven't found the brooch."

"Let me see what I can sense," I told him. I closed my eyes, cast my senses out and tried to get a feeling for the missing brooch. I picked up on a barrage of emotions, many of them angry, and turned automatically towards the strongest source of left-over emotions. I opened my eyes and found myself drawn towards a set of closet doors. "Did you get a chance to check the closets?" I asked him, pointing to the one that had the strongest vibrations.

Julian went over and opened the doors I pointed to. A blast of energy slammed out, and I took a step back, but it was too late. Magick rushed out of the closet and hit me with a solid punch to the solar plexus. I winced and noticed that Julian had a similar reaction. And now that the doors were open wide, I could see why.

Leilah had set up the walk-in closet as a sort of magickal work space. The left-over vibrations that emanated from the area were chaotic, and sour.

He walked over and flipped on a nearby light switch. The closet was illuminated by a simple bulb in the ceiling. An old desk had been made into a work surface, and Leilah had covered it with a black lace shawl. In the center of the desk were her tools.

I moved closer but did *not* touch anything. A long, obviously sharp athame, and a copper pentacle were arranged on the desk. I noted a dark red glass bottle with a fancy faceted stopper, a miniature iron cauldron, a pair of fabric poppets, and assorted candles that had been burned down to various lengths; and notebooks and papers.

There were several spiral bound notebooks tossed carelessly on the surface of the desk, and also a few sheets of paper. I bent over and squinted at the notes that she'd left out. "These are astrological correspondences. Notes on the most opportune time for magickal workings," I said.

Julian reached out and picked up a poppet. "Well, this is new."

"Maybe you shouldn't be touching that." I pulled my sweater's long sleeve over my own hand, reached up and took the doll from his. "Leilah does like her poppet magick." I cautiously replaced it back on the work surface.

"Holly, look at these." Julian pointed to one of the pages. There on the upper corner of the page was a sketch, a very detailed sketch of the amethyst pin we were looking for. Julian scanned the paper. "She appears to have used the pin's magick to amplify a spell for someone named Raelyn."

"Oh crap," I breathed. "I overheard Leilah offering to do magick for Raelyn to bind her fiancé to her."

I ran my fingers over the sketch on the paper. It was a good likeness. I pulled my cell phone out of my purse and took a few photos of Leilah's altar set up, and was attempting to get a clear photo of her notes, when I bumped the phone into the bottle on the desk. It fell over, and some of the liquid leaked out from around the stopper. "Damn it," I swore. The potion was thick like molasses, and from the smell, that had to be one of the ingredients. A little began to run down the sides of the bottle.

"Use this." Julian passed a handkerchief to me, and I blotted up the small spill.

I tried to avoid skin contact with the potion, but in my efforts to wipe my fingerprints from the bottle, a little got on me anyway. I replaced the potion bottle and tried to wipe the stickiness from my fingers with his handkerchief as best I could. Out of curiosity, I held the linen up to my nose and sniffed. "Cherries, molasses and something else…"

Julian leaned closer to smell the handkerchief for himself. "Cinnamon oil... and ginger, maybe?" His eyebrows raised. "Those are classic ingredients for love and attraction spells."

Well, whatever it is, this potion is *powerful*. My fingers are starting to tingle, probably from the cinnamon oil." I made another attempt to wipe any remaining potion from my fingers.

He sighed. "I wonder what sort of catastrophe Leilah is conjuring this time?"

When a noise sounded outside Leilah's bedroom door, we froze. The knob rattled. Someone was trying to get in.

Julian took my arm and tugged me out of the walk-in closet. He flipped the light off, and hurriedly closed the closet doors.

"Where do we go now?" I whispered to him.

He took the handkerchief, stuffing it in his pocket, and made a 'come ahead' gesture. I silently followed him across the room. We stepped into an adjoining Jack and Jill bath and then out the far door. I glanced over my shoulder in time to see the housekeeper had unlocked the door and was carrying a stack of linens into Leilah's bedroom.

Silently, he took my hand, pulling me through to another guest room. He waited a moment and then eased the door open to the hallway. We'd gone about ten feet when I heard Aunt Faye, Thomas and all the ladies from the historical society walking up the stairs to the second floor.

At the sound of the voices, Julian hurried down the hall away from Leilah's room, and to the opposite wing. He opened another door and tugged me inside. He shut the door softly behind us and flipped the lock.

"Why are you locking the—" He pressed a hand over my mouth: A warning to be silent.

I nodded and he slowly removed his hand. We stood chest-to-chest as we listened to the approaching tour group discussing the architecture of the home. As I stood there, I smelled molasses, ginger, cinnamon and cherries. I had a second to worry about whether or not skin contact with that potion was a bad thing.

"I think I should go wash my hands," I whispered. "You didn't come into contact with any of that potion, did you?"

"I don't think so," he said, and pulled the handkerchief out of his pocket. He studied it, and then allowed it to drop to the floor.

My eyes followed the handkerchief as it fell slowly

to the carpet. I was still standing chest-to-chest with him, and suddenly I wanted to kiss him so badly that I couldn't breathe, or even think about anything else.

I wanted to see what his mouth tasted like, and I didn't give a damn if anyone heard me outside the door. Fascinated, I started to lean in.

He caught my arms at the elbows and I stopped. We both froze, our gazes locked for a heartbeat, then two, then three. My heart was beating so hard I was surprised that he hadn't heard it. He released me, and shakily, I took a small step back.

Out of desperation I looked around, anywhere, other than into his eyes. Over his shoulder I noted that the bedroom was spacious. A sitting area was situated nearest to the door and across the room, and a King size bed took up the far wall. The room was made up in burgundy and gold, had a masculine quality. From the vibration, I knew it to be his room, and it was, without a doubt, the biggest, fanciest room I'd ever been in, in my life.

Heavy brocade curtains were drawn against the afternoon sun. High above the bank of windows, a little half moon shaped window allowed some light in, and it gently illuminated the space.

"Do you think the tour group will come down this way—" I started to say, and then Julian pressed a finger to my lips for silence.

Sure enough, a moment later and I could hear the group. It sounded like they were right outside of the door. Someone rattled the doorknob behind us, and I jolted. After a moment they seemed to stroll off down the hall. Slowly he slid his finger away from my mouth and rested his hand on my shoulder. I stared up at his unusual eyes, and he gazed down into mine.

"Julian," I whispered as we studied each other. With no warning, he dropped his energetic shields, and I got hit with a blast of his emotions. To my astonishment, I discovered that my fascination with him was *not* one-sided.

I'd had no idea he'd been so skilled at cloaking his feelings. But now they were free, and an energy seemed to wrap around the two of us, binding us together. I gasped as I felt it, and wondered if he was being affected as well. "Julian?" I started to speak, but I never finished my sentence.

Before I could form another word, Julian reached out, cupped the back of my head with his hand, and tugged me forward. I tilted my face up, he swooped in, and I found myself being thoroughly kissed by Julian Drake.

Finally! I thought.

"Holly," he murmured, tugging my head gently back by my hair. "I dream about this hair," he whispered. When he ran both his hands through it, my heart leapt hard against my ribs.

I tilted my head back farther and opened my mouth to him. His tongue slid over mine, and he slowly wrapped one arm around me, pulling me closer. As our magick intertwined, I could *sense* all of his emotions bubbling below the surface. Kissing him was different, more intimate, as we were both empaths, and I gasped, unused to the sensation of magick combined with attraction.

We stood in that little beam of sunlight, our tongues warring with each other, and my clutch bag hit the floor with a muffled thud. Simultaneously, our hands rushed over each other, trying to touch, and to sense. My cardigan went flying, and I strained to get his jacket off him.

Now his mouth teased and tormented mine, and it made me want him. Badly.

Desperately.

I'd locked away any sort of real sexual passion for over six months. And as Ivy had warned me, keeping any strong emotion bottled up meant that it would be impossible to control if it ever broke free. Now thanks to the potion it was loose, and I *reveled* in it.

I wanted him right then and there in that bedroom, despite the group of people touring the house. It was crazy. It was irresponsible, and it was reckless. Even as some part of my brain recognized what was happening...

The rest of me didn't give a damn.

He cruised his mouth over my cheek, and nipped my ear. "You smell like cherries and spice."

"The potion," I murmured as he kissed his way down my neck.

"What?" I felt him smile against my throat.

"I think it's the potion." I panted, trying to kiss his mouth. He evaded my kisses with a smile, but allowed me to shove his jacket off his shoulders.

He pulled me to him again, and nibbled on my ear. "It's *not* the potion." His voice was low and sent shivers down my spine.

I nodded and thought, *KISS ME!* Maybe he picked up on my request, because he gripped my hair with one hand, and dipped me back. I sucked in a harsh breath when he stopped just shy of kissing my lips and instead detoured, working his way across my face with soft, slow kisses. His free hand glided down, and tugged on the tip of my breast. "Dear Goddess," I moaned.

"Be quiet," he whispered. "They'll hear us."

I finally realized that there were, in fact, several women right on the other side of the door. As they continued to chatter, oblivious to what was happening on the other side of the locked door, Julian nudged me further away and deeper into the room.

His mouth had finally covered mine, and I followed blindly where he led. I was desperate to slide my hands down his chest. I yanked his shirt aside, and I heard his shirt buttons pop. I purred in appreciation at what I felt beneath my fingertips.

I'd wanted to touch him for weeks. Now I could.

He was lightly furred and his muscles were well defined, and he reacted to my explorations with some shudders of his own. I hesitated when I reached the top of his waistband. He'd started tormenting me again with softer kisses on the side of my mouth. No matter how I strained to kiss him, he moved at the last second... A butterfly kiss on my cheek. A slow sweep of the tongue over my ear. A quick nip, but never a direct kiss on the lips.

I didn't like the teasing. To make my point, I nipped at his chin, and slid my hands down and over him, measuring his thickness and length. *Oh my.*

Julian's reaction was immediate. His kisses went from teasing and tormenting to explosive. Now it was all open-mouthed kisses, dueling tongues and teeth. He tugged at the side ties that secured my wrap-around dress and I felt it flutter open. Julian yanked one side of my bra down, and I hissed out a breath when he latched onto my breast.

He pushed me back against a closet door, and I threw my head back, reveling in the feelings: *desire, passion, excitement, and the thrill of the forbidden.* Whether the feelings came from the potion, from him, or from me...I really didn't care.

This coming together was magnetic, hypnotic and unstoppable.

And I only wanted more.

I ran my hands over his chest again as he suckled my breast, and then I buried my hands in his dark hair and yanked his mouth back up to mine. I kissed him hard, nipping at his bottom lip.

"I want you," he whispered, pressing up against me.

The closet doors shifted slightly behind my back.

"I want you too. So, so much." I whispered between kisses.

"I want you right here." His voice rumbled in my ear.

"Yes," I gasped, and surrendered. "Whatever you want. *Anything.*"

At my words, he reached down, ran his hand over the back of one thigh and yanked it up so I was completely open to him. I hung on to his arms as he pressed himself closer to me still. Pinned between the closet door and Julian's lower body, I felt his erection clearly through his slacks and my panties. I gasped.

With our eyes locked on each other's, he moved his lower body against me in a smooth sort of rolling motion.

"Please," I heard myself whimper. "*Please* Julian." I strained towards him.

He began to kiss his way down my throat, shoving the dress out of the way, and off my shoulders. It fluttered to the floor with a little rustle of sound. He reached out past me, and I heard the door slide open. He firmly took ahold of both of my hands, stretched them up over my head and back. He nudged me a few steps back, pressing the back of my fingers against something smooth. "Hold on," he growled in my ear.

The clothes bar, I realized. I nodded my head, took ahold of the rack built into the closet, and gripped it.

He kissed his way across my chest, and lower to my

belly. Out in the hall people were still chatting and laughing. He yanked his shirt off, and dropped to his knees in front of me. I gulped. "What are you going to —" I managed to whisper, right before I felt him shred my panties. "Oh!" I gasped.

"Quiet." He warned me. I looked down my own body to see him staring up at me. Those incredible eyes seemed to glow in a wild combination of brown and blue. His eyes never left mine as he pressed my thighs apart, dipped his head, and tasted me.

I couldn't help it, a little scream escaped. He stopped immediately. "Don't make another sound," he growled. "Or I'll find something to gag you with."

Those words should have been a dose of reality. It should have made me say: *Stop, what are we doing?* Instead it only made me more desperate.

"Open for me," he commanded.

I did, and was rewarded as he laved me with open mouth kisses, stabs of his tongue and the barest edge of his teeth. I squeezed the bar in the closet and hung on for dear life.

One of his large hands held my thighs apart and the other reached up and tested my readiness for him. I felt one flinger slip inside. When he added a second, I began to shake. His fingers stretched me and massaged a spot deep inside that had me going wild. My head bounced off the inside of the closet wall once, as I strained to hold onto the clothes bar, and not to cry out. His fingers began to move faster and faster, he growled against me, and I came.

I came so hard I saw spots before my eyes. At some point I must have let go of the bar because I found myself, kneeling over Julian on his bedroom floor. I gasped for breath as he rolled me over to lie on my back. Somehow, we'd landed between the closet and the bed, and he stretched over, rooted in a nightstand drawer for a second, and pulled out a foil wrapped condom. He opened it, and reached down to unbuckle and unzip. He knelt between my legs and shoved his pants aside.

I tried to focus on him: his beautiful face, the fall of that dark hair across his brow. I reached out, but he remained right out of my grasp. "Do you want this?" he asked, as he rolled the condom over his impressive erection.

I looked into his eyes, and was utterly lost.

Why are you lost? My inner voice wanted to know. I ignored it and focused on the incredible, gorgeous man kneeling before me.

"Don't tease me." I whispered, straining to touch him.

Again he evaded my touch. "Holly, are you sure?" he asked.

Are you? Some part of my mind wanted to know. *He's giving you the chance to say no... This could all be because of that stupid potion. Are you absolutely sure?*

"Holly?" His voice was rough, low and desperate.

"Yes Julian," I said. "I'm sure."

He reached down, gripped me behind one knee, and pulled me closer to him. I slid across the lush carpet and his hips forced my thighs farther apart. I felt the tip of him press against me and I gasped again. Our eyes locked, and I started to tremble.

"Now," he said, pushing his way forward, and he filled me so completely that my back arched off the floor.

I couldn't help but cry out, and Julian silenced me by dropping down and covering my mouth with a kiss that went on and on.

Somewhere in the back of my mind I knew the tour group was right outside his locked door, maybe a dozen feet away. I struggled hard *not* to shout at the feelings he gave to me, so instead I took my frustrations out on his back. I dug my nails in, raked them down, and heard him hiss out a breath in pain. And still he moved faster, rolled his hips deeper.

He lifted his mouth, and the eyes that met mine were glittering and wild. "You do that with your nails again and I'll retaliate," he warned.

I ran my hands down and over that exceptional butt of his. He hadn't completely undressed, and for some reason that was incredibly hot. I wound my legs around him tighter, and deliberately dug my nails into his butt instead.

"That's it," was all the warning I got.

He pulled out, flipped me over, and yanked me up on all fours. I gasped, and then he was sliding so deep inside that I dropped my head to the floor and moaned into the carpet. I stayed there, head down, collapsed for a while. From this angle he stretched my core so tight that it bordered on pain, but every stroke was incredible.

I felt his hand tangle in my hair and he pulled me back up and to my knees. I leaned back against his chest— still kneeling on the carpet. He wrapped his other arm around my torso, pulling me closer so I was half sitting in his lap. When he bit me at the nape of my neck holding me firmly in place, it was exactly right. Exactly what I wanted.

It was incredible, this way. It was almost *too* much. I'd thought I was experienced. But with Julian Drake I discovered that what I'd known before was *nothing*. Lost in his sensual spell, I threw my head back as he played with my breasts, and I came again, taking Julian with me this time. It seemed to last forever, and finally, we collapsed on top of each other on the carpeted floor and tried to catch our breath.

I don't know how long we lay there, but all I could think about was: *How soon could we do it all over again?*

Julian turned to me and kissed me softly. He whispered my name over and over, as I tried to catch my breath, and his hands were soft and gentle as he passed them over my body.

"Again," he said.

I stared at that handsome face, and everything inside

me clenched. I nodded my head. "Yes."

It was like we couldn't stop.

But why couldn't we stop? Some sane part of my mind wondered.

Julian rose to his feet and pulled me to mine. An impatient flick of the wrist and the bed spread was tossed off the bed, and he pushed me gently back. I sighed when I hit the firm mattress. With a few quick moves he shoved his pants completely off, and reached into the nightstand again. Silently he set a few more condoms on the bed next to me, and I reached out, took his shoulders and rolled, pushing him onto his back.

"My turn," I whispered against his chest. I slid my mouth over his body, returning the favor he'd bestowed on me at the start. His hands gripped tightly in my hair as he shuddered while I licked, nibbled and kissed my way down.

When he could stand it no more he rolled me under him. He whispered things that had me blushing while he dealt with another condom, and then he surprised me by gently easing himself inside. Our eyes were locked on each other as he slowly buried himself deep. He caught my hands in his, stretching them up and over my head. He kissed my forehead and eyes, and our fingers intertwined as he took me again, leisurely and carefully this time.

As the light coming in through the little window above us changed, and the shadows shifted, we moved together. I knew as he gazed down into my eyes that this was much more than a rogue spell we'd been caught up in.

Our emotions intertwined and added to the intensity. Empathically, I could sense his soul, and I *knew* who he was: a quiet, gorgeous man, who had suffered in the past. Like me, he'd walked too far into the dark side of magick once before, but he'd worked hard to become the person he was today. His emotions were intense, and they ran deep.

His feelings for me were new and unexpected, but they were *real*. Captivated, I wrapped my fingers around his as he began to thrust deeper and move faster. He kept me just at the edge until I was ready to beg for release, and then we both surrendered to the orgasm together. It hulled us out, and afterwards sent us both crashing into sleep.

CHAPTER TEN

It was fully dark when I woke up, and I slowly came to the realization that I was sprawled across a very fine chest. I breathed deep and recognized the scent. *Julian.* I sighed and burrowed closer.

Reality came crashing in about ten seconds later.

I was practically naked in Julian Drake's bedroom. And we'd spent the past few hours having sex... all kinds of crazy, mind-blowing sex. "Oh boy," I said. I sat up slowly, tugged my bra back into place, and scanned my surroundings. I reached for the nightstand, patted around and clicked on the bedside lamp.

Julian sat up. I watched as his eyes cleared, and could tell the exact moment clarity returned to him. "Holly." he reached out a hand to my hair, and I jumped slightly. "Are you alright? Did I hurt you?"

I took a swift mental inventory. I was a little sore, but otherwise, fine. "No," I whispered, leaning my face into his hand. "Of course you didn't hurt me."

He pulled me over to him and I snuggled against his

shoulder for a few moments more. When he pressed a kiss to my forehead, I flashed back to raking my nails down him. Concerned, I sat up.

"Oh shit," I said. "Let me see *your* back." I reached out and nudged his shoulder towards the light so I could check. Lines of red scratches started below his shoulder blades and ended at his waist. "I did a number on your back," I said, appalled at what I'd done. "Julian, I'm so sorry."

"It's fine." Julian waved away my concern. He pulled me close, leaned back against the headboard, and held me.

"What the hell just happened to us?"

"What *didn't* just happen?" He pressed a kiss to my hair.

"Well, I suppose we sort of jumped each other's bones."

"You hopeless romantic," he said, dryly.

"I've never felt anything that intense in my life," I whispered to his chest.

"Why, thank you," he said earnestly.

The blood rushed to my face, and I wasn't sure if I should be horrified or thrilled with myself. "I can't imagine what you must think, after what I did to your back." I said softly, unable to meet his eyes.

"Holly," he tipped my face up to his. "Are you sorry this happened?"

The past few hours replayed in my mind, and I struggled not to be embarrassed. I glanced over the side of the bed, saw our clothes thrown everywhere and used condoms beside us on the bed. My stomach lurched. "Oh god." *At least we used protection.* I thought.

Julian quickly worked out what I was reacting to. "Let me clean that up," he offered, and he gently set me aside and rolled to his feet to deal with the mess.

I tugged a corner of the sheet up over my lap, reclined back on the pillows, and watched him. Now that his shields were down, I could sense he was concerned and that doubt was beginning to form in *his* mind. He was wondering what I would do, and worried how I would react to everything that we'd done.

Well, that made two of us.

He walked over to what I guessed was a bathroom. A light went on and he moved out of view for a few moments. I heard water running and then he came back with a glass of water. "Here," he said, holding it out to me.

I sat up against the pillows a little higher to sip at the water. "Do you think we activated a love spell in Leilah's room?"

Julian reached down to the floor. "It's possible." He picked up his shirt and held it in front of him.

"Oh," I said in a small voice. His empathy made him vulnerable to intense emotions... as mine did for me. "How do *you* feel about that?" I asked, setting the water aside.

Julian sighed. "You're not to blame for any of this." He turned away and shrugged stiffly into his shirt.

"I'm not trying to place blame," I said, as he continued to keep his back to me. "Please don't turn away from me, Julian." I held out a hand to him.

He glanced over his shoulder and studied my face, and came back to sit next to me on the bed. "I can sense your distress, Holly."

"What you're sensing is me being *embarrassed*," I said softly. "I've had a few different sexual partners. But I've never experienced anything like what has happened between you and me. I've never reacted like that with a lover before..." I trailed off and tried to psych myself up.

"You're a gorgeous, successful, older man, and I can't imagine what you'd see in me. I'm... well... I'm sort of damaged goods."

"Why would you think that about yourself?" he asked.

"There's a lot you don't know about me. Some of it isn't very good."

"I doubt you've done anything that—"

"I got pregnant."

He blinked, but other than that showed no reaction. "When?"

"Last fall." I tried to keep the tremor out of my voice. "But I lost the baby."

"That's why you came back to William's Ford," he said, pulling me close and tucking my head under his chin.

"No one else knows except Autumn." I burrowed

closer, taking the comfort. "I didn't have the courage to tell the rest of the family."

"I'm sorry, angel," he said.

"Julian, I'm no angel," I said. "I've been very attracted to you for a while, but I figured you didn't think of me that way."

"I've wanted you since that day at the antique shop," he said.

"Really?" I asked, looking up at him. "I thought you were simply being kind and trying to be my friend."

"I *was* trying to be kind, but when you looked up at me with those big sea-blue eyes..."

"Oh god," I covered my face with my hands. "Did I tell you, you were pretty?"

"You also said I was sexy," he said with a hint of a smile. "You had a concussion, I didn't hold it against you."

"These last few weeks of working with you, has—"

"Been torture," Julian finished, and ran a hand through my hair.

"Yes," I said on a sigh. "I kept telling myself you're my boss and that I had to stop thinking of you that way, to stop dreaming over you."

He chuckled. "I've been shielding my feelings from you. It wasn't easy, Holly. Considering that we've both admitted to being attracted to each other... we can rule out being ensnared by a love potion, don't you think?"

I nodded. "Part of me can't believe I'm here with you, like this," I said. "And another part of me hopes that *you* don't have any regrets."

He tipped my face up to his. "No regrets." He kissed me soft and full on the mouth. "And I want you all over again."

My heart stuttered. "Ah..." I managed

"Do I need to prove to you, how badly I still want you?"

"It's not that." I put my hand on his chest to stop him. "It's only that I'm not sure I'm up for another round right this minute," I admitted. "We may need to let things recover."

Julian dropped a kiss on my nose. "Let me take care of you, Holly." He took me in his arms, stood, and carried me towards the bathroom.

"I could get used to this, being carried around." I said, resting my head against his shoulder.

The bathroom was as decadent as the bedroom. Done all in beige, cream and brown, a double vanity with acres of counter stretched along one wall. A huge soaker tub was opposite, and a glass door shower big enough for several people took up the far end of the room. Julian set me on the counter, and I hissed when the cold granite met my backside.

"Cold?" he asked with a mischievous grin that melted my heart. I'd never seen a playful side to him before, and it was endearing. With a few efficient moves he started the water in the tub, and he laid out a huge fluffy bath sheet.

I made a calculation to the depth of the water in the

tub, and figured my hair would end up soaking wet. I sighed and shifted to get down from the counter.

"Where do you think you're going?" He caged me in with his arms.

"I was going to get my purse. I need something to tie my hair up with, a hair scrunchy. If I get my hair wet it's going to explode out everywhere."

"I'll get it." He kissed me. "You stay right there."

I watched the water rush in the bathtub and swung my feet. He returned and handed over the scrunchy. I bundled my hair up as best I could and secured it to the top of my head. "Yeesh," I said, turning to face the long mirror over the counter. I'd done my best with my hair, but sloppily bundled on top my head was not my best look.

I saw his face in the mirror when he shut off the water and stood behind me.

"You're beautiful," he said. He kissed my right shoulder. "I like the tiny crescent moon tattoo, I noticed it before, but was too... distracted to tell you."

I blushed. "It's the family crest," I managed to say without stuttering.

He smiled at the rising color in my face and slowly unhooked my bra. My breath caught in my throat as the bra dropped and he ran his hands over my breasts.

"I don't think I can..." I began.

"Let's get you in the tub," he said, and scooped me up. A second later he was lowering me into the water, and it felt like heaven.

"That feels good," I said and leaned back.

"If you need anything I'll be right outside." He handed me a bar of soap and a washcloth and left, leaving the door slightly ajar.

I pulled my knees up and dropped my forehead on them. The past few hours flashed back through my mind, and I shivered in reaction. I began to wash and wondered what in the world would happen now.

Where did we go from this? Besides one coffee, we hadn't ever even been on a date. His father would never approve of me, and my family would likely be horrified. What about my job... what about... I pressed the washcloth to my face and groaned.

Not everything needed to be decided upon today. First things first, I needed to get out of the tub, get dressed and figure out how to discreetly exit the Drake mansion. When I entered the bedroom again, I was wrapped up in a towel and my clothes and his were laid out on the now neatly made bed.

Julian smiled when I walked in. "I'll be right back," he said, and went to the bath to clean up. Grateful for the privacy, I slipped my bra back on and realized that my panties were gone. I vividly recalled him ripping them off me, and I blushed, hard. I searched around the room but couldn't find them.

Shrugging, I slipped my dress on, secured the side ties and stepped into my shoes. I went to try and repair my hair in the bedroom mirror and discovered how decadent it felt to walk around in a dress with no underwear on.

I added my thin cardigan, repaired my hair and face with the cosmetics I'd had in my purse, and sat on the side of the bed to wait. Julian emerged from the bath, and my heart gave one hard jerk when he strolled out with only a towel slung low over his hips. I must have made a noise in reaction because he stopped and considered me as I sat there.

"I'll only be a moment," he said, and went to his dresser. I nodded and watched him drop the towel and step into a pair of dark briefs. He walked slowly over to me and reached for his clothes.

I gulped. Loudly. I'd never watched a man get dressed before. It was oddly intimate. When Julian picked up the fresh shirt I suddenly remembered why he needed one in the first place. I said the first thing that popped into my mind. "Sorry about the shirt."

He raised an eyebrow. "I'm not." Leisurely, he slipped the shirt on, but didn't button it. "Did you find all of your things?" he asked.

I slanted a look up at him. "Nope."

"Really, what are you missing?" he asked completely straight faced.

"The panties you ripped off me."

He bent over, his arms on either side of me on the bed. "Does that mean you have nothing on under that dress?"

"I have my bra on," I said tartly, leaning back on my elbows.

Julian made a low growl in his throat, He hovered above me, and stared.

"What are you doing?" My voice was breathy.

"I want to remember you here on my bed, just like this."

"If you keep talking like that we'll never get out of here, and I need to get back home," I pointed out.

He lowered his forehead to mine, and sighed. "I know."

When he stood and continued to dress I was torn between relief and disappointment. "Julian," I said, and waited until he looked me in the face. "This was incredible. I won't forget it, and I do *not* regret it."

He stayed where he was, his eyes intense. "Saying things like that makes it harder for me to let you go."

I stood up and went over to him. "I didn't ask you to let me go. I only asked you to take me home."

He pulled me close. "I want to see you again, soon."

"Yes, I'd like that." I said into his shoulder.

"You know we need to keep this private," he warned. "Especially at work."

"I know," I sighed in his arms. "Also, neither of our families would approve."

"We'll figure it out." Julian said, releasing me from his embrace. "Are you ready?" he asked.

When I nodded yes, he took my hand and led me to the door. He unlocked it, but before Julian opened it, he kissed me one last time.

Getting home was surprisingly easy. Julian and I

went out of his room and down a set of back stairs as silently as possible. It was almost as if we were alone in the house, even though I knew there were servants, and his cousin and father. We eased out through the kitchen, across the darkened brick courtyard, and around to the garage where the cars were housed.

Before I knew it we were pulling up at the curb in front of the manor. I couldn't kiss him goodbye and I settled for a quick squeeze of his hand before I exited the car. "Good night, Julian," I said and gave a casual wave.

He nodded and drove off.

I walked down the driveway and into the manor, when I shut the garage door behind me the contrast in mood from the somber, formal Drake mansion, compared to the happy and animated atmosphere of the manor, was shocking. At the Drake mansion there'd been only formality with little sense of fun. Here at the manor, it was loud, noisy and chaotic.

As if to prove my point Morgan scrambled past me, chasing Merlin up the kitchen stairs. My nephew was wearing a play football helmet and brandishing a rubber sword. The cat wailed and Morgan gave a toddler version of a battle cry. Autumn came down the steps past Morgan, hauling moving boxes and admonishing him to stop chasing the cat.

Aunt Faye was arranging a vase filled with forsythia blossoms at the island in the kitchen, and Lexie and Bran were seated at the table, loudly debating paint swatches for the new baby's room.

I set my purse down and went to the fridge for a bottled water, uncapped it and took a swig.

"Hello, dear." Aunt Faye sounded calm in the center of the pandemonium. "How did everything go? Did you get lucky?"

I choked, coughed and spit water out of my mouth. "What?" I asked horrified.

Aunt Faye frowned and handed me a dishtowel to mop up the spill. "Did you and Julian have any luck finding the brooch?"

Oh my god, pull it together girl! "Some leads," I managed to say. "I'll tell you more about it later."

Aunt Faye nodded and I left, going up the kitchen stairs to escape to my own room. Once I got to my room and locked the door, I dropped onto my bed.

I closed my eyes and thought back to Julian holding me in his arms while we cuddled after... well after everything. I played back the events of the afternoon in my mind, the search for the brooch, accidentally unleashing that love or possibly lust potion. I trembled, remembering the pleasure he'd given me, and admitted to myself that *if,* indeed the potion had pushed us together, or gotten the ball rolling— so to speak— the rest had been all him and me.

I had no idea what to do next in regards to the missing brooch, or with Julian Drake as my lover— not to mention my boss. My life had now become extremely complicated.

One thing I knew for certain.
I already missed him.

***

I woke up the next morning to the strong fragrance of roses. I rolled over, opening my eyes, half expecting my grandmother's ghost to be sitting at the foot of my bed. But instead I found Merlin sprawled at the foot, in a nest of blankets. I released a slow breath and sat up in bed. My body was a little sore and stiff this morning, and when I remembered why, my stomach gave a little lurch in reaction. I scrubbed my hands over my face and tried to recall the dreams that had haunted me through the night.

They'd been strange and weird, and none of them had been about Julian. I'd dreamt of my mother sitting on her bed and writing in a journal. But she'd appeared different, maybe younger? Though the dream image was soft and fuzzy, it was the emotion behind it that made me uneasy.

Frustrated with the vague apprehension the dream had given me, I staggered off to the bathroom. I had the day off and had decided while I was in the shower to see what real, physical information I could find on Irene Bishop and her amethyst brooch. As I dressed for the day I checked my cell phone, hoping for a text from Julian.

I was disappointed that there was none. I tugged a

simple, cotton skater dress in purple down over my hair and reached for a pair of tights. When I sat on the side of my bed to pull up the tights, I discovered rug burns on both knees. Now, fully awake, I realized why my knees had been stinging in the shower.

I had a moment flashing back to how I'd gotten those rug burns, and my stomach tightened. I went and found a couple of adhesive bandages and covered the skinned knees so they wouldn't stick to anything while they healed. I decided to switch out the tights for a pair of comfortably soft gray leggings instead. I picked up my mother's crescent pendant from my dresser and fastened it on. The person looking at me from the mirror was noticeably different. My eyes were clearer, my skin was flushed, and my aura seemed brighter and more vivid. Living in a house with Witches, and Seers, someone was bound to notice.

"Good grief," I said, making a face at my reflection. "Maybe I should wear a sign that says 'Recently Laid'."

I checked the time, it was close to nine am. Hopefully most of the family would already be gone for the day. To play it safe I decided to stay in my room and give it another half hour.

I straightened up my room, made my bed— which annoyed the cat, and picked up the towel, to dump it in the hamper. My phone signaled a text, and I checked it. It was from Julian.

Good morning, Angel.

I smiled down at those three little words and my

heart ached. I sat on the side of my bed and wondered what to reply.

I miss you, seemed too needy, *Hey Handsome,* seemed a bit too shallow. *How's your back?* Was way too slutty, and using an emoji was a cop-out. I finally settled for:

Good morning, Julian.

I stretched out on the freshly made bed and waited to see if he would respond. Merlin took that as an invitation and joined me, walking up my chest. He started rubbing against the cell phone, marking it with his scent as I held it up. I rubbed Merlin's kitty ears and he began to purr. Another text came in:

What are you doing, right now?

I couldn't resist teasing him a bit. I texted: *I'm lying in bed with a gorgeous beast.* Then, I aimed the phone at Merlin, quickly took his photo, and hit send.

Ha!

You asked...

I'll think of you today.

I sighed over that. Then sent: *I'll think of you too.*

***

I was a basket case when I went to work at the museum the following day. I hadn't heard from Julian since the morning before, and the enormity of what had happened came slamming home when I parked my old car in the museum staff parking lot and sat, surveying the building.

I was sleeping with my boss.

He was nine years older than me, was wealthy, successful, and respected at the museum. I was merely a college student working part time.

The facts didn't sound very pretty, they actually sounded reality-TV-tacky. If people at the museum found out, it could go one of two ways. Either I'd be the opportunistic slut, or he'd be the predatory boss. Even though *neither* of those scenarios were true... people wouldn't care. My reputation, such as it was, would be trashed and Julian's career could take a major hit. I dropped my head to the steering wheel and groaned.

For comfort, I touched a hand to my mother's crescent moon pendant. I had it waxing side out today, as the moon was growing towards full. And I realized as I ran my fingertips over the pendant that I couldn't sit and hide in my car. I needed to get up and go forward.

"Suck it up, Buttercup," I told myself. I gathered my things, climbed out of the car, held my head up high and marched toward the main doors of the museum.

I had purposefully dressed up today, and my petal pink midi-dress came down to my shins, and swished satisfactorily. I'd added a thin, soft gray cardigan and had paired the dress with neutral low-heeled shoes. I'd considered trying to do something different with my hair but instead I let it air dry and finger-combed it into long curling cables down my back. Up-dos were always a risk, and coaxing it into long curls was about the best I could do.

I walked to the entrance, passing the pretty saucer magnolias that were in full bloom. I couldn't help but stop and admire the candy pink petals. Magnolias were associated with the element of earth, and in the language of flowers, the blossoms symbolized sweetness and perseverance. I reached up and cupped a blossom in my hand.

"May I?" I asked the tree, keeping my voice low. "I could use some perseverance today."

I felt a little tingle of power from the tree, and I waited. When the branch shivered, I knew that I had permission, so I snapped a single blossom from a low branch. "Thank you," I whispered, and having taken comfort from the tree, I tucked the flower behind my ear, put my shoulders back, and strolled inside.

I greeted people as I waked up to the offices on the second floor of the building. Eventually these would all be moved once the expansion of the museum was complete. Now the new building was a nearby structure of iron beams, but in another year it would be complete.

I pushed open the door to Julian's offices and went straight to my desk. His door was closed, so I figured he was out or somewhere else in the building. Even when he was working, he typically kept it slightly open. I tucked my purse in the bottom drawer, powered up the computer, and checked my in-box for files, or messages.

I'd barely begun going through the departmental emails on an upcoming fundraiser when Autumn stuck her head in the door. "Hey Holly."

I glanced up. "Hi."

Autumn had her straight, brown hair casually clipped up on the back of her head. As was her habit she was wearing a bright color. Today it was a clover green. She let herself in and came over to perch a hip on my desk. "Nice touch with the magnolia. I love that color pink on you," she said, adjusting her glasses by the frames.

"Thanks, I couldn't resist the flower, and the dress seemed like a good springy choice today."

"You look good, Holly," Autumn said. "It's nice to see you *blooming*."

I rolled my eyes. "That was a terrible pun. Tell me why you're really here, because I know it's not to compliment my outfit."

So, this weekend..." she trailed off.

"I already told you I'd help you paint."

Autumn's green eyes seemed to sparkle. "Yeah, I know, I still wanted to make sure that you were good with the weekend long marathon of cleaning and painting. I didn't want to assume."

"I'm looking forward to it." I knew Autumn was anxious to get her hands on the house. She wanted to move in as soon as possible. But before she could, some work needed to be done. To make her smile I rubbed my hands together. "That master bedroom is going to be gorgeous when I'm done with it."

"You still think the vintage blue-green we picked out is the best choice?" Autumn asked nervously.

I was opening my mouth to answer when Julian opened the door from his office. I managed not to react. I hadn't known he was in there.

"Good morning," he said, and it was so polite, so smooth, that I don't think anyone would have ever guessed that we were anything other than co-workers.

Autumn nodded. "Hi Julian. I was making sure Holly was still available to help me paint this weekend."

He came out and walked over to my desk. Today he was wearing a spring gray suit with a white shirt and a patterned tie. I was struck all over again with how attractive he really was. His dark hair was casually styled but still perfect. Self-consciously I tucked a wayward curl behind my ear.

"That's right. Don't you close on your house this week?" he said casually. I wasn't surprised he knew. In a town like William's Ford, news of the old bungalow returning to the Bishop family had been quite the topic of discussion.

Autumn grinned. "Yep, I get the keys tomorrow."

"That's exciting," Julian said, and I could tell that he meant it.

"And she's dragooning any innocent bystander into service," I said. "You may want to run now." I glanced up at Julian. "Save yourself."

"Ha, ha," Autumn said. "Bran said he'd help. But Violet has a big wedding she's doing flowers for, Ivy has to work, and Lexie can't be around the paint fumes, *and* she needs to keep Morgan out from underfoot." Autumn blew her bang out of her eyes, and shrugged. "It's amazing how fast people scatter when you need a few extra hands to paint and scrub."

I was silent. I knew Autumn was hurting over her separation from Rene. They'd quarreled over her buying the house, and she hadn't heard from him in weeks. Because of that— Autumn didn't feel right asking Marie for help with moving in. Besides the support of the family, she was doing this on her own. I knew she was proud of that, but I could also feel that deep down inside she was lonely, but determined to move forward with her life. I glanced at Julian.

He focused on my cousin and tilted his head slightly. *He was picking up on all her conflicting emotions too.*

"What time do you want to get started?" I asked her.

"Saturday morning, 7:00 am," Autumn answered.

"I'll be there," I assured her.

Autumn's smile lit up the office. "Thank you." She hopped off my desk. "I'll let you get to work." And with a wave to Julian she strolled out of the office and shut the glass door behind her. I cringed as she tripped in the carpeted hallway but managed to catch herself. She smiled and kept moving.

Julian slipped his hand in his pocket. "I like your cousin. She's full of energy, intelligent, and a hard worker." He motioned me to follow him and I trailed after him into his office. He went to sit behind his desk.

"Well, she can really use the help." I took the chair across from him. Unsure of my next move, I kept up the conversation about Autumn's house. "I love her dearly, but the thought of her up on a ladder alone makes me nervous," I said.

"She does have a tendency to trip and bump into things," Julian said with a wry smile. "I wonder if that's because she so busy 'seeing' everything else that she gets distracted?"

I sat back in my chair, surprised at his insight. "Probably," I said. "I've never thought about it like that before."

Julian rested his hands on the desk. "Can't she afford to hire painters?"

"She's putting every dime into the purchase and kitchen and lower bath renovation. She can't afford the extra expense of painters coming in to repaint the upstairs."

"Smart," Julian nodded. "Invest your money in the big renovations and then do whatever else that you can, yourself."

"Exactly," I said, and then I caught myself. Here we were having a relaxed conversation. And there was no awkwardness, no hint that we were anything more than co-workers and casual office friends. *So why was the fact that this wasn't awkward... awkward?*

Our eyes met and held. "I like the flower." He

smiled.

"Thanks." I blushed.

He sat back in his chair and kept his expression sober. "I was wondering... the upcoming fund raiser for the museum next week and auction?"

"Yes?" I knew he'd been working on acquiring items for the auction for a while. I had a stack of phone call messages to go through on my desk about donations.

Julian's gaze held mine. "I'll need you there, as my assistant to help me keep the bids on the auction items, and the donations in order."

"Sure," I said, feeling a little shimmer of pleasure at him wanting me to be with him. "I'd be happy to help."

"It's formal. As my assistant you'll need to dress accordingly."

Oh jeez, a society type of thing! I realized, and felt uneasy. "I'll try to wear something that won't embarrass you," I said, then immediately regretted the words.

"Holly," the mild tone was in direct contrast to the raised eyebrows and disapproving look.

"I apologize, that came out snarkier than I intended." I cleared my throat. "I'll ask Autumn what would be appropriate. She's going too." When he continued to study me silently I stood up. "Well, I'll go work on those emails."

I left the office door slightly open behind me and went directly to my own little desk. I'd managed about two minutes of work before the phone on my desk rang. I glanced over. It was Julian calling me.

"Yes?" I said politely.

"Check your cell phone," he said softly and hung up.

I frowned at his office door and pulled my phone out of my purse.

I saw I had a text message and I tapped on the screen.

You look beautiful today.

I smiled. *Thanks. So do you.* I sent back. I set the phone down, took a deep breath and tried to focus on the task at hand. Julian exited his office on his way to another meeting, nodded politely to me, lowered his shields slightly, and left.

I was able to sense the desire radiating from him. He'd let me get just a taste of it as he left the office, and it was enough to have my stomach clenching in reaction.

Neither his facial expression nor mannerisms were anything but professional or polite. He glanced back at me, smiled, and casually strolled off down the hall, and I was left in the office a quivering mess.

I licked my lips against a mouth that had gone suddenly dry.

I wanted him all over again.

CHAPTER ELEVEN

I stood on the porch steps of the bungalow while my cousin struggled with the old lock. I hunched my shoulders against the sharp, and cool, late March breeze and shivered in my old gray sweats and zippered hoodie. There was no point in wearing anything nice today. I had tied a scarf around my hair and held two new plastic buckets filled with cleaning supplies.

Aunt Faye was standing behind me, holding a box filled with other household supplies, and she was dressed casually in jeans and a velour zippered jacket. Lexie held onto Morgan by the back of his coat with one hand and carried a new ceremonial Witch's broom in the other. Ivy strolled up the steps carrying two new gallons of paint, and finally Bran was hustling to join the rest of us and was carting a mop, tools, and more supplies.

The wind blew Autumn's hair in her eyes, and the door finally relented and swung open. The rest of us waited while Autumn was the first to step inside of her new home.

Lexie handed her the broom. Its handle was made from an old Rowan tree branch and was naturally protective. "A new broom sweeps clean," Lexie said.

"Welcome to my home," Autumn said. "Won't you all come in?"

Once the family had filed in, we waited in the living room while Autumn moved the broom across the threshold and swept any dirt out the front door. "I sweep away bad luck with this Rowan broom, all negativity will depart at the sound of my tune," Autumn chanted. "My home is a safe haven and surrounded with light, warded and secure all day and night."

Autumn swept the broom's bristles one final time across the threshold and then placed the broom next to the inside of the front door. She closed the wooden door firmly and traced an upright pentagram with her fingertips in the center of the door. "As I will it," she said.

"So mote it be," the rest of us chimed in.

"Welcome home, dear," Aunt Faye said. "May you know only happiness and contentment here."

"Blessed be," I added.

Ivy set the paint cans down, making a little thud, and the spell was over. "Okay people, I have an hour before I have to get cleaned up for work. Let's get this party started!"

"New house!" Morgan yelled and scrambled for the stairs to go explore.

"I'll go give the bathroom the once over and keep an eye on him while he's upstairs." I volunteered.

"Morgan John." Lexie's firm voice had Morgan freezing on the stairs.

"Yes, Mommy?" he said smiling innocently through the spindles on the staircase.

"Behave yourself," she said.

In answer he smiled and hopped up the stairs one step at a time. I followed him and together he and I checked out the three empty bedrooms and bathroom. Morgan decided he wanted to sit in the hall and race his toy cars up and down the hallway, and since he was in my line of sight I went straight to the lone bath in the bungalow and got to work.

I unzipped the hoodie and draped it over the newel post. I pulled on some disposable latex gloves and scrubbed the hell out of the bathroom. The little sink was serviceable but not original to the house. I knew Autumn had plans to replace it. The Greenes had added a little white open cabinet next to it. At one time it held baskets I imagined for storage. I wiped that down too.

While it was probably okay, I still wanted to make sure it was clean for the family to use over the next few days as Autumn prepped the house before she moved in. The penny tile on the floor needed to be mopped, but that might as well wait until we were done with all the painting.

The old claw foot tub was amazing and huge. I wiped down the chrome ring above the tub for the shower curtain, then I had to balance myself on the rim to scrub the inside of the tub out.

"Whatcha doin'?" Morgan asked.

"Scrubbing the bathtub." I glanced over at my nephew, and he stood in the doorway with his head cocked to one side.

"You're funny," he said, and dashed off.

"Thanks." I blew an escaped curl out of my eyes. I supposed me dangling over the edge of a tub did look silly to an almost three year old. "Stay where I can see you," I reminded him.

"Okay," he called back.

I rinsed out the tub, scrubbed down the white subway tiles that wrapped around the lower half of the bathroom walls, and then I scrubbed the sink and toilet. I kept an ear out for Morgan who was singing and chattering as he ran from bedroom to bedroom. I scowled at the floral wallpaper. Testing, I pulled on a loose corner and a big section peeled right off. "Ha!" I said. "Your days are numbered, old ugly 80s wallpaper!" I wiped down the mirror over the sink last and peeled off the gloves to dump in a little trash bag.

"My name's Morgan John. I live next door," I clearly heard my nephew say.

Who was he talking to? "Morgan?" I called, and walked into the hallway. I didn't see him and followed his voice as he continued to talk.

"I'm going to be a big brother," he said conversationally. There was a pause, and then he responded. "I get a new room, the baby is gonna have my old room."

I hurried forward with the bucket and trash bag, and came to a halt in the doorway of the master bedroom. Morgan sat on the floor cross-legged and was talking to an empty, open closet. His face was tipped up as if he was speaking to someone.

"Morgan," I called him.

He smiled at me. Then to my astonishment, he turned back to the closet. "That's Holly," he said.

He was seeing something or someone that I could not, I realized. The closet was empty, of course, but there was a definite presence in the room. It felt feminine, amused, and kind. I caught the faintest whiff of perfume on the air. The scent was floral, yet I couldn't identify it.

"Who are you talking to Morgan?" I asked as I went over to him.

"To 'Reen," he smiled at me. "I'm gonna go play. Bye 'Reen!" He waved at thin air and got up and began to hop across the floor.

'Reen. I jolted a little bit. *Could he be trying to say 'Irene'?* I slanted a look towards the closet.

The happy feeling in the air became sad as Morgan bunny hopped out and down the hall. *Was Aunt Irene's ghost still wandering the bungalow?* Testing, I spoke out loud to whoever might be listening. "Hopping is his new thing." I flinched when the closet door began to close. It shut with the softest of clicks.

Morgan sang a new song he learned from preschool loudly and off key out in the hall.

"Great-aunt Irene, are you here?" I asked.

My heart raced as the closet door re-opened, and the floral smell intensified in the air. "Autumn is moving in," I explained as happy emotions flooded the room. "I'm sure you'll have lots of company in the house over the next few days."

"Holly?" Autumn called from downstairs. "If you're finished, can you bring the cleaning supplies down to the kitchen?"

"On my way," I called back. I wondered how Autumn would take sharing her new house with the ghost of our great-aunt? "I'll talk to Autumn privately," I whispered to the room. "I'll tell her you're here."

I went out in the hall and took Morgan by the hand as he continued to bunny hop loudly all the way back to the first floor landing. Bran scrubbed down the mantle and fireplace, Lexie mopped up the hardwood floors in the dining room, and Morgan decided to sit out of the way on the big square of the bottom landing. He settled in with his trucks while I carried the bucket into the kitchen.

"Thanks," Autumn said, taking the bucket.

I set the trash bag aside in the corner. "We need to talk later, you and I," I said.

Autumn pulled out a stack of cloth rags and tossed one to Ivy. "Okay, what's up?"

Ivy snagged the cloth and, dragging a bucket with

her, proceeded to climb bodily into the original lower kitchen cabinets on the left hand side of the kitchen. They were deep, and she all but disappeared.

"Where's Aunt Faye?" I asked.

Autumn smiled. "She went to go get doughnuts."

"Typical." Ivy's voice was muffled from inside the cabinets. "She always disappears when there's cleaning to be done.

I pulled Autumn farther away from the dining room so our conversation wouldn't be overheard. "You have *company* in the bungalow." I said.

Ivy yanked herself out of the cabinet. "You mean like mice?" Her eyes were huge as she sat by our feet.

"No, I think it might be Great-Aunt Irene." Quickly I told them both what I'd sensed, and what I'd overheard with Morgan.

Autumn put her hands on her hips. "What sort of floral scent?"

"I couldn't identify it."

Autumn smiled. "Was it lilacs?"

I thought about it. "Maybe."

"Well that makes sense. I felt something too the first time I walked in here this winter. Then I smelled lilacs." Autumn pulled a pair of gloves on with a little snap. "Well, the old girl will just have to get used to me, won't she?"

I raised my eyebrows. "You're taking the news remarkably well."

Ivy snorted with laughter. "Autumn is used to

ghosts. After all, Grandma Rose has been keeping her entertained for years."

Autumn grinned and dipped her cleaning rag in a bucket of soapy water. She wrung it out and proceeded to the big pantry. She pushed up the sleeves of her old sweatshirt, hunkered down and began wiping down the old wooden shelves. "Let's get to work, Blondie."

I joined her and started on the opposite side of the pantry. "Will you keep the pantry when you renovate the kitchen?"

"That's the plan," Autumn said. "The contractor comes over next week with the final plans for the lower level reno. All of the cabinetry on the left side of the kitchen stays. The few pieces on the right, we'll take down, save, and reuse in the expanded space when we bump out into the existing dining room. So I'll be roughing it with a mini fridge and microwave in the smallest upstairs bedroom for the next few months."

Back to back, we worked in the pantry. I scrubbed at the tongue in groove knotty pine paneling. "Well you can always mooch a few meals at the manor. You can walk right over."

"That was part of my master plan." Autumn said in a dramatic voice.

I laughed as she attempted to add a sinister chuckle to her statement, and to my horror a piece of the wall shifted. "Oh, no!" I stopped and put the cloth down. "I hope I didn't damage the paneling."

Autumn spun around and she ran her hands over the

section that was wobbly. "You didn't damage anything, Holly. The section is loose."

"I'll go get a hammer," I volunteered." You've got nails in the tool box, don't you?"

"Holly broke the house," Ivy snarked behind us.

Autumn went to try and shift the board back into place and instead the whole section came off in her hands. "Hey, look at that!" she said, setting the panel down on a shelf. "It's like a little built in niche." Autumn reached in the newly revealed space and pulled out an old cookbook.

"What was that doing in there?" I asked.

Autumn opened it up. "I guess it was forgotten. I wonder if it's been there the whole time the Greenes lived in the house?" My cousin flipped through the pages. "It's dated from the 1940s. Look at all the vintage recipes!" She sounded excited, and shifted so I could study the pages and kitschy illustrations with her.

"There's a lot of notes written in the margin," I said.

Autumn flipped to the front of the dusty book. "Wow, looks like it was a gift from Great-Grandma Esther to her daughter Irene. She dated it *Winter Solstice, 1948.*"

I felt a little shiver. *The book belonged to Irene? Why had it been hidden? Had Mrs. Greene found it and stashed it away?* I wondered. *Or had Irene hidden it before she died?*

Before I could say anything, Ivy pushed her way into the pantry to see. "That's cool." She took the vintage cookbook and thumbed through it. "Maybe you could save it, Autumn, and then display it when the kitchen reno is finished. It'd be neat to have it on a stand where you could see it through the glass fronted cabinets."

Autumn smiled. "That's a great idea. A little Bishop family history, *and* it'll go with the vintage vibe I want to reproduce. I'll go and store this in a bedroom closet until the lower level reno is finished." Autumn took the book, wrapped it in a paper bag, and took it upstairs.

Aunt Faye arrived with doughnuts a short time later, and everything came to a halt. The family crowded around the counters, laughing and talking, and I told myself to stop being paranoid. If Autumn wasn't concerned about the possibility of sharing the house with a ghost, or wasn't curious as to why the cookbook had been stashed behind the paneling... then maybe I was simply overreacting.

Ivy left to go home and clean up. She was on shift at *Enchantments* today. Bran and Aunt Faye went upstairs to start taping off the baseboards in the bedrooms and hall in preparation for painting. Lexie carted drop cloths upstairs to protect the floors, and Morgan decided they made a fine tent.

By lunchtime Morgan had gone from adorable to annoying. As we set up to start painting upstairs, he was bored with the drop cloth tents, and his toys, and had himself a nice little sulk going. When he realized that his mother had to go in and work at the police station, it got ugly.

"Have fun with that." Lexie gave Bran a kiss goodbye as Morgan started to whine.

Bran ran a hand down Lexie's hair. "You're not supposed to be around paint fumes anyway."

"I know, I really wanted to be able to help out more." Lexie said.

"No worries Lexie." Autumn carried in brushes and rollers. "You and my soon-to-be-niece can help me work in the gardens, planting flowers in a few weeks."

"I'd like to do that," Lexie said. She patted her son on the head. "Morgan John, give me a kiss goodbye."

Morgan threw himself at her legs and started to cry.

"I'm not going to war," Lexie said wryly.

By the time she'd managed to pry herself free, Morgan had gone to full meltdown. He dropped to the floor and lay there sobbing as if the world had ended.

Bran stepped over his son as he lay on the floor, ignoring the tantrum, and began to pour the paint into the tray. My lips twitched as Morgan sniffled and raised his head, wondering why no one was paying attention to him.

Aunt Faye sat neatly on the floor and began painting the warm ivory color Autumn had selected above the taped-off baseboards.

Bran began cutting in around the baseboards with the pretty blue-green color Autumn had chosen for the master bedroom. I dipped the roller in and started rolling the paint on the walls. After a few moments the difference from the olive green color to the vintage robin's egg blue was impressive. I kept working until I had one wall mostly covered.

"Hey Autumn!" I said. "Come and look at your new paint!"

Autumn poked her head in the room. "Oh wow," she said. That's *much* better."

Before she could say anything else, a knock sounded on the front door. Autumn went to go see who was there, and Bran winked at me. "I called out the troops," he said.

I smiled in response when I heard the voices. Then I went down the steps to watch as the coven poured into the bungalow, bringing noise, laughter and energy into the house.

Theo and Zach stood dressed in old jeans and shirts, holding new paintbrushes, cans of paint, and rollers. Violet O'Connell, her blonde and purple hair pulled back in a ponytail, carried in a few more gallons of paint, and had plastic drop cloths folded under one arm. Marie Rousseau brought up the rear with a big gift basket.

"What are you all doing here?" Autumn asked, obviously shocked.

"We heard there was a painting party and didn't want to miss it." Theo smiled at her and gave her a hug. When Autumn held on, Theo murmured to her, and whatever he said had my cousin laughing on his shoulder.

Zach nudged his partner aside, and enthusiastically

hugged Autumn next. "You think I watch all that HGTV for nothing? Girl, show me that horrible old paint color and turn me loose!"

Violet set the paint down and eyed the staircase wall. "Please, promise me I get to paint that horrible pink over with this nice ivory color. Faye said it was what you'd chosen for downstairs."

"But I thought you had wedding flowers to do today..." Autumn said to Violet.

"I finished them, and Mom took over at the flower shop so I could come help you out." Violet tugged on her dark purple sweatshirt. "You didn't think I'd leave a friend hanging, did you?"

Marie handed Autumn a huge gift basket. "Here, I know how hard you've worked and saved to buy a house of your own."

Autumn's eyes filled with tears. Rene and Marie were brother and sister, and since my cousin and Rene had parted ways— Autumn had been unsure where that left her friendship with Marie. "Thank you." My cousin's voice was thick with emotion as she handed the gift basket off to Violet's waiting arms.

"I'm sorry I can't stay to help today," Marie said. "I have several tattoos scheduled. But this basket has some things you'll need and a gift card for the local hardware store. I'm sure you'll be able to find something to use it on."

Autumn and Marie embraced, and with a bawdy laugh and a wave to the coven, Marie promised to come visit Autumn next week.

"So, Autumn," Violet said after dropping off the basket in the kitchen. "Where do you want us to start?"

"I can't believe you're all here." Autumn grinned at them. "But if you want to help, the living room and stairwell walls need to be painted. The kitchen and dining room we can leave as they are— because reno starts on them next week."

Theo brushed his dark hair aside. "We brought painter's tape." He pulled a roll of it off his wrist where he'd worn it like a bracelet. "I'll start taping off the woodwork."

I came all the way down the stairs. "Hi everyone."

"Hi Holly." Violet gave me a quick hug. "You feeling better these days?"

"Yes, thanks." I said.

Theo grinned at me. "How's the new job at the museum working out?"

"It's good." I said and left it at that.

"Working there will look good on your résumé in the future." Theo pulled off a long piece of tape and competently ran it along the baseboard.

"Hey gorgeous," Zach said to me as he patted my shoulder. "Good god." Zach scowled, as he took in the rose color that was also on the living room walls. "What were the Greenes thinking?"

"It's a mystery," Autumn said straight-faced.

"Let's get to work," Theo suggested, and he, Zach, and Violet divided up the work between them, and I went back upstairs to paint the master bedroom with Bran.

Aunt Faye ordered pizza to be delivered for lunch and everyone dug in, standing in the kitchen or sitting on the dining room floor. Morgan found plenty of people to talk to now, and he went from person to person, or played in the empty dining room, when the painting resumed.

By late afternoon, the master bedroom, upstairs hall, and one of the bedrooms were finished. Autumn left the smallest of the bedrooms alone, as she was planning on using it as a makeshift kitchen during the renovations.

Zach, Violet, and Theo had obviously performed some sort of magick because they were cleaning up from painting and removing the tape when I came back down stairs. The warm ivory made the entire first floor look larger. The maple woodwork of the staircase now gleamed in contrast with the ivory paint.

The drop cloths were folded up and the left over paint was taken to the basement for storage. Bran decided to take Morgan home, as he was starting to get cranky again. Bran picked up the little boy, and he dropped his head on to his father's shoulder. He started towards the front door and Morgan waved goodbye to the group.

Autumn held the door open for them. "I swear, as soon as the weather breaks I'm taking out a section of iron fence between the yards. Then it will be a quicker trip back to the manor."

Violet went to the front porch and stood with her. "What section of fence?" she asked. Autumn and Violet walked over to the side of the porch, discussing the yard and Autumn's future plans for opening the fence, creating a passage between the yards.

"Bye 'Reen!" Morgan said, and waved at the empty staircase.

"Morgan," Bran said patiently as they left. "Mr. and Mrs. Greene have moved away. They don't live here anymore."

"No, no," Morgan pouted. "Reen."

I felt the hair rise off the back of my neck. But no one else seemed to connect *Reen* with Irene Bishop, one of the previous owners of the bungalow. I waked back upstairs and considered the new paint on the master bedroom walls.

Aunt Faye said that Irene was a 'complicated woman', and that the magick she worked was 'borderline'. Finding the cookbook like that made me uneasy. I walked across the room and opened the window a bit wider to help the smell of the paint dissipate. I'd never had the chance to touch the book Autumn had found. I had no way to 'read' it, to use psychometry and to try and see what —if any— sort of vibrations might have come from it. I wondered if I should go look for it now. But it made me uneasy.

Besides, Autumn deserved to move into her new home without any drama. I glanced over at the bedroom closet and then switched off the light in the room and went back downstairs to join the rest of the Coven.

***

Later that evening, Autumn and I began moving a few things into the bungalow. Ivy and Cypress had arrived, and between the four of us we loaded up my cousin's car and then she drove it next door. We carted a few bags of groceries, then her mini fridge and microwave, into the Bungalow. I set up a little card table in the smallest of the upstairs rooms and plugged the appliances into a power strip.

"Be careful of the walls, Ivy," Cypress warned her room-mate as they hauled folding chairs up the stairs.

"Yeah, yeah," Ivy grumbled.

Cypress and Ivy brought the chairs into the room and set them around the card table, creating a makeshift kitchen.

We all went back downstairs for the small dresser Autumn had bought second-hand. It was heavy, but she and I were able to maneuver it up the stairs. Cypress and Ivy brought up the four drawers, and Autumn arranged everything as she preferred and set the microwave and little fridge on top of the sturdy dresser.

"We have a similar set up in our dorm room," Ivy said.

"And we put our groceries in the top drawer of the dresser," Cypress chimed in.

Autumn grinned at them. "I did the same when I was

living at college." She picked up her groceries and loaded soda, water, milk and juice in the fridge.

"So what's on the agenda for tomorrow?" Ivy asked as Cypress started to poke around the other bedrooms.

Autumn folded the empty bags. "Stripping the wallpaper off the bathroom walls, and if it goes quickly I want to try and get the walls primed for painting."

Ivy cringed. "I guess I'm on for tomorrow, since I didn't get to help paint today."

"Thanks, Ivy." Autumn slung an arm around her shoulders. "I appreciate the help."

"You still hoping to officially move in on Tuesday?" I asked her.

Autumn nodded. "Yes, that's my day off and since Aunt Faye surprised me by hiring movers. Tuesday is definitely *the* day."

Cypress popped back in. "Will you have the bathroom ready by then?"

Autumn went to go look at the only bathroom, and the rest of us followed along. We stood crammed in the bathroom while my cousin explained her plans for removing the wallpaper on the upper sections of the walls and painting the old plaster.

"You know," Ivy said, thoughtfully, "black walls would be *awesome* in this bathroom."

"No." Autumn said.

"No, seriously." Ivy gestured broadly. "Hear me out. With the random black penny floor tiles, against the white subway tiles, black walls would be amazing."

"I already have the paint I chose for the bathroom here in the bungalow," Autumn said.

Ivy raised an eyebrow. "What color is it?"

"It's a historic preservation color," Autumn said, "called 'Nostalgia'."

I choked back a laugh as Ivy made a face. "Nostalgia?" Ivy said. "What sort of name is that?"

"I was with her when she bought the paint," I told Ivy. "It's pretty, a sort of gray with blue tones."

Ivy narrowed her eyes at the bathroom walls. "Hmmm, I can kind of see that in here."

"Well thank god," Autumn said, tartly. "I would have been so upset if you didn't like the color that I chose to paint *my* bathroom."

Cypress laughed. "So you'll do blue-gray towels in here?"

"I already bought them," Autumn said. "They're in a box at the manor."

Ivy was studying the oval shaped rod above the tub. "Well I hope you bought a couple of shower curtains. To use the shower in the tub... that's probably going to take more than one curtain to keep the water contained —" Ivy stopped speaking and sniffed the air. "Do you guys smell that?" she asked.

A soft floral scent flowed through the room. *Lilacs*, I realized. I slanted a glance at my cousin to gauge her reaction.

"Hi, Aunt Irene," Autumn said conversationally. "We're talking about re-doing the bathroom."

Cypress pushed her back firmly against the door. "You didn't tell me the house was *haunted*." Her eyes were wide as she looked around.

I'd assumed since Ivy hadn't had a strong reaction to the possibility of a ghost in the house that Cypress wouldn't either. But watching my friend, I realized I was way off base. Clearly, the experience she and Ivy had gone through with the campus haunting had left an impression on Cypress.

Autumn reached out a hand to Cypress and rested it on her shoulder. "Cypress," she said. "If anything, this is a residual style haunting. I think the house has simply held onto the memories of my ancestors."

"Cy," Ivy took her hand. "You know I'd never invite you into a place where you'd be interacting with malevolent ghosts again."

Cypress licked her lips. "I hope y'all don't mind, but I think I'm going to head back to campus."

"No, I don't mind." Autumn's voice was soft, comforting. "You go ahead."

Cypress bolted. She took off down the stairs and went right out the door.

Ivy sighed. "I'm going to go after her."

"Go," Autumn said.

"I'll be back in the morning to help you with the bathroom," Ivy said. "I promise."

"See you at eight o'clock."

Ivy gave me and then Autumn a distracted hug. "See you tomorrow." Ivy clattered down the stairs almost as loudly as Morgan had done and was out the door and hurrying to catch up with her friend.

I stood in silence for a few moments studying my cousin. "Autumn," I said, "I think you better fill me in on *everything* that happened on campus with Ivy and Cypress."

Autumn nodded, and she moved out of the bathroom. She started going through the upper level and shutting the windows we'd cracked while we'd been painting. "I thought they had talked to you about it," she called as she worked her way through the rooms.

I moved to the hallway. "Judging by the reaction Cypress just had, I'd say they left out a lot." I frowned as I recalled what they'd told me about their experiences. "They'd made it seem so exciting..."

Autumn took my arm and we started down the stairs together. "Exciting, sure. But that old bitch Victoria Crowly did her best to try and kill Cypress."

I stopped on the bottom landing. "They *never* told me that."

Autumn began closing windows and shutting off lights on the lower level. "Ivy pulled her out of the way of a falling tree. According to Nathan it was a very close call."

My mouth hung open. "I had no idea..."

Autumn nudged me out the door and locked it behind us. "Come on. I'll buy you a beer and tell you all about it."

I shivered in my sweats and zipped my hoodie closed over my t-shirt. "Make that a Margarita instead."

"Deal. Come on," Autumn said.

I tugged on my sweats "I don't think I'm dressed appropriately."

"It'll be fine," she said as I climbed in the passenger seat. "It's not prom."

I tugged the scarf from my hair and my curls sprang free. "Well then, I want some nachos too."

"That does sound good." Autumn backed out of the drive and cranked up her car stereo. "Look at us… a couple of single Witches out on the town, on a Saturday night. Whoo Hoo!"

Her good mood was infectious. "Be afraid, William's Ford!" I said.

With a wild cackle, Autumn sped off down the road and headed for downtown.

CHAPTER TWELVE

We ended up at the same Mexican restaurant Autumn had first taken me to when I'd come back home from Kansas City. We sat across from each other in a cozy booth, digging into a plate of loaded nachos and sipping at our Margaritas.

I unzipped my hoodie, and Autumn started to laugh.

"What?" I asked.

"Oh god, I didn't notice your t-shirt today, I was too busy painting." Autumn wiped her eyes with a napkin. "That's hysterical."

I glanced down at my chest. The old shirt was white but now it had splatters of robin's egg blue and ivory paint on it. The faded red letters printed across were still easy to read: *Only 2% of the world has Red Hair. So I'm basically a majestic unicorn.* "Ivy gave it to me," I explained.

Autumn laughed harder. "Of course she did."

"So explain to me what *really* happened on campus with Ivy and Cypress last year."

"Most of what I know came from Nathan," Autumn said, sipping at her drink. "Ivy played everything pretty casually."

"Wait," I frowned. I was shocked at the thought of my goth-loving dramatic sister, keeping anything remotely low-key. "*Ivy* downplayed it?"

"Which should tell you something." Autumn sent me an arch look.

"Good point." I munched on a nacho.

"I asked Nathan about it on Halloween night." Autumn helped herself to a chip. "He came over to celebrate with the family."

"*Nathan* celebrated with the Coven?"

"Why does that surprise you?" Autumn wanted to know.

"Well, Ivy made it seem that he was very discreet when it came to his magickal tradition."

"He is," Autumn said, "but he seemed to enjoy himself when he was passing out candy to the neighborhood kids. And he ended up staying for the Coven celebration afterwards. Between the trick-or-treaters and the Samhain celebration I had a chance to talk to him privately."

I leaned forward as Autumn relayed to me what Nathan had told her about the interactions Ivy and Cypress had experienced with the ghost of the university's founder. What I heard shocked me, and I was starting to get a better understanding of why Cypress was skittish around ghosts.

I kept my voice low, using the cover of the other restaurant patron's chatter for cover. "Ivy banished the ghost of Victoria Crowly from the dorm, and then *bound* her to the grave?" I sat back, with a deeper respect for Ivy's magickal prowess. "Holy crap," I said. "Blood magick. That's hard-core."

"Yes, I know." Autumn gave my hand a squeeze.

I shook my head in amazement. "She acted like it was a group effort in a little rainstorm..."

"Not according to Nathan," Autumn said. "Ivy was the one who did all the 'heavy lifting' so to speak— and all on her own."

"Maybe she needed to," I said, considering.

"How's that?"

"Ivy made a comment to me when I first came back to William's Ford about learning to stand on her own with solo magick," I said.

"Standing on your own is overrated," Autumn grumbled as she scooped up another nacho.

"Hey." I reached out to her. "Are you okay?"

She scowled. "Yeah sure. Why wouldn't I be?"

"You never talk about what happened with Rene," I said.

"No, I don't." Autumn set the glass down with a peevish snap. "But hey, I'm still standing, aren't I? Tonight is supposed to be a happy night. I bought my own home, and we started painting... I'll be moving in in a few days. Even though I'll be moving in *alone*."

"Autumn, are you aware of how angry you really

are?" I said as jealousy and resentment rolled off my cousin.

"Damn empaths," Autumn grumbled.

"Talk to me."

"I guess I wasn't what he wanted after all." Autumn lifted her eyes to mine, and her green eyes shimmered with unshed tears. "There's not much to say... Rene's already moved on with someone else."

"He has?" I sat back. "How do you know?"

"His new bitch of a girlfriend sent me pictures of the two of them from social media." Autumn caught herself, and blew out a breath. "It was a nasty slap to be sent photos of Rene with another woman— seeing them draped all over each other, smiling and laughing at some fashion show type of thing."

"Rene used to model professionally, maybe he was simply working the event?" I offered.

"Trust me," Autumn sighed unhappily. "I know the difference between posed photos and candid shots." She took out her phone and pulled up the file. She handed it over for me to see.

I scrolled through the photos. "Wow," I managed as I studied the woman with closely shorn hair, amazing features, and glowing cocoa brown skin. "That's one tall, uber thin woman." I cringed slightly when I saw that Rene had his hands on the woman's ass.

"She's a professional model, exotic looking, and drop-dead gorgeous," Autumn said, bitterly.

"How did she get your email?" I asked.

"Obviously she has access to Rene's phone," Autumn said.

"Oh," I handed her back the phone. "I'm sorry."

"He wanted me to move to Chicago with him," Autumn said softly. "Live in a penthouse overlooking the lake. Go to fashion shows in New York... You know, do all the jet-set type things."

My heart broke a little as Autumn sniffled. "That doesn't even sound like him..." I frowned. "A jet-set life? What the hell was he doing in William's Ford for so long then?" I asked. "Why did he even open a business here?"

"As a sort of a test run, he told me." Autumn rubbed her forehead. "I found out that he'd been tired of the model and actress types he'd been dating, and he wanted to go somewhere quiet, regroup, and reconnect with his sister."

"And then you two met."

"Yeah, we did. I gotta tell you Holly, getting involved with a gorgeous Creole man, who was a Hoodoo practitioner, was absolutely the last thing I ever expected to do." Autumn signaled the waiter. "What the hell," she said and ordered a jumbo margarita, and a tequila shot.

"Ah, hey there cousin, you might want to slow down."

Autumn passed me her car keys. "You're driving home."

I ordered a soda and held the keys. I listened while

Autumn talked about her breakup with Rene, and watched as she proceeded to get slightly drunk.

"Do you know what it's like to date someone who is prettier than you are?" Autumn asked a couple of margaritas later.

"No. I don't." I thought about it. "I guess that'd be hard."

"Everywhere we went women made fools of themselves over him. But I got used to it after a while. He said he was crazy about me... It's not like we even had a fight," she said. "Rene just gave me this ultimatum to leave and go with him to Chicago, or else. He went all dominant on me."

"He did *not*."

Autumn giggled. "No, not like fifty shades dominant — more like 'I'm the man and I'm telling you we are moving'." Autumn scoffed. "Why he *ever* thought I'd fall in line with that shit, is beyond me."

"Had he ever had any luck *persuading* you to do something you didn't want to before?" I asked. "I know Cypress is able to do a sort of glamour on men. Guys fall all over her, they'll do whatever she wants. They always have."

"Honey don't get me started..." Autumn gestured with her big margarita glass, and a bit sloshed over the sides. "He tried that sexual compulsion mojo on me once, to try and get his way."

I blotted up the spill. "He did?"

Autumn took a big sip through her straw. "Yeah, I

busted his chops for it too."

"Well good for you!" I smiled.

Autumn sighed. "It wasn't easy let me tell you... He used that glamour mojo to make it to the top of his field. *And* he used it on women who came into his salon and spa. They practically stood in line to get in the door."

Oh god, I realized, feeling horrified. *Did Autumn have any idea of how unethical that sort of thing was?* "You know what you're describing, right?" I asked her — but she kept talking over me.

"He's like sex on a stick, Holly. The deep rumbling voice, that body, those pale green eyes." She sounded almost spellbound, then she shook it off, and drained her drink. When she raised her hand for the waiter, he appeared a moment later with another large margarita and a tequila shot. Autumn downed the tequila, sucked on a lime and then reached for her new drink.

"Maybe you should slow down," I suggested. "Can I get a pitcher of water?" I asked the first waiter that passed by.

"I'd never met anyone like him. Probably never will again." Autumn said sadly.

"Hey," I took the margarita glass away from her. "You need to listen to me. You do realize what you're describing to me, right? I said again. The waiter came back with a pitcher of ice water and two glasses. I poured my cousin a water. "Drink this."

Autumn shoved the margarita aside. "I should

probably listen to you."

"Yeah you should. So shut up and—"

"Here's the funny thing though." Autumn cut me off again. "He made me wait *months* before we ever slept together."

I shook my head. "You're kidding right?"

"No." Autumn held onto her water glass. "He told me *I* wasn't ready, and that *I* needed to have better control over my powers first."

"Why?" Despite myself I was curious.

"I vamped him once accidentally and another time during sex. He didn't like that I could do that."

My curiosity was peeked. "You drained his energy *and* his magick?" I asked, wanting to be clear.

"Apparently." Autumn mumbled into her water glass. "After that, we didn't have sex very often. He said I depleted his energy too much... that it wore him down, made his immune system weak."

"I beg your pardon?" I said, offended on behalf of my cousin.

"Yeah." Autumn raked a hand through her hair, pulling the ponytail loose. "You know how shitty it made me feel when he said that?"

"Do you know if Rene had ever been involved with a Witch before?" I asked her. "It's very possible that his power relied on *him* taking energy from other women."

"Well shit." Autumn gaped at me. "So all the time he made me think I was some out-of-control energy leech, always vamping him... He'd been draining the energy of the women who were *attracted* to him at his spa and salon?"

"That'd be the perfect cover, wouldn't it?" I said. "He could toss the lure out there, they'd come running in, and then he'd be able to easily feed on their fascination."

"Like little frustrated-housewife-energetic-happy-meals, on legs." Autumn said, her hands beginning to shake.

It was painful for me to watch her put all the pieces together, so I reached across the table and laid my hand on hers. I connected with her empathically and sent her some calming energy. Much like what Ivy had done for me once. "Be calm," I said.

Autumn took a few ragged breaths. "So that would make him sort of an incubus— for lack of a better word?"

"It's only a theory," I said. "But it fits, and being around a strong-willed Witch, like you... he wasn't able to take any energy from you personally during your ah, *intimate* moments."

"Oh my goddess." Autumn was a little green around the gills. "I thought that sex... if you wanna get all metaphysically technical, was supposed to be a sort of energetic exchange?"

"It is." I agreed. "But if we follow this line of thought, and Rene had no way to 'feed' when he was around you, then his personal energy would diminish and..."

Autumn dropped her head in her hands. "Oh my Goddess, I'm a fool."

"No, you're not." I said.

"I thought I loved him, Holly." Autumn lifted her head and met my eyes, they seemed to glow a bright angry green. "I wanted to stay close to the family, settle down here in William's Ford, get married, maybe raise some babies eventually..."

I thought about the vision I'd had the first time I walked in the bungalow. "Don't worry," I said as my cousin wiped her eyes. "You'll have *all* of those things someday."

Autumn held up her water glass. "Thanks for letting me talk this out with you."

"You've done the same for me." I reminded her.

Unexpectedly a warm wave of energy rolled over my shoulders. It skittered down my spine and hit me in the root chakra, and I felt all my feminine muscles clench in reaction. I saw movement out of the corner of my eye and glanced up.

Julian.

"Hello, Holly." Julian smiled down at me, then he nodded to my cousin. "Autumn."

There he stood, my secret lover looking very GQ in dark slacks, a button down shirt, and a black leather jacket. And here I sat, in gray sweats, and an old paint splattered t-shirt. *Talk about two different worlds...*

I was so wrapped up in him that it took me a few seconds to realize that he wasn't alone. His cousin

Duncan Quinn was standing at his side. I hadn't seen him in almost three years. Duncan looked good in dark jeans and a casual shirt. A heavy denim jacket made his eyes look a brighter blue. Duncan's aura was a strong healthy color. There was no lasting taint from the Grimoire that I could detect.

"Hi Julian," I said, glancing at my cousin to see how she would react to her former boyfriend.

"Hey Julian," Autumn said, then shifted her eyes over. "Duncan." She nodded.

"Mind if we join you?" Julian asked, and before I knew what he was about, he slid right in to the both next to me.

"How goes the house painting?" he asked as his thigh touched mine.

Duncan slid in the booth next to Autumn, and if she was uncomfortable with that, I couldn't tell.

Autumn sat back with a happy sigh. "We got a lot more accomplished today than I expected."

Duncan smiled at her. "Which room is painted blue?"

"How did you…" Autumn began, and then glanced down at her paint-splattered sweatshirt. "Oh, ha."

Julian's hand was resting on his leg, perilously close to my own knee. I felt the slightest touch of a fingertip along my leg and I trembled. To cover it, I dove into the conversation as if painting was of the utmost importance. "The master bedroom is robin's egg blue," I said. "The whole downstairs is now this great ivory color."

"Well, except for the part that I'm having torn up." Autumn smirked at me.

"What contractor did you hire?" Duncan asked her casually.

"Kenneth Construction," Autumn said with a slight slur.

"He has a solid reputation." Duncan nodded.

We all chatted politely enough about the renovation plans. Well no, Autumn chattered on and I tried to pay attention. I jumped when Julian ran one hand over the outside of my thigh. His shields were down, and desire simply radiated from him.

Fortunately for me, Duncan was so busy staring at Autumn, and she was so busy swaying in her seat that neither of them noticed anything going on with Julian and me. I had no idea what emotions Julian was able to pick up from me, but after ten minutes or so of close contact with him, I was desperate for some relief. Under the table I poked him in the leg.

"Stop that," I whispered the words.

Julian's lip curled slightly on one side, so I knew that he'd heard me... but other than that he had no reaction.

"We'll let you two finish your nachos," Julian said and shifted to rise from the booth.

"See you at work, Julian," Autumn said too cheerfully.

Julian scanned the table and narrowed his eyes at my cousin. "How much have you had to drink, Autumn?"

"Juz a few margaritas," she said, then laughed.

"I'm driving. Don't worry." I told him.

"I think you should let me help you get her to the car," Julian offered.

I studied my cousin as she sat there grinning up at Duncan. "That's probably a good idea."

Duncan stood. "I'll go settle the bill." He walked off, and Autumn leaned her head back against the booth and shut her eyes.

"What made her drink so much?" Julian asked me. "I've never even seen her drink before."

I slid out of the booth. "She was telling me about her break up with Rene Rousseau."

I could see that Julian was about to ask for details, but Duncan came back.

Duncan seemed to realize how far gone my cousin was and to settle the matter he reached in and slid her across the bench. "Hey there." Autumn said, smiling at him.

Duncan smiled back. "I'm taking you home, Autumn." He pulled her to her feet, looped an arm under her shoulder and navigated her out of the restaurant.

I grabbed our purses and followed. I didn't even have to point out which car was hers. Duncan opened the passenger door and put Autumn in the car. As I hovered nervously behind them, Duncan reached over competently and buckled her in the seat.

Autumn beamed up at him. "You never made me

feel like shit about myself in bed, you know that?"

Duncan froze, his face a few inches from Autumn's. "Er... thank you," he said.

"You were the best lover I ever had." She yawned and shut her eyes.

"Well, fuck me." I breathed, horrified by Autumn's tipsy confession.

Julian tried to squelch a laugh at my words, but it escaped anyway. "You alright there cousin?" he asked Duncan.

"Yeah." Duncan slowly shut the car door on a now sleeping Autumn. He shifted his eyes to me. "Can you get her in the manor by yourself?"

"I'll have Bran give me a hand," I said. "Thank you, Duncan."

Duncan nodded to Julian and I and walked off across the parking lot. He started up his blue pickup and left.

Alone in the parking lot with Julian, I could hear the local church tower chime the hour. It was midnight. I was surprised when he sighed— it felt wistful.

"What is it?" I asked, concerned.

"Duncan still loves her," he said.

Shocked, I tipped my face up to him. "He does?"

"For some people, there's only one." Julian said, staring down in my eyes.

I cleared my throat. "I guess I better get her home."

Julian walked me around to the drivers side of the car and gallantly opened the door for me. I slipped in and rolled down the window so I could speak to him.

"Thank you, for your help."

"Of course, Angel."

I made a face. "I've told you, I'm no—"

He leaned his face in close to mine. "You're my angel."

I waited to see if he'd kiss me. It was in his eyes, and for a split second we leaned in towards each other, then the honk of a horn from another car in the lot reminded us both where we were.

He eased back and I nervously licked my lips. "Ah, do you have a ride home?" I asked.

"Now that you mention it," Julian said, with a rueful grin. "No. I rode with Duncan."

I started the car. "Well hop in the back, I'll drop you off on the way."

Julian nodded and slipped in the back seat. "It's lucky for us she doesn't drive that old pickup truck anymore. Otherwise I'd be sitting in the bed of the truck."

I started to laugh at his dry humor. "True," I said. I looked over my shoulder and backed out of the space to head home. Autumn snored lightly as I drove down the dark streets.

"She's out cold," Julian said, petting my curls that had fallen over the driver's seat.

"Yeah." I sighed at the feeling of him stroking my hair. "I think I *am* going to need your help getting her in the house."

Five minutes later I pulled up and parked in the

driveway. Julian solved any problems by scooping Autumn up and carting her inside. My cousin was oblivious, and as the rest of the family was asleep, we decided to put Autumn on the downstairs family room couch, and I took off her shoes and covered her with a throw.

Julian and I slipped back outside, and I drove him home in Autumn's car. I pulled up around the back of the mansion and put the car in park, but left the engine idling.

"Come inside," Julian said. "Be with me tonight."

"I really want to," I said.

"But?"

"How will we get in and out of the house without being seen?" I asked.

"Good point." Julian groaned and leaned his head back against the headrest.

"I don't suppose we could park in the garage?" I joked.

Julian snapped his head up. "I'm not having sex in the car like some horny teenager." He seemed offended.

I tried a smile. "Well, I was only—"

He reached over and pulled my face close to his. "What I want to do with you, would take more room than a car seat would allow." His voice was almost a growl.

Oh my.

He kissed me. A soft, full, on the lips kiss, then he lifted his head. "*Soon*, Holly."

I let out a slow breath. "How soon?" I asked.

"Tomorrow morning I have to drive out of town for a meeting, and to pick up some items for auction. Would you like to come along?"

"Sure," I said, pleased at the chance to spend some time with him. "But won't that raise a few eyebrows?"

"Not necessarily. Tell your family, you are coming with me to the art museum in St. Louis. I *do* have a meeting with the community events director, there."

"What time do you want to leave?"

"We should be on the road no later than nine."

I leaned forward and kissed him on the mouth. "I'll look forward to it."

He opened the car door and climbed out. "Goodnight, angel." He shut the door softly.

"Goodnight." I put the car in gear and drove back to the manor. I parked Autumn's car, let myself in and went to check on her. She was still sound asleep on the couch. I left her purse beside the couch. I slipped upstairs to my room and threw myself on the bed.

I flopped down and lay there, my mind racing. *Would we have a chance to even be alone after his meetings, or would tomorrow simply be strictly business? I hadn't asked what to wear... What if I wore something casual and he showed up in a suit and tie? I could wear a dress, something casual but still business appropriate...*

I stripped and headed for the shower, mulling over my choices for something appropriate to wear. Maybe

I'd luck out and a nice long shower would help me relax. But I doubted it.

***

To my shock, when I came downstairs at a quarter to nine, I found Autumn sitting at the table the next morning only looking slightly worse for wear. She was wrapped in a robe of Aunt Faye's and was sipping from a large mug of tea, and her hair was wet and drying on her shoulders. Aunt Faye bustled around the kitchen, as she and Autumn discussed the best way to remove old wallpaper from the walls.

"What spell did *you* use to avoid a hangover?" I asked Autumn, as I joined her at the table.

"I have a few home remedies for such things," Aunt Faye announced airily.

"It works too." Autumn held up a glass that looked like it had held tomato juice. "That is if you can keep it down." She burped.

I laughed.

Aunt Faye handed me a mug of tea. "I found your cousin on the couch an hour ago, rousted her up, and stuffed her in my shower."

"With my clothes still on," Autumn groused.

"Woke you up, though. Didn't it?" Aunt Faye said with a crafty smile.

"Wow, 'The Revenge of Aunt Faye'." I made air quotes.

"You look lovely this morning, dear," Aunt Faye said to me. "I love that little black and white dress on you. Do you have to be at the museum today?"

I smiled and did my best to sound casual. "Julian is picking me up in a bit. He has meetings in St. Louis and we have to go and pick up a few more items for the auction."

"Will you be home for dinner?"

"I don't know," I said.

"Well no worries, I'll leave you something you can heat up." Aunt Faye waved and strolled out, announcing she wanted to take her tea on the front porch.

I waited until I heard the door close behind her and poked my cousin. "How much do you remember about last night?"

Autumn cleared her throat. "Pretty much all of it."

"Do you remember talking to Duncan?" I asked gently.

Autumn's face went red. "God, did I talk to him about how good he was in bed?"

"You did." I sipped at the mug of tea to hide my smile.

I watched her face as she played back through her memories... then she groaned and laid her head down to the top of the table. "Someone shoot me now."

"I can call Lexie," I teased. "She's armed. Maybe she can taser you or something, that ought to put you out of your misery."

Autumn held up her hand and waved it weakly.

here, Officer."

"I wouldn't worry about it, too much." I patted her head. "He seemed to take it pretty well."

"How in the hell am I going to face him at the auction next week?" Autumn wanted to know. "The Drakes are *all* going to be in attendance, the event is even held in the Presidential Suite of the Drake Building on campus."

"Speaking of," I said, picking up my mother's enameled crescent moon pendant. "I've got to go help my boss at the event, and he said it was formal. I'll need you to help me figure out what to wear."

Autumn lifted her head and studied me. "Are you going on a *date* with Julian?"

"No," I said patiently, sliding the pendant back and forth on the chain. "I'm accompanying him on his meetings."

"You look pretty fancy, Holly."

I glanced down at my short sleeve jersey dress. It was a simple, fit and flare dress that hit right at the knees. The collar was crochet and white, contrasting against the black. "I've seen you wear dressier clothes than this to work."

Autumn shrugged and sat back in her chair. "That's nice that he's taking you along to the museum in St. Louis. It'd be good for you to make some contacts there."

"Yes it will."

"Okay," she said. "Once I get through the next few

days, and get moved in, we'll take a look at what you and I have, and figure out what we are both going to wear to the auction."

"I'll want to look good, because chances are I'll be running into Leilah, and probably seeing other notable families in town." I dropped the pendant and tried to stop fidgeting. "I'm only going to be assisting Julian with tracking the bids on the auction items, and keeping notes on any separate monetary donations. I'll be *working*, not mingling."

"I get it." Autumn yawned. "Oh, and by the way; Ivy, Nathan, Aunt Faye, Lexie and Bran are all attending too."

"They are?"

"Face it kiddo, we *are* a founding family. That makes us 'notable'. The Bishops will be out in force that night. Leilah won't be able to get anywhere near you."

"I'm not afraid of Leilah Drake Martin," I said, firmly.

"Good." Autumn stood and stretched. "I'm going to go, get changed, and work on the bungalow. See you later."

"See you later." I smiled, praying that I was projecting serenity and casual confidence. I picked up my purse to see if I had everything I might need for the day. I double-checked that my brush, a few cosmetics, my cell phone, not to mention a few foil wrapped packages, were safely zipped inside of an inner pocket my purse.

I wasn't sure what would happen today while Julian and I were out, but I wanted to be prepared— which was why I was also wearing a red lace bra and matching panties under my dress. I was really hoping that he'd meant it when he'd said, *Soon.* Last night.

I heard a knock on the door and calmly went to go greet Julian.

CHAPTER THIRTEEN

I spent a pleasant morning at the St. Louis Art Museum. While Julian took his meeting, I strolled around admiring the exhibits. The first item I wanted to see was the marble statue entitled, 'Reclining Pan'. The Italian sculpture was dated 1535 and was attributed to Francesco da Sangallo. I found the statue and walked around, admiring it from many perspectives as possible.

Going to see the statue was a sort of local mini Pagan pilgrimage, and the 'Great God Pan' was stunning, from the top of his head to the tips of his goat feet. The statue had a sort of lazy sexuality about it; perhaps since Pan would forever be grinning, with his head thrown back and his impressive physique on display. He wasn't a safe homogenized deity, and I smiled at the reed pipe in his hand and the grape clusters around his feet.

Then again, I smiled to myself, *some things weren't meant to be comfortable, or easy.*

My lips twitched when I overheard a young mother

gasp and hustle her children out of the wing where Pan was displayed.

A skinny teenager standing alone, dressed all in black, smirked at me. "Look at the little Christians run from one of the old Gods." His voice cracked.

The teenage boy reminded me of Ivy, back when she was in high school. "It's stunning, isn't it?" I murmured, and left him alone so he could spend some time with Pan.

I wandered around, and the Oceanic exhibit gave me chills. I was a little horrified when I overheard some college student talking about a local legend of how the exhibit was haunted by the spirit of the effigy figure displayed inside the case. The little information panel on the glass also mentioned the local lore about how at night the figure was thought to scratch the glass of the display... *from the inside*. I also noted that the little plaque stated that inside the statue was the actual skull of a Malakulan man the figure represented.

There was an aura of horror and fascination coming from the display. And I wasn't sure if I was picking up on the general creepiness that had folks coming to see it for themselves, the horror of the visitors, or possibly the mood of the exhibit itself. While the museum was clever to play up on the local story, it still made me uneasy. I quickly walked away from the Oceanic section and went in search of the Egyptian exhibit instead.

I was studying the Mummy mask of an Egyptian

noble woman when I *sensed* more than I heard Julian step up beside me. "She's beautiful," I said, staring in awe at the gorgeous funerary mask, the stunning colors and touches of gold and glass.

"Her name translates to 'Twice Beautiful'." Julian said. "The Museum fought for years to keep her, and in 2014 they won," he said.

I tore my eyes away from the mask and glanced up at him. Today he wore a tailored navy blue, two button suit. The suit was cashmere and seriously stylish. He'd worn it with a classically white shirt, and his tie was a pearly gray. For a moment I wondered what was better looking, the dark haired man waiting for me, or the priceless artifacts all around us. "Are you finished with your meeting?" I asked.

"I am." he smiled at me. "Did you want to look around some more?"

I stepped aside so other visitors could see the mask. I wandered over to a sarcophagus that was on display. I waited for Julian to join me. "It's a beautiful museum, but I'd rather spend some time with you, alone." I kept my voice low.

The random patches of blue seemed to glow against the brown of his eyes. He placed his hand gently at the small of my back. "Miss Bishop," He nodded politely, and with the barest of touches, he guided me from the building.

We spent the rest of the morning picking up a few donated items for the fundraiser; a big gift basket of local wines and some gorgeous hand made jewelry. I enjoyed spending time with Julian. And while I wasn't sure if this was our first official date, it did feel like one.

He announced he knew a great place for lunch, and surprised me when we stopped outside of William's Ford at a little mom and pop style diner for lunch— a diner where they knew him on a first name basis. I'd been half expecting some fancy French place where I would have no idea what food to order. Seeing his relaxed and open smile as we took our seats made me realize that I'd let the outer package, the wardrobe and his elegant manners, throw me off.

Julian tugged his tie off and rolled it up to stuff in his jacket pocket. "Better," he sighed as he picked up a laminated menu and passed it to me.

"What do you recommend?" I asked. The diner was loud, noisy, and smelled pleasantly of fries and bacon.

"It's all good, but I'm having a burger," he said.

A tough looking young man, covered in tattoos and multiple piercings, strolled up to our table to take our order. He and Julian chatted as if they were old friends, and when Julian introduced us, the air went heavier.

He was nervous. Julian was wondering how I would react to his friend.

I smiled up at the man. "Hello Diego, nice to meet you," I said.

"I'll be back with your drinks." Diego said, and walked off towards the kitchen calling out our food order.

"How did you two meet?" I asked casually. Like the diner he'd chosen for lunch, meeting Diego was another pleasant surprise. As was seeing Julian Drake being so casually friendly with someone from such an obviously different background.

"Diego and I met in rehab." Julian said, watching me for my reaction. "He got clean from drugs and I had a chance to pull myself back together after the grimoire damn near destroyed my life."

"Do you still expect me to think less of you, because of that?" I asked gently.

"No." Julian reached for my hand. "My father came up with the idea of telling people I'd been abusing drugs. But whether it was drugs or power, I was *addicted,* and in many ways the damage it inflicted on everyone around me was the same as if I'd had a substance abuse problem."

He'd never touched me in any way that could be construed as affectionate *in public* before. It was a simple gesture, holding my hand on the table-top, but it felt huge. "I understand that, Julian." I said and laced my fingers with his. "More than many other practitioners would. I know exactly what happens when magick takes you over, and how hard it is to fight your way out of its thrall."

"I know you do." Julian gave my hand a squeeze. "When I came home, it was simpler to let people think I was recovering from substance abuse as opposed to dark magick."

He gave a lopsided grin. And my heart simply melted... until I realized, *he wasn't grinning at me.*

A heavily pregnant young woman waddled towards us. "Julio!" she yelled. She had long black hair pulled back in a braid, a gorgeous Hispanic complexion, and to my surprise, she planted a big kiss on Julian's mouth. "Mmmmwha!" she made a happy noise when she lifted her mouth from his.

Not sure what was happening, I let go of his hand, sat back and allowed my clairsentience to do its thing. I scanned them both. *They weren't lovers,* I knew, even as I narrowed my eyes at them. *The vibes were all wrong. But there was affection... a sort of love even...* and it made me a little envious.

"Hi Nina," Julian laughed. "Let me introduce you to Holly."

"Hello," I said cautiously as Nina made herself at home on Julian's lap.

"Hi!" She twinkled at me, and now there was such a happy, playful vibe coming from her that my shoulder's dropped, and I couldn't help but smile in reaction.

"Get your hands off my woman," Diego said easily as he dropped off our drinks.

"My baby daddy is a jealous man," Nina said to Julian. "You should be careful."

"I'm not the jealous type, but if you don't get off that man's lap, I may start noticing pretty red heads." Diego wiggled his eyebrows at me.

"Secretly, I've always liked men with tattoos," I said, playing along.

He threw back his head and laughed. "*Bruja* or no, I could get into all these curls..."

Somehow he knew. I didn't know much Spanish but I did understand that *Bruja* translated to *Witch*. I studied Diego's face, as he smiled down at me, and his emotions were easy to read. While he enjoyed teasing Nina, he was totally in love with her... and he was both nervous and *thrilled* about becoming a father.

"How's my goddaughter?" Julian patted Nina's bulging baby belly. "How's she doing these days?"

Goddaughter? I thought. Fascinated with Julian and his interaction with Diego and Nina, I leaned back in my chair and watched.

Nina rolled her eyes at him. "I've told you, we're fine."

Diego tugged Nina to her feet, slipping an arm around her. "The doctor says next week, maybe sooner."

"You should be home resting. You shouldn't be on your feet all day," Julian said.

Nina rolled her eyes. "Men! You sound like this one!" She glared at Diego. Her name was called from the kitchen. "I'll be back with your orders." She planted a kiss on her boyfriend's cheek, and Diego gave her butt a playful swat as she waddled off.

Julian got up. "Give me a second, Holly," he said.

"Sure." I watched as he went after Nina and

followed her to the kitchen. Sure enough, now he was talking to both of the cooks too.

"He's a good man," Diego said, drawing my attention back to him.

"Yes, I know he is."

"He won't tell you, but he's helped me since I got out of rehab a few years ago," Diego said in a low voice that went no farther than our table. "It was Julian who pushed me to go back to tech school, he even found us an apartment close to campus that we could afford." Diego stopped talking as Nina and Julian came back carrying our lunch. Nina kept trying to carry both plates, and Julian insisted on carrying his own food.

"Here you go." Nina slipped my club sandwich smoothly in front of me.

"Thank you," I said, and I watched Julian dive into his hamburger with enthusiasm.

"He's never brought someone to meet us before," Nina said.

"Oh?" I said, looking archly at Julian. He sat with his burger, and I thought I detected a slight blush.

"No, he hasn't," she said. "I'm relieved to see he found someone like you. You be good to him, you hear?"

I smiled at her, and watched the interaction between the three of them with interest. While they talked and joked, Julian tried to convince Nina that Juliana was a fine name for a girl, and she had plenty to say about that. After the couple left and we finished our food,

Julian glanced up at me a little self-consciously.

"I like your friends," I said.

"I hoped you would."

I was getting a clearer picture of Julian Drake— and he definitely wasn't the person most people thought he was. The more he let me see who he *really* was, the more fascinating he became. "You know," I told him, "I was attracted to you before, but after today, seeing you with Diego and Nina... I think I'm starting to fall for you Julian."

He wiped his hands on a napkin deliberately and gave me a look that spoke volumes. "Angel," Julian breathed. "That sort of honesty is dangerous at times."

I met his gaze. "I'm not afraid of you, Julian."

"I know a place where we can go," he said softly. "If you're sure?"

"I just so happen to be *prepared*, if such a thing were to occur," I said.

"We're leaving." Julian stood up and grabbed my hand.

***

Julian paid the bill and gave Diego a one armed hug and kissed Nina on the cheek. His jaw was tight when we left the diner, and when he opened the car door for me, I wondered what he was going to do next. He reached across the seat and took my hand. He held it gently as he drove, and I realized he was holding himself back.

Which I admit, sort of scared me, but thrilled me at the same time.

We stayed silent as he drove across the river towards William's Ford, and he took an exit I was unfamiliar with. The area was rural, and within ten minutes we were turning down a gravel road. The trees were thick as we traveled along the drive, and were brushed with young green leaves. Eventually we came to a charming little 'A' framed cabin in a clearing. Julian stopped at the security gate, punched in a code and the gate swung open. He drove through and the gate shut automatically behind us.

"What's this?" I asked as Julian pulled his car around to the back of the building.

"A hunting cabin," Julian answered. He shut off the car and came around to open the door for me.

I stepped out, and Julian selected a key, took my hand and I followed him up the back steps. He opened the door for me, I walked in and discovered a pretty little one roomed cabin. The cabin was small but the steep pitch of the roofline made it seem bigger. There was a neat kitchenette, a leather sofa and sturdy coffee table facing a brick fireplace. An antique wooden rocking chair sat beside the hearth, and a queen size bed was tucked against a far wall. Julian locked the door behind us and set the keys on the kitchen counter. He walked over and clicked on a lamp.

"It's pretty," I said, looking at the room that was all

wood beams and honey-toned wooden logs.

"There's a bathroom to the right if you'd like to freshen up," Julian said.

I nodded and went to use the bathroom. The walls were paneled in old barn wood, which contrasted with the high end finishes in the bathroom. A granite counter, fancy shower, and stone floor made the little room rustic and modern all at the same time.

When I emerged from the bathroom, Julian had removed his jacket, and there were now several sturdy jar candles lit across the mantle of the fireplace. He stood barefoot by the bed, and folded the quilt back neatly.

The candles were probably meant for power outages — not romance, but it didn't bother me in the least. I walked over to him and set my purse on the little nightstand by the bed. I stepped out of my flats and toed them out of the way.

Julian buried his hands in my hair, and pulled me close. I rested my head against his chest and sighed. "I've waited all day," I said. "Kiss me, Julian."

He began to cruise his mouth across my hair, then down my face. "Holly?" he murmured close to my ear.

"Yes?" I sunk my hands in his gorgeous hair, and pulled his mouth down to mine.

"Are you recovered from the last time we were together?" He nibbled his way down my neck.

"Yes, I'm fine." I smiled against his hair.

He nudged me around with the gentlest of touches,

and slowly unzipped my dress. He gently pushed the dress off my shoulders, and I turned to him to see his reaction as I stood there in only my red bra and panties.

"My god, have you had that on all day?" His voice was ragged.

I smiled. "Yes, Julian."

"You have no idea what those two little words do to me," he growled. He slowly unbuttoned his shirt. I froze, captivated by the intensity in his eyes, and watched him. The shirt was dropped to the floor, and then he reached for his belt buckle.

I gulped as he unbuckled, unfastened and then unzipped his trousers. He stepped free of them and now he stood in only a pair of dark briefs that strained against the proof of his desire. For me.

"Are you sure?" Julian asked me.

"I'm here, aren't I?" I reached for his hips, tugging the briefs down, and he allowed it. When I would have reached for him, he took my hands.

"I'm waiting for your consent."

"I have red lingerie on and condoms in my purse, Julian," I said, my voice going up in frustration. "How much more consent do you need?"

"Angel," he said patiently, and I stopped and met his eyes. "If you had any idea of the things I want to do to you, *with* you..."

He's nervous, I realized. *He's nervous that he'll hurt me.* "You won't hurt me," I said confidently, even as I trembled. There was an energy about him. He was practically vibrating where he stood.

"No one can hear us out here," Julian said, and he stepped to me and unhooked the front clasp of my bra.

"Good." I managed as the bra dropped to the floor.

"No one will disturb us." Julian bent down and kissed the tip of my breast. "You can scream as loud as you want when you come." He moved to the other breast.

I dug my hands in his hair and held him to me. "Okay," I managed.

My knees began to shake when he calmly pulled my panties down my legs. He raised back up to my mouth and kissed me deep and long. "Lie down on the bed," he invited me.

I lay on my back on the cool white sheets. The bed was surprisingly high off the ground, and my feet dangled over the edge. Julian pulled the condoms out of my purse, and tossed the purse aside, watching me the whole time.

My breath caught in my throat as he rolled a condom on, and he reached down, took ahold one of my legs and pulled me so that my butt was close to the very edge of the bed. I relaxed my legs and allowed them to dangle off the side of the mattress, and they fell open for him.

I grabbed ahold of the sheets and hung on as he guided my legs up, wrapping them around his waist. The bed was tall enough that I was at the right height for him to remain standing, and slowly, deliberately, he slid inside of me. When he pressed in to the hilt, my back arched. He scooped his hand under my hips and lifted me higher. He rolled his hips once, and I let out a little scream of pleasure.

"You can do better than that," Julian said, and ran his fingertips across that bundle of nerves at my core.

"Julian!" I shouted at the combination of sensations, as he rubbed and tormented that spot while thrusting deep at the same time. He was relentless.

"I'm going to take you over and over again," he said. "As many times as you want."

"*Yes, Julian,*" I managed, and those two words made him growl low in his throat and thrust harder and faster. I wrapped my hands in the sheets and held on for dear life. My orgasm had me screaming loud and long.

I fell back to reality a few moments later, only to discover that Julian was still standing between my thighs, still deep inside me, and still hard.

"Julian?" I said, out of breath from the orgasm. "You didn't come?"

He smiled at me, and gently nudged me back further to the center of the bed. "Oh, no... I'm in no hurry. And I have plans for you." He joined me on the bed. In one smooth motion, he rolled to his back and guided me with his hands so that I was arranged over him.

I threw my head back and shuddered as he pushed his way deep inside of me. "God!"

He ran his hands over my breasts, and then he ran them around to my back, and fisted them in my long hair. Delighted at being in control, I braced my hands on his arms and rode him as hard as he'd ridden me. I bent over and kissed his mouth, and our tongues met and danced. Soon, he was shouting with his own release.

Afterwards, he pulled me over to spoon with him on our sides. My eyes fluttered once as he wrapped me in his arms. He rested his chin on top of my head, and we dozed off.

I woke up a short time later and found that Julian was kissing my shoulder. I wiggled my backside closer to him. "I'm not finished with you yet, Angel," he warned, lightly biting my shoulder.

And happily, he wasn't.

***

A few hours later and we realized we had to go back. We took a shower together, dressed, and I helped him put the cabin to rights. It was oddly intimate, and I hadn't expected it to be. But there was something about stripping the soiled sheets and remaking the bed together that had me struggling to keep myself composed.

I was tucking my end of the sheet in, when my fingertips felt something at the foot of the bed between the mattress and the box springs. I yelped, and yanked my hand back in surprise.

"What?" Julian smiled at me. "I promise you angel,

the only thing that bites… is me."

"Very funny," I said. "There's something under here," I told him.

Julian frowned. "Let's see." He walked over and lifted up the corner of the mattress and discovered a small cloth bag. He lifted it up. The velvet bag wasn't more than six inches in length, and maybe four inches wide, and it was full. Whatever was in it was bumpy and heavy.

"What the hell is that?" I said.

"Only one way to find out." Julian's voice was tense as he opened the drawstring bag and dumped the contents on the fresh sheet.

Several vintage diamond rings and antique hairpins tumbled out and sparkled in the light. I saw a flash of soft purple among the tumble of jewelry. "Oh my Goddess," I breathed. "The amethyst pin is here." I reached for the old crescent moon pin that had belonged to great-aunt Irene.

"Don't touch it," Julian warned. "You don't want your fingerprints on anything."

"You're right." I nodded, and using the edge of the sheet, I pushed the jewelry apart so I could study the cache. "Julian, these are the items that were stolen from *Obscura*," I told him.

"Are you sure?"

"Positive," I said.

"Leilah," Julian hissed. "She must have hidden them out here."

"Does she have the security code for the gate?"

"She does. My father let her have a party out here over the winter."

"What do we do now?" I asked. "Should we call the police?"

Julian ran an aggravated hand through his hair. "That could be problematic."

"There's a bit of an *understatement*," I said, tossing up my hands. "How are we ever going to explain how we found them? 'Oh, hello officer, my secret lover and I spent the afternoon doing the *wild thing* and afterwards we went to remake the bed, and found the stolen jewelry?'"

Julian started to chuckle. "Holly," he said, walking over to wrap his arms around my waist. "I adore you." He kissed me.

"Don't distract me." I pulled my mouth free of his. "I'm trying to think."

Julian smiled at that, and pulled me so that my head rested against his chest.

From the circle of his arms I studied the jewelry on the bed for a few moments. "I have an idea," I said. "We'd be outing ourselves to someone, but I know that we could count on them to be an ally— of sorts."

"Alright, what did you have in mind?" he said.

"Do you trust me?" I asked.

"Always, angel." He tipped my chin up, and I found myself gazing into those unique eyes.

I rose to my tiptoes and kissed him. Then I went to

my purse and took out my cell phone. While Julian used a clean pillowcase to pick up the items and put them back in the bag, I punched in a familiar number.

"Hello?"

"Hi, it's Holly," I said. "I need your help."

***

Julian and I sat side by side on the leather sofa in the cabin with the contents of the bag lying out on the little coffee table in front of us. The person I'd trusted had come right over when I'd called, and at the moment they were rooting through the items while wearing latex gloves.

"You did the right thing to call me," they said.

"I hope so," Julian said seriously.

Gloved fingers picked up the amethyst crescent pin. "The brooch's magick has been activated."

"Yes," I sighed. "Leilah is using it to empower a love spell."

"Well that's *not* good." Gingerly they set the pin down, and stripped off the protective gloves. "What I want to know is, what the two of you were doing out here in the first place?" Aunt Faye stepped back and planted her hands on her hips.

"You're a sharp woman Aunt Faye," I said. "I'm sure you've already figured that out." I kept my gaze level, refusing to be embarrassed.

Aunt Faye narrowed her eyes at me, then slid her

gaze to Julian. "I *knew* it," she said, sitting in the rocker. "This started that day, you went to search the mansion."

I cleared my throat. "I think you of all people would understand why Julian and I want to keep our relationship private." I said to her.

She leaned back in the chair with a smile. "My dear, you can relax. I've been quite fond of this young man ever since he saved my life a few years ago."

Julian shifted beside me on the couch. "I only helped get you and Autumn out of the mansion, and away from Rebecca."

"Don't downplay your role," Aunt Faye said. "I've been keeping tabs on you for the past few years Julian. I know exactly what you do with your spare time."

I opened my mouth to defend him, but Aunt Faye barreled on.

"You've tried to keep your volunteering at the rehabilitation center quiet, but you've made a difference Julian, and people are taking notice."

"It's nothing," Julian said, and shifted on the couch.

"I doubt that Mr. Vasquez thinks that." Aunt Faye smiled. "You are paying his tuition, and from what I understand he's at the top of his mechanics classes."

Julian crossed his arms defensively. "Diego deserved a second chance—"

"Oh I couldn't agree more." Aunt Faye cut him off.

How on earth did she know about Diego? I wondered.

"You have an ally in me." Aunt Faye met Julian's eyes. "Do you understand?"

Julian smiled. "Yes, I am beginning to."

"You two are both adults. We all know that various members of the families will not be comfortable about the idea of you two being involved. But frankly, that is none of their damn business."

I sat back, and for the first time since I'd called to ask for her help, relaxed. "Thank you Aunt Faye," I said.

"I can see that you two have feelings for each other, and I simply want to say, that you can *both* trust me to be discreet."

"Thank you Faye," Julian said.

Aunt Faye leaned forward in her chair. "Now, we have some work to do. Between the three of us I think we can easily break the spell Leilah cast." Aunt Faye's silver eyes seemed to light up.

I felt both resolve and mischief coming from her. "What did you have in mind?" I asked.

"Do you know who Leilah targeted with the spell?" she asked.

Julian draped his arm around my shoulders. "Yes, we do. We found her notes the day we searched the mansion, and Holly took photos of them. So we know not only *who* she targeted, but exactly *how* she cast the spell."

Aunt Faye was literally rubbing her hands together. "Well don't keep me in suspense!" Aunt Faye said.

"Who's the poor sap that Leilah bewitched?"

"Erik McBriar," I said.

"Ooooh," Aunt Faye drew the word out as if it were delicious. "Did she really? I thought that narrow-minded young man was engaged to some girl who has a predilection for posting photos of herself all over social media."

"Duck face," Julian said straight-faced, and made me laugh.

"Yes, he is engaged." I explained. "But from what I overheard back at the antique store, Ginny was against them getting married. And then a few weeks ago in the university library, Raelynn told Leilah that she was having trouble with him."

"Such as?" Aunt Faye's eyes were bright as she waited for the details.

"Well he'd postponed the wedding, and were arguing about her going on a trip for Spring Break."

"Tell me simply *everything*."

I filled her in with what details I'd learned about Raelyn hiring Leilah to do spellwork on Erik McBriar. Then when I finished, Julian explained what we'd learned from the notes Leilah had left in her room. He mentioned the potion we'd found, but to my relief, left it at that.

"You know I hate to say this..." Aunt Faye began, "but it seems to me Erik McBriar is actually receiving a bit of karmic payback for pressuring you into quitting the antique store."

I raised my eyebrows. "Aunt Faye!" I said, shocked.

"Oh, please." Aunt Faye raised one elegant eyebrow at me. "He pressured you into quitting because he was *afraid* of Witchcraft, and intolerant of other belief systems. And I am frankly, still offended at the comments he made about you staying away from his sister and her young family."

"I'm still offended, too," I said. "But this is a nasty, and very manipulative spell that Raelynn had Leilah put on him."

"Well, it seems to me young Mr. McBriar is about to learn a valuable lesson," Aunt Faye said. "I doubt he'll dismiss the Craft so casually, again."

I never knew the old girl could be so.... ruthless, I thought. *And here I'd thought I was the only Witch in the family who struggled against her dark side.*

"I heard that," Aunt Faye said.

"Heard what?" Julian said, looking from my great-aunt to me.

"Aunt Faye's a telepath," I explained. "She can hear your thoughts—"

"Especially when they're directed at me," Aunt Faye cut in.

I shook my head. "I can't imagine Erik McBriar would be happy if he ever found out that three Witches did magick on him."

Julian tugged on one of my curls. "I imagine he'd be even more unhappy finding himself bound to a girl who used spell craft to coerce him into marriage," he said, matter-of-factly.

"You've got a point," I said to him.

"He'll get over it," Aunt Faye predicted.

"Aunt Faye?" I asked. "Can the energy of the amethyst crescent be used to break the manipulative spell, only? What if that magick all backfires on Raelynn instead of Leilah?"

"You can't pay someone else to cast a spell for you — or to throw a hex, and still keep your hands clean. That's not how it works." Aunt Faye insisted. "If Raelynn requested the spell and paid for it; then she's as culpable as the Witch— in this case Leilah— who physically cast the spell."

I nodded. "Then they would both receive in return whatever sort of energy they sent out."

Aunt Faye smiled, and it was as thin and sharp as a razor. "Karma can be a bitch, dear."

"Look, I don't like Leilah, or Raelynn for that matter, but we are talking about unleashing a boatload of negative energy onto them. The fallout could be bad. I've worked hard to stay away from the darker side of magick. This makes me nervous."

"My dear," Aunt Faye got up and came over to sit next to me on the arm of the couch. She took my hand. "Magick is many shades of gray. It's not as simple as good or baneful or light or dark... It's about balance."

"So we're working to restore that balance." I glanced at Julian and remembered when he'd once said almost the same to me, about working to balance the scales.

"Balance is good," I said. "I can work with that."

Aunt Faye used the cast off glove to pick up the brooch. "Trust me, I know exactly what to do with this. We can restore the balance, break any enchantment against Erik McBriar, *and* teach Leilah and that Raelynn both a valuable lesson."

"When did you want to get started?" Julian asked.

"Why wait?" Aunt Faye said. "Let's go take a walk in the woods, find a natural clearing and work a little spontaneous magick."

EPILOGUE

We didn't have to walk very far. Julian was familiar with the woods around the cabin, and he found us a clearing fairly quickly. I'd never seen Aunt Faye work magick before, and she was much more of a practical Witch than I'd realized.

She didn't need fancy tools or a bunch of herbs or stones. Instead she worked with the natural energy of the spring woods that was all around us. The three of us focused our intentions and individual powers on breaking the spell, and I had no doubt that it worked.

I held Julian's hand as we finished up with the ritual, and we all smiled when the sun came out from the afternoon clouds. As the light shone down on us, the birds began to sing louder, and a doe and two fawns stepped into the clearing. They stopped and watched the three of us for a few moments, then slipped back into the trees.

Aunt Faye went back home, taking the cache of stolen jewelry with her, leaving Julian and I alone, and we lingered at the cabin a bit longer.

Aunt Faye wasted no time and immediately gave all of the stolen items to Lexie. Lexie wasn't happy that the only information Faye would give her was that an 'anonymous' source had located the jewelry and had wanted to turn them over to the authorities.

Lexie did her thing, filled out her reports with the police department, and after lots of paperwork, eventually the stolen jewelry was returned to the Chandler's at *Obscura*. Once the insurance paperwork was cleared up, Aunt Faye was able to purchase her sisters' pin back and cleanse the item. She's locked it up in a safe place and has informed me that it's going to stay tucked away until she's confident that the brooch is completely clear of any magickal residue.

I heard Erik McBriar had called off his engagement with Raelynn. William's Ford was buzzing over the juicy gossip for weeks. Apparently their breakup was sudden and unfortunately very public. Rumor has it that she threw a nasty fit and screamed obscenities at him in the middle of a restaurant, and then she stormed off...

Only to clip three separate cars in the parking lot on her way out.

Fortunately for the owners of the cars, the restaurant's security cameras caught the whole thing. Unfortunately for Raelynn, the police picked her up and she's been charged with three different counts of leaving the scene of an accident, or maybe that's a hit and run? In an interesting turn of events, Raelynn had carelessly let her car insurance coverage expire, so she's also in trouble for driving without insurance.

Hello karma.

After running into Erik McBriar a few times at The Black Cat Coffee House, I discovered while he made an effort to be polite, he didn't look too good. I actually felt sorry for him, and figured I should chalk that up to my psychic empathy. I've always hated seeing anyone suffer... even Erik McBriar. I'm not sure what the lasting effects of that spell will be for him, but I hope he recovers from it, and from the hit his pride took from such a public break up with Raelynn.

Oddly enough, Leilah failed several of her classes at the university and is now on academic probation. Julian informed me that their father isn't too pleased, and Thomas took many of her privileges away, including her car, until she can learn to act more responsibly. Apparently Leilah threw a fit over that, so Thomas informed her that if she doesn't straighten out, he'd cut her off without a cent.

Bran and Lexie had their baby girl, who surprised us all by arriving a few weeks early. They've named her Belinda. She's a sweet, tiny little thing and has dark blonde hair and blue eyes, like her mother. Morgan is fascinated with his sister, and has announced that it's okay if the baby has a pink room, because his new room — which used to be Autumn's— is blue.

Autumn has been content at her new home. Even living in a construction zone hasn't fazed her. Ivy was home for the summer, but she and Nathan did take a trip to the east coast. Ivy finally got to see Salem, Massachusetts and visit the place where the Witch trials were. She also met Nathan's family. She hit it off with his sister Hannah. I'm pretty sure they've been keeping in touch.

We still work together on my telekinesis, or PK, once a week. Ivy has had me doing small things as witchy exercises. I actually managed to make a cat toy roll back and forth across the floor with my powers the other day, without being angry or upset. I was calm and centered, and Ivy says it's good progress... besides, the cat was thrilled. Merlin keeps dropping more cat toys at my feet, hoping I'll make them move all by themselves.

***

So the wheel of the year rolled on, Lughnasadh, the first harvest, came and went, and I prepared to start my final year of college. Ivy moved back to Crowly Hall with Cypress, and I decided to keep living at the manor. I stacked my new textbooks on the marble topped table my mother had used as an altar, hoping to empower them for knowledge and success for the new semester.

I heard Morgan run down the hall and shout at the top of his lungs to Bran that the baby was awake. Of course the little boy's shouting only made the baby cry louder. A few moments later I heard Bran go tend to the baby. I smiled and tucked myself into the window seat of the turret with a contented sigh. The light of the full moon streamed in through the turret window, and as I watched, the full Holly Moon rose higher in the eastern sky.

It made me a little wistful, and I wished Julian could have been sitting there with me. Aunt Faye has kept our secret, and though it hasn't been easy keeping our relationship quiet, being with him was definitely worth the effort.

Lost in my own thoughts, a solid *thump* from behind me had me spinning in surprise. I checked to see where Merlin was— and he was sitting in front of the old armoire. The cat was frozen in position and was staring at the large piece of furniture. Curious, I stood and began to walk across the turret towards the armoire, and Merlin jumped against the furniture like he was trying to get inside.

Merlin meowed at me as if asking for help, so I walked over and pulled open the door. I chuckled when Merlin hopped straight inside.

"What are you doing, kitty?" I asked him.

Merlin was digging, not unlike a dog, at a stack of quilts that were arranged at the bottom of the cabinet. Ivy and I had been using the armoire for the storage of heavy winter blankets and other than that— the armoire had been more decorative than useful since we'd taken over the room.

I knelt down before the cabinet, shooed Merlin out of the way, and lifted the quilts out. Once the quilts were on the floor, he hopped back in and started pawing at the center of the bottom panel. The bottom of the armoire was wooden and appeared solid, but I had a *feeling*... Out of curiosity I ran my hands over the bottom panel and found in the back center of the cabinet a small button. I pushed it and the bottom popped up, releasing from a catch. Merlin hopped out and sat beside me.

"What the hell?" I'd never known there to be a hidden compartment in the piece, and I slowly lifted the panel back. Its hinges squeaked and folded out, similar to an old secretary desk. Holding my breath, I peered inside the secret compartment and found a single hardback book.

As soon as I touched it I knew it had belonged to my mother.

Using the fold out section as a desk, I set the book down and opened it. Merlin climbed up and sat next to the book, as if lending feline support.

It was a journal, I realized after a few moments. The first entry was dated 1986. I did a little mental calculation. My mother would have been twenty-four years old, and as I flipped through the pages I began to see that the gentle and serene mother I'd thought I'd known had once been a passionate, and often angry, young woman.

I scanned through the entries, many which spoke of Bran as a baby, and how my mother had raised him as her own. There was plenty in the journal about her frustration with her younger brother, Arthur.

"Wow." I raised my eyebrows at a particularly scathing section of what my mother had thought about her parents— my grandparents Morgan and Rose— and their refusal to yank her brother, Arthur, back in line, as he basically had ignored his own child.

Merlin nudged my hand with his head. "If I'd have known this book existed a few years ago," I said to the cat, "I might have had an easier time understanding the secrets my mother had kept."

When the family secret of Bran's biological parentage came to light after Autumn had arrived in William's Ford, the family had been at odds. Bran, I'd learned in my senior year of high school, was actually Autumn's half brother. Technically, he was my *adopted* brother.

Biologically Bran, Ivy, and I were cousins. But since my mother had adopted him, we were also siblings as well. Many years before, Arthur had fled William's Ford with Autumn and her mother, giving up all parental rights to his son, and that was when my mother had made it official, and Bran became *her* legal child.

It had been shocking at the time to learn the truth, but seeing it all through the eyes of my mother as a young woman gave me a very different perspective. I flipped to a new page and found an entry that mentioned my great-aunt Irene.

"Oh, hello." Suddenly very interested, I began to read.

Spring Equinox 1986.

If anyone can help me, it will be Aunt Irene. She will understand.

I love him; but no matter how we try, we can't find a way to be together. I love him and I want to be with him. I am tired of hiding and keeping our affair a secret. He isn't happy with his wife, but yet he refuses to leave her.

I've told him I don't care if he ever divorces Yvonne. I'd go anywhere, live anywhere. We could leave William's Ford and raise our boys together.

He can't get from her the kind of passion we share. Why, why won't he leave her? He says he loves me... but still he won't leave his wife. I have to do something, I don't care if love magick is forbidden. Thomas Drake is my soul mate. There has to be a way for us to be together.

Irene will know what to do.

"Oh my god," I breathed. "Mom was once secretly in love with Thomas Drake?"

Merlin gave a soft meow. The cat lifted a paw to the journal and batted at the pages, almost as if he wanted me to keep reading.

I gulped and tried to get the mental image of my mother and Thomas Drake having a passionate affair out of my mind.

But this all made a horrible sort of sense.

Autumn had seen Thomas after my mother's burial at the cemetery, and she said that he'd been visibly upset. The night the Blood Moon Grimoire had been recovered, Thomas had turned over the cursed Grimoire with relief and he'd told Autumn, *he'd done it for Gwen...*

"Oh. My. Goddess." My mind whirled as I realized how everything was fitting together. "She would've only been a couple years older than me when she wrote this..." Merlin nudged the back of my hand with his head again, so I steeled myself and re-read from the beginning of the entry. Very carefully this time.

"Wait a minute," I said out loud. "*Our* boys? Did she mean Bran and Julian?"

Fascinated by what I'd found, I continued to read...

I waited until everyone was asleep and then I walked through the gardens and over to Aunt Irene's bungalow. I let myself in the back door, and Irene was waiting for me, sitting at her kitchen table, as if she knew I was coming. While she's not a Seer like Aunt Faye, Irene simply 'knows' things. Irene held my hand, looked at my palm and read my fate.

I am both heartbroken and hopeful at what she read there. Irene told me that while I may love Thomas, that the Drake and Bishop lines were not meant to be joined in this generation. She warned me that working a love spell would have a terrible consequence for both myself, and Thomas, and our boys.

"*You think you're so clever?*" she said. "*That no one would know about you and Thomas? You are a fool! "Thomas is the heir! Silas Drake would never allow his son to be bound to a Bishop woman!" I sat there and shook with fear as she warned me that I was putting myself and Bran in terrible danger by continuing the affair.*

Irene insisted that Silas, would seek vengeance if he discovered that Thomas and I had ever been together— and that his revenge would likely be aimed at Bran.

That terrified me. Thomas' father is cruel, and insane. He cares nothing for his daughter, Rebecca, and is instead obsessed with only the magickal lineage that passes from father to son. That unbroken male line of power of the Drake family. Silas is the one who insisted Thomas marry Yvonne, Silas pressured them to conceive a child almost immediately, and it is well known that the old man is a magician of the darkest sort. A true sorcerer.

Irene's blue eyes burned when she made her prophecy. "Mark what I say!" Her hand seemed to heat up where she clasped it onto mine. "Gwen, you cannot change what is fated."

I knew the truth when I heard it, and I dropped my head on her kitchen table and cried. I cried for Thomas, I cried for our boys, and I cried for what can never be. After a time she rinsed out a tea towel with water and told me to wipe my eyes. I sat there, my shoulders shaking as Irene took my hand again, and with her next words, I went from sorrow to hope.

She foretold that I would have two daughters someday... Twins, she said. Though she would not live to see them born herself, she foretold that my girls would be strong and gifted Witches. One light and the other dark, two halves of the same coin. She warned that I would have to wait, that the girls were not destined to be born into this world until we'd reached the second half, of the final decade of the century.

My heart had been broken... and yet now, I had hope.

I sat in her kitchen until the early hours of the morning. When daylight broke I got up to leave the bungalow, and I made a vow. I would never see Thomas Drake again, and I promised my aunt that I would name one of my twins after her.

My hands shaking, I gently closed the journal. "Holy crap! I'd always thought mom had *despised* Thomas Drake," I said to the cat.

As soon as the words left my mouth, I *felt* the truth. My hands resting on the cover of the book allowed me to feel my mother's emotions as if she were still here in the room with me. "I wonder if she'd only been angry and hurt?" I said to myself. "But maybe her hatred had actually been directed at Thomas Drake's father, Silas."

Deliberately I took my hands away from the book. The emotions coming off the journal were intense, desperate, sad, and angry. And it gave me a sudden insight as to how unrequited love could easily turn to hate over time.

"Oh, Mom," I sighed sadly. "I'm so sorry you went through all of that. But I'm glad you had your Aunt

Irene next door to go to for guidance."

Because certainly, I thought. *My Great Aunt Irene, no matter what Faye said, had given my mother excellent advice, and she'd very correctly prophesied mine and Ivy's birth. Light twin and dark twin... she'd been right on the money.*

Now I knew why my middle name was Irene. Mom had kept her vow. I put everything back where I found it and closed the armoire doors. Merlin leaned against me, so I scooped him up and carried him to the window seat. I settled back on the cushions and he snuggled into my lap.

I sat under the light of the Holly moon, and considered. There was no way that Autumn buying the bungalow, Irene's brooch popping back up— only to be stolen by Leilah, and finally returned to us— was a coincidence. I glanced over cautiously at the armoire. Now I'd found my mother's journal, and my instincts were shouting at me.

There was something bigger at work here. Something that I couldn't yet see.

Time was running in a circle, and like my mother before me, I too had become secretly and passionately involved with the heir to the Drake line.

I could only hope that my story would have a happier ending.

The End

Turn the Page for a sneak peek of the continuation of
Autumn Bishop's story
Spells Of The Heart

By Ellen Dugan

Coming June 2017

Spells Of The Heart

I pulled into the driveway of my bungalow, parked the car and sat grinning like a lunatic. I still couldn't believe it. I, Autumn Bishop, Witch, and Seer of the Bishop family line, was a homeowner.

My 1920s Craftsman style bungalow was painted a bright cheerful yellow with white trim and a gray roof...and it was conveniently next door to my family's manor home. I climbed out of my car, smelling the roses that were still in bloom along the driveway, and walked up the short curving sidewalk to my front porch.

The porch steps were lined with pots of colorful annuals, and I noted as I went by that they needed a good soaking. The September temperatures were still warm, and we'd been having a dry spell. Still, the shade and coolness of the covered front porch was welcoming, as was the white painted bench and small table that I'd added to create a seating area.

Today would mark the important step for me. As of this afternoon, the lower renovation would be complete.

My newest contractor Mr. Brown had called me at work to notify me that everything was ready to go in the kitchen.

This was a huge milestone, as I'd been using an upstairs bedroom as a makeshift kitchen since I'd moved in. All that was left to do now was to finish the new lower level bathroom. I was currently on my third contractor, and my bathroom tile had been on backorder for weeks. Which had been another delay in a string of frustrations and postponements with completing the lower level renovation.

My first contractor had mysteriously quit after the tear out portion of the kitchen had been completed. He'd left me a note saying the crew was too nervous in the house to continue working in it. So I'd gone for a second company, and I'd had to wait a month before they could get started. They managed to do the framing, wiring, drywall and the floors… but they too had walked off the job before the reno was complete. They even refunded some of my money since they wouldn't finish the job. And they refused to tell me why.

Finally I'd hired a third contractor, and once again had to wait weeks for him to schedule me in, but now things were wrapping up. The kitchen was mostly done, and all of the pieces for the new bathroom had arrived. A perfect vintage bathroom sink, antique medicine cabinet, old repurposed light fixtures… were all ready to go. It seemed like a good omen that the tile and sink had arrived for the new bathroom just before the appliances were scheduled to be delivered and installed.

Crossing my fingers for luck, I let myself in, sighing in relief at the air-conditioned coolness. I grinned at the empty but *clean* front room and walked straight to the back towards my kitchen. What I saw there made me misty.

The original cabinets had been painted a crisp clean white. I'd worked hard with the current contractor, and we'd managed to add similar style cabinets to the newly expanded kitchen. They blended in beautifully with the old ones. Glass fronted cabinets shimmered to the left and right of the old farmhouse style sink. The nickel-plated drawer pulls and cabinet handles were reproduction, sturdy, shiny and new. But they had the old *look* I'd been going for. My new white stove and dishwasher blended in exactly as I'd imagined with the lower cabinets.

The fridge had a funky retro look— but was energy efficient and brand spanking new. It shimmered white, and while it had cost me a pretty penny, seeing it in place in the kitchen made me realize I'd been exactly right to splurge on it.

The tile floor was new as well— there'd been no way to salvage the old floors, and it was laid out in a soft gray and white checkerboard. The floor tiles were arranged in a diamond pattern, and they too had a retro look. The kitchen backsplash was soft gray subway tile with black trim, and the countertops were a solid surface composite material that was a warm smoke, slightly darker than the tile on my floors.

"It's perfect!" I said, and since there was no one to hear me, I squealed in delight.

I ran around for a good five minutes trying everything out. Opening drawers and cabinets, turning on the stove, flinging the refrigerator door wide...It was *exactly* everything I'd hoped for.

"Vintage pieces combined with modern convenience!" I said out loud, and ran my hands over the glass-fronted cabinets. "I'm so glad we salvaged as much of the original materials as possible." I strolled over to the new glass back door, delighted at the afternoon light that streamed in. I turned and took in everything from a different angle. The kitchen was large, warm and inviting, and I could hardly wait to add pops of bright color to it with my plates, and red accessories.

Pumped, I went to check on my newly completed bathroom and stopped still in the doorway. "What the hell?"

While the plumbing had been roughed in months ago, the new toilet, vintage medicine cabinet, and antique sink lay on the floor, exactly where they'd been when I'd left in the morning. The shower tiles had been delivered, but were still in their boxes, sitting inside the unfinished shower stall. Nothing had been installed and nothing had been done.

I grabbed my phone ready to call the contractor, but before I could punch in the numbers, I saw a note attached with blue painter's tape to the back of the uninstalled toilet.

I yanked it free. *Dear Autumn,* it began.

The kitchen appliances have been installed, and this concludes our business here. I have refunded your money on the bathroom that we were contracted to put in— but were unable to finish. You will find my check in your mailbox, because I'm never setting foot in this house again.

By the way, you may want to call a Priest.
Sincerely, Gerald Brown.

"Son of a bitch!" I shut my eyes. I stomped back in to the living room to face off with the roommate that had become a major pain in my ass. Even though she was dead.

"Damn it Aunt Irene!" I yelled. "That's the third contractor you've scared off!"

A light, ghostly laughter drifted down the maple staircase.

"What is *wrong* with you?" I asked, tucking the note in my pocket.

Originally, I'd been surprised and then pleased when I'd learned that the bungalow had originally been built for another Bishop. First Franklin Bishop and his wife had lived here, and then they'd given the home to my great-aunt Irene.

Irene, a Witch with— according to family legend— a penchant for less than ethical spell-casting, had lived in the bungalow alone until the early 1990s. After she'd passed away, the house had been sold to a different family.

When the house had gone up for sale earlier this year, I had jumped at the chance to have it, thus putting the bungalow back in Bishop family hands after thirty years of different owners. *I mean how perfect was that?* I loved the architecture, the gardens connected with the grounds of the manor, I had my own place— and it was right next door to my family!

And yes, I'd realized pretty quickly I wasn't *alone* in the house. Not only am I a Witch and a Seer, which means I can *see* the past, present, and future. I'm also a psychic sensitive so I'm *also* able to see, hear and interact with ghosts stuck in this realm— whether I like it or not. Which truly hadn't bothered me. I've dealt with some pretty incredible things since I moved to William's Ford a few years ago.

However, at the moment, if it would have been possible, I'd have throttled my dead relative. I marched to the front door, yanked it open and checked the mailbox on the outside of the house. Sure enough, an envelope was inside. I tore it open and found a check from Mr. Brown.

I shut the door behind me and sat on the floor of my empty living room, feeling frustrated, angry and disappointed. I dropped my head in my hands and let a few tears fall. "I am so *angry* with you right now." I said, to whoever was listening. "Aunt Irene, why are you doing this to me?"

I sat there glaring across the room at the door of that unfinished bathroom and the scent of lilacs wafted through the air. That was Aunt Irene's calling card of sorts. I sighed. "Maybe I can finish the bathroom myself." *I watched those shows on HGTV... tile work didn't look too hard...*

Suddenly, something skidded across the floor. I jolted when an old cookbook came to a stop directly in front of me. I recognized it as the one I'd found hidden behind a panel in the kitchen pantry, months ago.

"What is that supposed to mean?' I asked crossly.

I waited, but nothing else happened. I picked up the old cookbook and frowned at it. "I had this packed up," I muttered, wondering how she'd managed to get a physical object downstairs. "Is there a recipe in here for banishing Witch-ghosts?" I flipped through the pages like I was searching for one. "Because if there is, I'm gonna use it."

As if in answer, there was a thud from upstairs.

Shaking my head, I stood and went into the kitchen. I decided to set the vintage cookbook inside one of the glass-fronted cabinets for now. As I closed the cabinet, I caught a figure reflected in the seeded glass. I didn't jump, but I did hold very still and study her. *It was an older woman with salt and pepper hair. She was wearing a simple blue dress, and was smiling at me.*

I rotated slowly. Even though I knew she wouldn't be there when I turned around, I looked for her anyway. The house was silent, and I was alone. "Is allowing me to finally see you, a way of saying you're sorry?" I asked quietly.

There was no answer.

A knock on the backdoor had me clutching my chest and spinning in surprise. My cousin Holly stood on the back porch, her red-gold curls exploding all around her face. She waved at me through the glass door. I flipped the lock on the door and let her in.

"I came to see the finished kitchen and bath. Give me the tour!" She smiled and gave me a hug.

"The kitchen is done, but the contractors walked off the job. Again." I pulled the note out of my pocket and handed it to her.

Holly read the note, and snorted with laughter. "I'm sorry," she said, trying to maintain a sober expression. "I'm not laughing *at* you. But this line about calling a priest...That's funny."

"What the hell am I gonna do, Holly?" I said. "The reno has taken twice as long as it should have because of all the delays and Aunt Irene's ghostly antics."

"I wonder why she's trying to hold things up?" Holly walked over to check the bathroom for herself.

"Where in the world am I going to find a contractor who she can't scare off the job?" I ran a hand through my hair. "What am I supposed to do, put in the contract, 'Please don't pay any mind to the ghost of the old Witch that used to live here'?"

"I have a suggestion," Holly said, coming back to stand by me.

"Lay it on me," I said. "Because at this point I'll consider anything."

Holly's eyes met mine. "There is a contractor we both know, who could roll with whatever Aunt Irene threw at him."

"No," I said realizing where she was heading. "Aw, hell no."

"Yes," Holly said just as firmly. "Autumn, you need to call Duncan Quinn."

***

Made in United States
Troutdale, OR
07/02/2025